MURDER

AT THE

OLYMPIAD

MURDER
AT THE
OLYMPIAD

A NOVEL

JAMES GILBERT

atmosphere press

Published by Atmosphere Press

Cover design by Matthew Fielder

Map courtesy of mapa-Jeff.Cartography.Square.site

atmospherepress.com

Puerto Vallarta

PACIFIC OCEAN

Bay of Banderas

Rio Cuale

0 km

1 km

2 km

CHAPTER 1

Rodrigo slowly backed out from the utility closet, banging the mop hoisted over his shoulder against the door. Turning around, he tried twice to prop it against one of the stools next to the bar, but each time it fell onto the tile floor with a clatter. In his right hand, he carried a bucket of water so full that it slopped over the edge when he set it down next to the counter.

"Watch what you're doing, damn it!" Antonio cried without looking over the ledge to measure the spill. "Did you inspect all the rooms?"

"Yeah."

"Well?"

"Number 201 has still got stuff in it. At least there are clothes on the hook and the towel is gone."

"And the key hasn't been turned back in either," Antonio said as he glanced at the rack behind him. "So the guy must still be around. Have you checked everywhere?"

"Not yet. Just going to."

"Well, get to it. He's probably sleeping it off somewhere. Wake him up and get him out of here. We're not running a fucking hotel!"

Antonio was tired and hot and anxious to close up. The temperature outside, even though it was after 2:00 in the morning had to be at least ninety degrees, and inside even three or four more despite the fans that just blew the heat around like the hot breath of desire. He turned around again, reached up to the console behind him, and switched off the music. The sudden quiet as the steady disco beat died out felt like relief from a throbbing headache he didn't know he had. Then, touching a switch on the wall, he turned on the fluorescent lights. The red glow from the recessed overhead lamps that had disguised every fault and feature with a romantic blur dissolved into a flood of stark white exposing the dark, uneven floor, the blemished and cracked gray walls. The unforgiving glare was bright enough to wipe away any illusions and ended the allure of this palace of dingy dreams. Farther on, there was the dark well of a staircase that led down to the level below. The steps behind him led up to private rooms.

"Make sure you check in the sauna and steam area," he shouted after Rodrigo, who was just disappearing around the curve in his descent.

Once on the basement level, Rodrigo walked across the dim corridor and stopped in front of the wooden enclosure of the sauna. He peered into the small glass window on the door, but the light was off and he could barely make out the shapes of the benches. Opening it up, the heat spilled out, sweeping over him. He could smell the combination of wood resin and sweat. But the room was empty.

He walked farther on to the glass door of the steam

room. Pulling it open, he entered the damp gloomy space, edged past the tile-covered bench on the right side, and then turned around a corner into the darkened back area. Condensation from the ceiling dribbled on his forehead and he wiped his eyes to get a better look. There was just enough light to see a shape stretched out on one of the side benches.

"Vamos, amigo, estamos cerrados," he said. And then repeated his words in English—louder this time. There was no response, so he moved closer. He could see now that the person was entirely naked and resting on a towel. He reached down and shook the man's shoulder.

"Wake up!" he said. "Get up!"

There was still no response.

Then, with both hands, he seized the man's dangling left arm and tried to pull him up. But the unexpected dead weight was so much that the man slipped onto the floor instead.

"Damn!" he shouted. "Damn! He's dead drunk!"

Retracing his steps, he hurried halfway up the staircase where he paused and called out to Antonio: "Found someone, but he's drunk, and I couldn't wake him up. What should I do?"

"Fuck!" cried Antonio as he walked around the edge of the bar. "I'll come down with you and together maybe we can carry him out. How big is he?"

"Couldn't really tell. Just lying there on the floor. It's dark you know."

"Okay, okay."

The two of them descended the stairs and Rodrigo switched on the overhead lights at that level.

"And when we're done," he added. "Make sure you

mop the floor in there. God only knows what..."

Rodrigo held the door of the steam room and then propped it open with a rubber shim that had rested inconspicuously against the wall. Antonio waited for him and together they edged around to the dark alcove. The man was still lying on the floor.

"Is this how you found him?"

"Well, yes; not exactly. I mean, I tried to get him up but couldn't. He's too heavy and out cold. That's why I called you."

"Okay, then you grab his legs and I'll take his shoulders and we can steer him out of here and onto one of the benches outside."

"Damn, that's a lot; dead weight," Rodrigo groaned, hoisting the man's ankles.

"Stop complaining! I've got him, so just back up and don't drop him... Come on, amigo. Wake up and help us out a bit!"

They struggled, half dragging the naked body out of the steam room, but instead of putting him on one of the benches or the worn couch at the side of the sauna enclosure, they just left him lying on his back on the floor.

"Okay, amigo, wake up. Last call! We're closed!" Antonio said, bending over and looking at the man's face.

"Definitely an American or at least a foreigner. Get a towel, Rodrigo, and cover him up while I try to wake him."

Antonio crouched down on his haunches and felt the man's face. It was warm, but there was no reaction. He grasped an arm, raised it up and then let it drop.

Rodrigo returned with two towels and placed them over the man's body.

"Do you think he's dead?" he asked suddenly.

"How should I know? Don't know how to tell," Antonio answered. "He's not cold. And not stiff."

"Feel for his pulse. I seen them do it on television. Feel his neck. That's what the detectives always do."

"Okay."

Antonio put his fingers around the man's neck and waited. "I don't feel anything. How am I supposed to know?"

"Those TV detectives can always tell right away."

"Yeah, but I'm not a detective! I think I'm going to have to call the police."

"That won't be good for business if he's dead. Do you think he stayed in the steam room too long?"

"Don't be crazy; it's not warm enough in there to wilt a flower. Probably just had a heart attack or something. But he's awfully young for that."

"Do you see those red marks on his throat? Looks like maybe he was strangled."

"He seems dead, so I guess he was. But you're an expert now?"

"Just what I seen on American shows. Bruises where you press down hard. I don't know nothing."

Antonio stood up and walked toward the staircase: "Stay there, Rodrigo, I'm going to call the Tourist Police. In case he moves, let me know."

"He ain't gonna move. For sure."

"Anyway."

Reaching the main floor, Antonio walked quickly around the bar and through the door in back leading into the small office that also fronted the entrance, where customers standing behind a wire grill, passed their money through and picked up keys to lockers or retiring rooms and a towel and plastic flip flops. It was also where he kept his cellphone. He dialed the number and a sleepy voice answered:

"Tourist Police."

"Is Captain Morelos there?"

"No. Sorry. He's been transferred to Oaxaca."

"Then can I speak to whoever is there?"

"You can tell me what's the problem. If I decide it's important, I'll pass you on to anybody."

"Listen. This is serious! I'm Antonio Lopez at the Olympiad Sauna. We got a customer that we can't seem to wake up. I think he might be dead."

"Did you try his pulse? Maybe he's just drunk."

"More than that, I'm afraid. You need to send someone around. Right away. I gotta close this place up."

"Okay, okay. I'll see if anyone is here, and I'll send them over."

"How about sending a doctor or maybe an ambulance too? So you can get him out of here?"

"We'll see about that when we get there."

The police car pulled up in front about a half hour later. A tired looking officer dressed in crumpled fatigues and a middle-aged woman wearing slacks and a sweatshirt and carrying a black bag—someone who might have been a doctor or the medical examiner but without a uniform—came through the open doorway, up the stairs, and rang the bell in the entrance alcove. Antonio buzzed them inside.

"I'm Captain Gonzalez," said the officer, pushing into the entranceway. "Just happened to be on duty and about to go home when you called. This is Señora Sanchez." He seemed peeved by the interruption to his day. "Where's the body?"

"I don't want no trouble; we never had no trouble here," Antonio said as he guided them to the staircase and then down into the basement level. He turned to look at them as they followed: "He hasn't moved since we took him out of the steam room."

"So you moved him?" the examiner shook her head as she was pulling on a pair of plastic gloves. "That's not very smart. Shouldn't have." She walked over to the body and crouched down, placing her fingers along the artery of his neck. She picked up and flexed his limp arm and then noticed the blotches on his neck.

"Do you think you could shine a flashlight on these marks?" she asked the officer. "I can't be sure and won't know until I have him back at the station, but it looks like he was strangled. You can see some bruising. And not too long ago. No signs of rigor yet."

Then standing and addressing Antonio, she said, "Do you have any identification for him? He looks like a foreigner. Could be about twenty-five years old or so."

"Use your pass key and go look in his room again, Rodrigo, and bring his clothes and anything else you find in his room," Antonio ordered.

"Just a minute," interrupted the woman. "I'm coming with you. And you're not going to touch anything, understand?"

"But I already have... awhile ago. And I don't need the key; I left the door open."

"Come along and be quiet," she said. "Just show me the room and stay out of my way! Anything else you did to corrupt the crime scene?"

Rodrigo was about to answer but thought she would just accuse him again.

The two climbed up the staircase to the upper landing in silence while Antonio and the officer remained below staring down at the body.

"I don't want no trouble," said Antonio in a tone that sounded more like a question than an assertion. "We never have no trouble here."

"Yes, you said that before. But looks like you've got a lot of trouble now. Not much else I can say right off. But certainly looks like a murder, and a foreigner too. Can't think of anything worse for you. We'll have to close your place down for a few days... maybe a week or two. Tomorrow, I'll send a team to look for fingerprints. And don't be surprised if you find a few things out of order."

"But officer, how long? We have to clean the rooms!"

"You're not listening very carefully. You need to think about how you can help us instead of mopping the floors. And when we're done here tonight, I want you and your helper to lock up. And plan to *stay* shut until I tell you. Don't have to tell you not to touch anything. And you'll have to come to the station of course... a lot of questions to answer... but later."

Approaching the row of cubicles on the second floor above the bar, Rodrigo led the medical examiner to the open door of 201. He switched on the single bulb light inside, which cast a weak glow around the tiny space, and let her step in first because there was scarcely any room to turn around. She entered and sidled along the raised wooden platform bed that was covered in some sort of plastic material and a crumpled sheet. The wall abutting it was mirrored up to the ceiling. Toward the far end there was a small built-in table. On top of it was a plastic water bottle, and above to the right was a wall hook with a pair of jeans and a T-shirt still hanging on it.

Taking both items of clothing down, she spread them out onto the platform and turned the pockets of the jeans inside out. Both in front were empty except for a few coins on the right side. Reaching underneath, she took a wallet out of the back right pocket. It was empty except for a vehicle insurance card. In the dim glare, she could make out the name "Jeremy Blackman" with an address in Los Angeles.

"Was the door to this cubicle unlocked when you came to check on him?"

"I don't remember, Señora; what I mean is, I always use my key, so I wouldn't know if it was or wasn't, would I?"

"Do you have some system of lockboxes? Somewhere he might have put money, credit cards, a passport?"

"No."

"And did you did find the room key anywhere on the body?"

"No. I didn't see that neither. It would have been on an elastic band. Guys put them on their wrist or ankle sometimes."

"You're sure it didn't fall off when you carried him out of the steam room?"

"Yeah, I'm pretty sure, but I'll go back and look again."

The medical examiner gave him an exasperated look but said nothing further. She backed out of the room and walked swiftly along the corridor and down the two flights of stairs back to where the body was stretched out on the floor. Rodrigo followed, staying carefully behind her.

"I've got an ID for him, some sort of insurance card from Los Angeles, but it looks very likely that he was robbed," she told Captain Gonzalez. "No cash, no credit cards, no passport. Whether that has anything to do with his death is, of course, for someone else to prove. And I looked, but there was no key inside the cubicle, as you can see, none on his wrist and there was nothing in his pockets. Maybe when you do a more thorough search, you'll find it." Addressing Antonio, she continued: "Did anyone turn in the key?"

"No Señora. Whoever did this I think has taken the key with him."

"Perhaps. We don't know that yet. Maybe it will turn up when we've done a more thorough search."

"As for the cause of death," she said, turning to the Captain Gonzalez, "I'll have a report for you tomorrow sometime once you get the body back to my lab. And I'll tell you definitively if it was murder or not. But it looks like it."

"Thanks, Señora," the officer mumbled. "I'll deliver the body as soon as I can get an ambulance here. In the meantime, can you give me the insurance card? If that's him and he's an American, I'll have to notify the Consulate."

"Good luck with that!"

"What?"

"You know as well as I do *what*; she makes trouble."

The officer turned to Antonio, who had moved away from the body, recoiling as if it was contaminated: "I want a list of names: everyone who entered today and, if you can, the time that this person arrived."

"I'm sorry officer, but we don't keep a list of names.

This ain't a hotel."

"Okay then, passport numbers or ID numbers for any locals will do."

"Might not be complete."

"Aren't you supposed to check everyone who enters? What kind of a place is this?"

Antonio took a step backwards and almost sat down abruptly onto one of the benches along the wall.

"I'm sorry, sir, yes, we usually check IDs for the age of the person. And we generally write down the ID number. But maybe if Rodrigo was at the window, he might have forgotten. He's not very careful sometimes. So you'll have to ask him. But listen: we never had trouble, here. And we have to be discreet, you know."

"Well, in this case, I think you've got considerable trouble... Hardly the time to be worried about anyone's reputation. Do you remember him—the victim—when he arrived and if he was alone?"

"I think maybe I was the one who checked him in. I seem to remember there was two of them: Americans, I think, about the same age... young, anyway. So if they actually came together, then one of them has obviously left alone. I can't tell you exactly when; probably Rodrigo checked him out. You know, it's very simple process. They just shove their towels and sheets into a hamper by the exit and return their shoes and keys. I'm not sure I'd remember anyone leaving specifically. Sometimes I just buzz them out without looking if I'm busy at the bar. But ask Rodrigo; maybe he..." Antonio was intentionally vague, not because he knew something and didn't want to say, but he figured if he sounded unreliable, the policeman would stop asking him questions.

"Then I'll want that list of those entries you have before I leave."

"I'm not sure I should give it to you," Antonio said after a pause. A look of dread spread over his face. "People who come here don't want to have their names known. It could cause terrible trouble for me if you investigate them. I'm sure you understand."

Gonzalez scowled and took a step toward him: "That's not my problem. If this is a murder, and I think it is, any one of your clients could be the killer. I need those ID numbers. You're to give me list before I leave. I don't give a damn about anonymous or about your business."

He then turned his gaze to the assistant who was sitting on a bench down at the end of the corridor. Rodrigo looked up anxiously when the policeman approached.

"Do you remember two Americans? The person lying here and maybe a friend of his? Did you see them together or check the other one out?"

Rodrigo stood up and stared blankly for a minute: "I never pay any attention to the guys here, whether they're American or not," he said, backing up against the bench he had been sitting on. "Never make eye contact, because if you do... I just work here; I'm not one of them!"

"I don't care what you are or aren't. Just tell me, did you see them together?"

"Not that I remember. But I do know that one American left earlier because I had to ask him for his towel. He'd left it in the locker area and I certainly wasn't going to get it for him. But he may not be the one you mean. We get lots of foreigners here."

"So that man you remember didn't have a room?"

"I guess not. I didn't check his key. But that wouldn't

be unusual. If two guys came together why would each need a separate room? But then this isn't a place where anyone wants to explain what they're doing or why. So who knows?"

"Do you remember what time it was? Approximately?"

"I don't know. Maybe around 11:00 or so. I usually go outside for a few minutes around that time. Get some fresh air. Could have been then or when I came back in."

"So you really don't know."

"That's right. I don't pay no attention. I just do my job without looking. I don't get paid to see things."

Gonzalez stared at Rodrigo for a moment and then decided that he kept repeating himself because of nerves and probably knew nothing more. But he would keep an ear open for anything suspicious about him just the same. He wasn't sure he could trust anyone here. And the whole place... maybe the late hour... and a foreigner murdered! He could expect nothing but trouble.

CHAPTER 2

The autopsy room in the basement of police head-quarters was painted a glossy, lime green with floor-to-ceiling metal cabinets lining one wall, a deep sink opposite, and, at the center, a gurney lit by a bank of overhead fluorescent lights. It was cool, almost cold, but Señora Sanchez wore only a thin, white surgical uniform with short sleeves. She was just peeling off her blue plastic gloves when the door opened and Captain Gonzalez swaggered in, glaring at her as if death was somehow her fault.

"I don't know how you stand this frigid room," he said, as he approached the shrouded body.

"You have to be cold-blooded to do this job," she answered, straight-faced at the half-intended joke. She hated all the morbid witticisms that her family and colleagues made at her expense, and she never allowed herself a smile when they did. She was the only one entitled to jest about death.

"Anything definitive about the victim?"

Sanchez walked over to the body and pulled the sheet back halfway, revealing the face and chest. The harsh light lent a bluish blush to his skin.

"You can see the bruises around the neck. Technically speaking, the hyoid bone was crushed against the vertebrae, causing almost immediate loss of consciousness and then death. My guess is that the killer was facing the victim and pressed his thumbs against his neck. I rather doubt that there was much of a struggle. He might even have been lying down when the murder occurred. Probably was, I think. And there wcrc no signs of any defensive gestures that I could discover. Nothing under the nails. But that may have been because he had consumed considerable amounts of alcohol, which limited his reactions. BAC level was over 0.5. Probably didn't even realize what was happening. Quick, but it took considerable force."

"Anything else?"

"Yes. There are some old contusions and healed fractures in the chest area. Several broken ribs; maybe a spinal injury too. Could have been an auto accident or some kind of serious fall. Some time ago. I don't know."

"Is that relevant?"

"No... But there's something else that is important. He recently had sex. I found semen in his anal cavity."

"Could he have been killed while having sex?"

"It's certainly possible. I'm not an expert on the various positions of male-to-male sex. But I'm sure you would know more about that." She allowed herself the flicker of a smile: she loved to question the masculinity of her colleagues upstairs who strutted around in high leather boots sporting their batons and pistols on their hips.

"Certainly not, Señora! Anything else?"

"I still have to run some more blood tests to complete the autopsy. Test for drugs if there were any."

"When can you have a full report?"

"Possibly in a few days. But I suspect I won't find anything else significant having to do with his death. It's just to be sure."

"All right, then. I'll expect something as soon as possible."

"And, of course, you'll try to get in touch with his American family through the Consulate. They might be better at finding them," she continued; there was something too insistent in his words, and she was delighted to remind him of his duty.

"I know my job, Señora. I'll call their office immediately. I just wanted to speak to you first to be sure of the information. I'll let the Americans notify his relatives."

He turned away, happy to exit the room but troubled nonetheless at having to deal with what he anticipated would be a hysterical reaction from the boy's family when they heard the news. And if they came to Puerto Vallarta, which they surely would, it would only get worse. At the least, there was the endless red tape and arrangements for shipping the body back to the United States. He was tired already as he calculated the bother when a foreigner was murdered. He hoped someone else, perhaps his superior could take over the investigation. That would be a relief—if only he was so lucky!

Gonzalez walked back to his office upstairs slowly, almost reluctantly. After checking the time, he dialed the American Consulate. He could practically compose the number by heart; there had been too many incidents of late. As the phone rang, he said softly, almost angrily: "So much trouble..."

After four rings, a voice answered: "Consulate of the United States; Fernando Reyes speaking. How may I help you?"

Gonzalez had passable English, but he responded in Spanish; best to keep it formal, he thought, and at a distance.

"This is Captain Gonzalez with the Tourist Police. May I please speak to the Consul General?" Of course he knew her name—they had a history of unpleasant encounters—but something made him want to avoid any hint of familiarity.

"Yes, Captain, I'll switch you over right away. May I inform Señora Pennyworth the nature of your call?"

"No, I think not," he replied. "Just let me speak to her, please. Right now." He was already angry without quite knowing why. Except that it often happened that he was short-tempered when it came to foreigners, an irony because of his position in the Tourist Police, something that did not escape him. He had never wanted to deal with people he didn't understand. And when he received this posting, it made him even more short tempered to be surrounded by the absurdities of Americans and Canadians who treated him like he was the alien, the unwelcome immigrant, the illegal, the bracero—and in his own country. But maybe, he thought, if he solved this case quickly, he might apply for a promotion into a better service—even the Federales and possibly in Mexico City. A murder case quickly ended would get him the attention he deserved.

After a brief hesitation and a click connecting him, she answered in English: "This is Amanda Pennyworth."

He replied in Spanish: "Good morning, Señora. Capitan Gonzalez here, from the Tourist Police. I'm afraid I have bad news. Last night we retrieved the body of a young American—at least he appears to be an American—from the Olympiad Sauna... perhaps you know what that is, over on Aveneda Cardenas in the Zona Romantica. I'm wondering if you could stop by the police compound as soon as possible. We have a preliminary identification, but perhaps you can find out more. I was sure that the Consulate would want to be informed."

"I can come within the hour," she said, switching into her precise Spanish. But then she hesitated. "Young, you say? Can I ask how he died?"

"We're not absolutely certain yet. Autopsy isn't complete." He hung up.

Amanda put the phone in its cradle and leaned back in her desk chair. She looked down at the neat piles of papers on her desk; one smaller on the right including finished work waiting for her assistant to send out, and the other stacked high on the left still demanding her attention. Most of these were requests for visas, although a few were probably communications from American business enterprises—either complaints about how the Mexican government was collecting taxes or sluggish and erratic service provided by the state-owned electrical, gas, and light companies. A murder, she thought, would certainly be a diversion from her routine.

And then she stopped herself. Why did she assume so quickly that it was murder? Maybe it was just some sort of accident. The officer had refused to say. But then, why were the police involved? And if it was something serious, she would have to be careful; her relations with the authorities had been strained at best. If only Captain Morelos of the Tourist Police hadn't been transferred back to Oaxaca several months ago, everything would be a lot easier. And that was only one reason she missed him. It had occurred to her that Captain Gonzalez had something to do with his reassignment. She knew that he disapproved of her and probably suspected their involvement. It would be just like him to interfere.

She started to get up but then settled back down for a moment, reluctant to leave off thinking about her brief affair with Romero. Completely against "company policy," because the State Department frowned on entanglements with locals, it had just happened and she had let herself become involved—or to be honest—encouraged him when he had shown an interest. After all, state wasn't a religious order and she had taken no vows other than to support her country. Nonetheless, the uprooted life, with new assignments to new places every three years, was hardly enough time to learn a new job let alone find someone permanent. It never surprised her when she went back to headquarters in Washington that she always heard the stale joke that the Department had invented speed dating, and to mix up the metaphor—all relationships necessarily had a brief shelf life.

Finally standing, she paused again to glance out the window. The morning sun had climbed over the mountain range that embraced the bay and the city of Puerto Vallarta and was shining through the remaining wisps of fog coiled up like gray tendrils of smoke emerging from the deep valleys cut into the steep green hills. It would be another hot day with no rain, perfect weather for the tourists who had jammed the lavish hotels and condos of the marina area. Why they preferred to stay locked up like wealthy prisoners in their expensive confinement had always perplexed her. Not because she couldn't understand that they wanted protection and the temporary luxury of a timeshare, but because she could never stand for such a sheltered existence herself. For that reason, she had chosen to live in the quarter adjacent to Old Town in the Zona Romantica, a small area of steep cobblestone streets, restaurants, and cafés and a vibrant gay nightlife. It was also the hub of the very large expat community that made the city an epicenter of mostly English-speaking nationalities: mostly Americans, but with a sprinkling of Brits and Canadians.

On the way out of the office, she stopped at her assistant's desk to say: "I've got to go to the police station, Nando. Not sure when I'll be back. But you can deal with anything that comes up."

Nando looked up from a document he was reading and asked: "Anything serious?"

"Could be a murder, I'm afraid. They think the victim's an American."

"Will you be back later?"

"Probably. If they have an identification, I'll need to start calling the United States to notify his family."

"And we can expect them to come to Puerto Vallarta, right?"

"Right!"

"And that will make trouble for us."

"Right again."

Amanda hailed one of the yellow taxis that always seemed to be parked in front of the Consulate and gave the driver the address. He turned to stare at her when she said, "The Tourist Police Station," and she could see he was curious. But she looked away, pretending to be preoccupied by the scene out the window. For the remainder of the trip, she watched the traffic stop and start along the dusty highway. Twenty minutes later, after crossing into Old Town, they arrived at the front entrance of the compound. She paid the bloated price—not bothering to argue about the "gringo surcharge" as she often called it—and walked through the gatcd entrance and entered the building.

Stopping at the front desk, she asked for Captain Gonzalez and then waited for the policeman to emerge through the double doors that led into the back part of the building with its offices and, she knew, a basement where there were several cells, a few interrogation rooms, and a small morgue.

"Ah, Señora Pennyworth," the policeman said as he emerged from the swinging doors, extending his hand. "Thank you for coming so promptly. Please, come back and sit at my desk. We can talk better there."

After he made way for her to enter, bowing slightly with exaggerated courtesy, she followed him along a corridor that passed by a large open work space with a scattering of cluttered desks. A knot of male officers standing by one of the large windows stared at her as they walked by and she thought she could feel their eyes assessing her movements. When they reached the end of the hall, Gonzalez stood in the open doorframe of a small office, so close that she had pass near enough to him to catch the scent of some variety of strong cologne. For a moment, she wondered if all of this excessive politeness was a disguised antagonism... or something else.

"Please sit down, Señora," he said, indicating the chair that was positioned in front of his desk. "We don't know much yet about your American because the autopsy has not been finished. But we are certain, at least, that he was murdered."

"And you are sure he's an American? Did you find anything to identify him?"

Gonzalez sat down opposite her and opened a solitary file placed in front of him on the desk.

"There was a wallet in his room with a name and address in Los Angeles on a card inside. A 'Jeremy Blackman.' I have it for you."

"And that's all you found? No driver's license. No passport? Nothing with a photograph? No money?"

"We are certain that he was robbed. His wallet was empty when we searched his room, except for this. The key, which he should have kept with him, was also missing. I can only tell you that he was found in the steam room in the basement, and as yet we have no idea what exactly happened. But we should be able to find the thief. We have a list of the IDs of all of the patrons at the sauna and my officers and I expect to find the killer quickly."

"Did he have a watch or was anything else stolen?"

"I have no idea. But you should not bother yourself with such details. Let the police find the man who did this. You just need to notify the family so we can eventually release the body."

Amanda had no doubt of the meaning underneath his confidence: "You do what's unpleasant and then stay out of my way; don't make trouble! We'll decide who is guilty.

And we certainly don't want your help."

Gonzalez pulled a small pad of paper from his desk drawer and took the insurance card from the file. He copied down the victim's name and address, and ripped off the top sheet. He passed it to her and then stood up abruptly.

"Thank you for coming so quickly. And please, you can be of help if you will notify the family, and once you find them, keep them from interfering. I'm sure you can do that. But when you speak to them, you must insist that we cannot release the body until all our examinations are complete. Do you understand?"

"Of course. There are procedures..."

Amanda took the paper, folded it without looking, and stood up. Gonzalez made no gesture to see her out of the station: quite clearly his polite attitude ended with the last sentence of the interview. And his meaning was clear enough even if she had no intention of acknowledging it: don't get involved. She had been warned.

Back at the office by early afternoon, Amanda ignored the insistent groans of her empty stomach. Sitting at her desk, she called Nando in and gestured for him to sit down. She knew the answer to all the questions she intended to ask him, but, at the same time, she wanted reassurance that she was making the right decision.

"It's a rather delicate situation," she began. "An American has been murdered in the gay bathhouse in the Zona... I'm sure you know about it. Certainly, it's no secret to anyone living in Puerto Vallarta, I'm sure, if *I've* heard about it. Anyway, we have his name and an address in Los Angeles. Could be his apartment or a house or, if he lives with his parents, theirs. Anyway, I need to inform someone as soon as possible and I have a choice: either I call them, just like that... a cold call with awful news. Or I wait to contact the local police and they can send out a team of grief counselors. I don't even know if his parents are still living, although the Tourist Police said he was young, so they probably are. Or maybe he lives with someone at the address we have... another man or a woman. But I'm guessing it's a man.

"You see the dilemma, don't you, Nando? If he's in the closet, I would be revealing his death in addition to something they may not know, and..."

"*Closet*? That word?" Nando interrupted.

"Sorry. It's just an odd American expression for hiding your sexual identity. I've never really thought about it, but I guess it assumes that everyone who's gay starts out by hiding... in the closet. And 'coming out' means to let everyone know."

A strange expression, she thought, and what a quirky mind she had to be explaining American slang at such a serious moment. Why, she wondered, did she always hide behind words when she confronted something she didn't understand? Maybe words were her closet?

"In any case," she started again, "if he has been leading a secret life of some sort, it might be news to his parents. Certainly not as terrifying as his murder. But who knows how people will react?"

"I see the problem," he said.

"Except there's more. If I can find a telephone number, then I can inform them immediately, awful as the news will be. Otherwise, there might be a long wait until the American police can manage to visit. And to complicate things, if he was living alone, then no one will be at the address we have, and we'll have to find his family in another way. You see... the delay."

"Yes, they will want to know immediately, I understand."

"What would you do, Nando?"

"I think you have already decided, Señora."

"Maybe, but I still want your advice."

"You could find a telephone number for the address and call. I'm sure that's what the police would do anyway, before they sent anyone out. Just to be sure they have the right person. And then you could decide how much to tell them depending on who answers. Maybe less of a shock if you do it."

Amanda didn't respond for a moment. She looked intently at Nando, thinking that this very ordinary-looking, middle-aged man, with stark black hair and a bronze complexion, someone who would never be singled out in a crowd, was the perfect employee—tactful, smart, and always willing to take up the slack in the duties of the Consulate. And someone who pretty much anticipated her thoughts.

"I agree," she said. "Why don't you place a call to the Embassy in Mexico City? I'll speak to the Ambassador or vice-Consul and they can contact the Los Angeles police to get the number. It'll speed things up maybe. The more official, the better."

"Won't they wonder why? Are you sure you want to involve them?"

"You're probably right. I hadn't thought of the consequences and I'd rather not explain just now since I really don't know much. Maybe I should call the Los Angeles police directly. Then we can decide how to proceed."

"All right, Señora. I will telephone the United States right now and when I have someone on the line, I'll buzz you."

He stood up and turned to leave the office.

"Yes, do that," she called after him.

Watching him through the glass in the upper half of her office door, she saw him speaking soundlessly, gesturing with his right hand as he talked. She glanced down at the pile of work to be done and opened the top folder. A few minutes later, her intercom buzzed and she picked up the receiver.

"I have someone from the Los Angeles Police Department, but she insists on some sort of confirmation."

"Okay, Nando," she said. "Put her through."

"Hello," she replied immediately when she heard the contact made, "This is Amanda Pennyworth from the American Consulate in Puerto Vallarta, Mexico. Who am I speaking to?"

"Officer Benson, LAPD. I can see from the caller ID that you are calling from Mexico. Your assistant said you needed information on a resident here."

"Yes, I'm afraid a young American has been murdered here in Puerto Vallarta. We have his name and an address in Los Angeles but no telephone number or any way to contact his family; no cellphone, passport, or other identification found on the body. I thought you could trace the location for me."

"Yes, if you give me the address, I can find a telephone number if there's a land line. Not so sure about that these days, though, especially if he's young. Probably only has a cellphone. But let me have it anyway, and I'll get back to you. Do you intend to call or do you want us to? Or if there's no telephone, we could send someone out."

"I'm not sure what to do," Amanda replied, hesitating. "Perhaps when we know the number, we can decide."

"Fine. I'll get back to you." The woman hung up and Amanda replaced the receiver absently into its cradle.

"Okay," she said to herself. But she knew this wasn't okay despite saying out loud what she knew to be untrue. She couldn't help herself, but she always managed to get caught up in a sticky web of complications. And she was afraid this would be the case. Being the bearer of doubly bad news—that one's son had died and in a gay sauna—would pile surprise upon grief for his family in a manner that she could only imagine. This had to be the worst part of her job: to inform someone's family of an accident or a death. It hadn't happened often, but it was always distressing. Certainly worse than the tedium of visa applications and complaints about stolen wallets or fraudulent promises of Airbnbs; this was a life and death matter—a death matter, she corrected herself. And here she was caught like a fly in a web watching the approaching shadow of her misery.

She was too nervous to concentrate, so she walked into the reception area where Nando was talking to a Mexican woman.

"I'll take care of this," she said.

"No need," Nando replied. "I'm just finishing. Just needs your signature when I'm done."

"I'm sorry. That's fine. Sure. I just thought..."

She turned around and re-entered her office, angry at her own impatience.

Just as she sat down at her desk, the intercom buzzed.

"For you, Señora," Nando said and switched the call to her receiver.

She was amazed that the Los Angeles Police had worked so rapidly to find the telephone number, but she was mistaken. Her surprise was even greater when a man's voice that she did not recognize explained in Spanish that the Tourist Police were close to solving the mysterious murder of the American.

"We have the names and addresses of all the Mexican visitors to the sauna. We've excluded the Americans and other foreigners because this seems to be a simple case of robbery and they are not likely suspects. I can assure you we'll make an arrest soon."

"That's good news," she replied, but not certain that this quick resolution would hold up. Things had a way of becoming complicated.

"And have you located his family yet?" the man continued.

"Is this Officer Gonzalez? I'm sorry, I didn't recognize your voice at first."

"Yes."

"Well, I've put in a call to Los Angeles and I'm waiting for some sort of result. I'll be in touch as soon as I know something."

"I hope that will be soon. It will look very bad for us if the body remains here... it would only be worse if we cannot catch up with the culprit. That is why we must work quickly."

"I will let you know as soon as I have any information."

He hung up, and Amanda sat for a moment still gripping the phone. It was clear to her that the local police were anxious to get rid of the body and hide the murder away as fast as possible. Allowing it to go unsolved would just fester into an outbreak of panic among tourists and bad publicity for the city. Even if it meant arresting someone who was innocent they would probably act quickly. Or worse, maybe arresting someone who had robbed the victim but hadn't killed him, which would utterly confuse everything. Would they even consider if there were two crimes instead of one, she wondered? There was absolutely no reason to conclude this yet, but if the murder and robbery were separate crimes with different motives, how on earth could the police, who were careening toward a judgment like a car running out of control on one of the twisting mountain roads to the north—how could they solve such a complicated case? Would they even be interested? And if she decided there were grounds to think so and she said something, her advice would most certainly be ignored. It would be best to put these questions aside. If she insisted on meddling, it was probably based on some exaggerated belief in her ability to solve mysteries. Let the Mexican police alone. As usual she was entertaining the preposterous.

This back-and-forth conversation with herself was a bothersome habit that often distracted her from paying attention to the brute facts of the world. She had a writer's imagination that couldn't be tamed but had no ability or patience to work out on paper the plots she invented. Too often her wild speculations led her to wander in dark corridors of fantasy, where all the doors opened into even deeper mysteries. To put it bluntly, she was probably inventing a complexity that didn't exist.

And yet... if Captain Morelos were here, she might have persuaded him to look more carefully at the circumstances of the murder. But that was no longer possible. And Gonzalez? Not a chance! The very definition of stubborn masculine arrogance!

A sudden awareness that the room was darkening interrupted her dreamy dialogue. Through the window behind her desk, she could now see that the city remained luminous in the fading day, changing colors as the sun washed the white buildings in burnt orange and the sky turned to a deep blue that shrouded the forested mountain in the distance in a black veil. Reluctant to switch on the light, she studied the obscuring sky. She realized, of course, that her brief reverie was an effort to avoid thinking about the delicate task that lay before her. Once the Los Angeles Police telephoned with a contact for the victim—his family, friend, or lover (it didn't matter who)—she would have to reveal what had happened. Break the news. What an appropriate cliché, she thought. Indeed, she would have to break something fragile—an illusion about the boy that would be shattered forever, when she conveyed the news of his shabby demise.

After several more minutes, and just as she was just preparing to leave for home, the intercom buzzed. Hesitating for a second, she cleared her throat and answered.

"There's a call from Los Angeles you were waiting for," Nando informed her.

"Thanks, Nando. And you should go home now. Don't wait around for me. Just switch all the incoming messages directly to my phone."

There was a click and she replied, "Amanda Pennyworth speaking."

"This is Officer Benson from the LAPD again. I wanted to inform you that the telephone number of your victim is, as I expected, a cellphone. The company has released the address of the owner, which is the same address you gave us in Los Angeles. So it must be the victim's. We are sending a team out now to check the property, and I will get back to you when I know more. I'm sorry I don't have anything more substantial to tell you. But I'll call you later tonight or tomorrow after our visit. Please let me have your cellphone so I can contact you directly."

"Thanks, Officer Benson," Amanda replied. She gave her the number, repeating it slowly, and then hung up. There was nothing more to do but catch a taxi back to the Zona Romantica to her apartment, take a quick shower, and then wander along the beach choosing among her favorite restaurants overlooking the sea. Tonight she deserved as much.

When she emerged into her bedroom an hour later, refreshed and, she had to admit, ravenous, she stepped into a flowered dress, put on a pair of sandals, picked up her purse, and walked out of the apartment, through the small garden in front of the apartment building, and onto the steep and broken sidewalk leading down toward the ocean.

It was only three blocks to the boardwalk—in this case the broad, undulating cement passageway called the Malecon—that followed the crescent curve of the bay that molded the city, its northern hotel area, the populous city center, and the Zona where she lived. The tropical darkness had fallen suddenly but the tips of rough waves of the ocean were luminous in the moonlight. Most of the restaurants she frequented were actually set out on the sloping expanse of shore. Tonight, she just chose the closest one. Walking on wooden planks set on the sand past a covered bar area and indoor settings that never seemed to have any clients, she emerged from the tent-like structure onto the beach where several tables were placed in the sand. Approaching the nearest empty one, she stood for a moment as the head waiter rushed over to her waving a menu.

"Hello, Miguel," she said.

"Señora, how nice of you to dine with us tonight. Please sit."

He made the elaborate gesture of holding her chair, clumsily because the legs were stuck in the sand, and when she was seated, reached over her shoulder to light a small candle placed at the center of the table. Its feeble light was just a trembling flicker in the glow of the city reflecting off the water which was the only real illumination. But it was enough to read the familiar menu.

Still hovering, Miguel inquired: "A margarita, Señora? I think I remember: limón with salt. Am I correct?"

"Indeed, and yes, please. And I'll have the Coco Shrimp."

"Excellent choice," he answered.

Of course Amanda knew that any choice she made would win his enthusiasm. But instead of offending her, she was delighted by his desire to please. She needed a calm interlude before the next phone call from the United States.

As she sat sipping her margarita and listening to the murmur of voices from the tables around her, she relaxed for the first time that day. Glancing around, she focused on a group of four women chatting enthusiastically—probably Americans, from one of the hotels in the marina area who had descended to the lively part of town for an evening of adventure among the natives. Two beach troubadours dressed in white with red bandanas around their necks approached them and began to sing in a broken harmony—something off-key, raucous, and indistinguishable. One of them strummed a guitar. Obviously uncomfortable, one of the women tried to wave them away, but the men just carried on with more enthusiasm.

Amanda wondered what the women would think if they knew about the strangled victim, the American boy lying in cold anonymity in the basement of the police compound nearby. Or about the place where his body was found? Would they be so giddy with delight in their search for authentic ambience? Would they even dare venture out on such an evening if they knew? Or would they shrink back behind the comfort and protection of one of the high-rise resorts with its private police, lush gardens, and gated entries?

To imagine such questions was to answer them. Which made her more eager for the police to solve whatever mystery was involved with the boy's death as soon as possible and without her. Otherwise, she knew she would be flooded with visits and telephone calls from worried tourists. Whenever a serious crime was reported (and the news spread quickly from the local newspaper to the hotels and bars of the city and eventually to the high-rise timeshares) there was always a worried response from visiting Americans—sometimes even from the large expat community. And the last thing she wanted was anyone's advice. With the smallest suspicion, the least infraction, fear itself would impel people to seek reassurance from the

Consulate. As if there was something she could do other than rehearse platitudes: "I'm sure the local police will solve the case immediately. There's no cause for alarm. The crime rate in Puerto Vallarta is far less than elsewhere in Mexico... or any American city for that matter."

In fact, it didn't matter *what* she said in response to such visits or phone calls, it was her tenor of voice that assured, and she had practiced and mastered the necessary tones to convey confidence and calm. It was one of the demands of her job. "Ways to master the sounds of poise and reassurance"—as she had afterwards dubbed one session in her training course.

Midway through her meal, she heard the cellphone stowed in her purse buzz faintly. It had been a mistake to bring it along, she thought, but an even greater problem if she missed an important call from the Los Angeles police. When she answered, she recognized the familiar voice of Officer Benson.

"I'm sorry to disturb you, but I thought it wasn't too late to call. We've been out to Venice and visited the address of the victim. It's a small apartment building, although no one answered the door. We were able to speak to one of the neighbors and she indicated that two young men had occupied the apartment for over a year. Where they might be now, she couldn't say, but she thought she remembered them waiting in front of the building with suitcases for an Uber—she imagined to the airport. Nothing more and she couldn't recall the exact date. So my guess is that the other American is still in Puerto Vallarta— at least that's a reasonable conclusion. We will probably enter the apartment if we don't hear anything further from your end. Perhaps we can find the location of his parents or other relatives in an address book or on a letter. I thought you'd like to know right away."

"Yes, thank you," Amanda replied. "I'll call the police here tomorrow morning and see if they've found anything else. I'll get back to you. Thanks again."

She turned off her cellphone, stuffed it back in her bag and stared down at her unfinished dinner. "But no thanks," she said softly to herself and looked around for Miguel to settle her bill.

CHAPTER 3

The next morning, she awoke with the sun streaming through the slatted blinds of her bedroom window, creating an irregular pattern of light and dark on the tiled floor. Like every day during the dry season, it promised to be hot and bright—perfect for tourists who would flock onto boats chugging out to the adventure park or to the sandy coves to the south. When she first arrived, she had taken several day-long trips on these "daiquiri cruises," as she called them because of their endless free drinks. For those who remained in town there were the souvenir shops that seemed to sprout on every corner, restaurants, and markets, or they could wander down to Los Muertos Beach to gape at the swimmers and sun bathers. Little would anyone suspect that this ominous-sounding name came from a long-past pirate raid in the area or that a very real corpse—an actual *muerto*—lay just a few blocks inland inside the gloomy basement morgue of the police station. She bolted upright suddenly and tossed off the covers as she pictured herself, lying pale and cold under a sheet on a steel necropsy table. For a moment she envied the ignorance of the tourists. It would be so much nicer to be oblivious... if she could. But death seemed so selfish that she could only think of herself.

She got out of bed quickly, as if to abandon such thoughts. And after a long, hot shower and breakfast, she took a taxi to the Consular Office arriving just as Nando was sitting down at his desk in the reception area.

"Good morning, Señora," he exclaimed. "A beautiful day, no?"

"We'll see," she replied. "That will depend, won't it, on what we can find out about our victim?"

"Do you know anything more?"

"Barely. I spoke to the Los Angeles Police last night and they located his apartment. It turns out that he probably came to Puerto Vallarta with his roommate or a friend. At least that's what they concluded. But nothing else. No information on his parents and that's a shame because they need to be informed as soon as possible. I'm worried about finding them."

"Of course; I understand."

Continuing into her office, she sat down at the desk and turned on her computer, arranging pencils and a notepad in neat symmetry beside the pile of work to which she needed to attend. She understood that this attention to the precise spacing in front of her was a sign of worry— an attempt to impose order on a worrisome situation. But somehow it made her feel in command and composed when she faced what she knew would be a very unpleasant task.

It took her several minutes to focus her thoughts on

the papers that had accumulated for her attention, but she gradually became absorbed in the busy work that always gave her so much pleasure. When she first joined the Service she had been warned that not everyone was cut out to be a Consular Officer, but somehow she found the changing demands of her job completely absorbing. She enjoyed the small victories in overcoming a bureaucratic snarl as much as confronting the inevitable misfortunes that happened to her countrymen on vacation. Perhaps it was just her penchant for solving crossword puzzles, looking up the meanings of new words and synonyms; her interest in math problems. This had made her a very critical (and often disappointed) reader of mystery novels because she regularly figured out the ending before trudging through the slush of false leads until the last evidence was revealed. She was only ever bested by Miss Marple, but then Agatha Christie didn't play fair, keeping the tangled skein of relationships explaining the murder stitched up in her inevitable knitting until she unraveled the surprise and implausible ending.

Toward noon, and with a rapidly diminishing pile of papers waiting for her attention and to be shuffled from left to right on her desk, the intercom buzzed and Nando forwarded a call from Captain Gonzalez.

"I finally have news for you, Señora. There are two interesting developments this morning. As you know, we will soon identify all of the Mexicans who were at the sauna during the murder and robbery, and we think they are probably all still in Puerto Vallarta. We shall interview each of them shortly and it's only a matter of time before we find evidence linking one of them to the crime. Then you may rest comfortably knowing that we have solved the case. But of course I shall inform you of our progress. Second is that a young American came to the station earlier today asking for information about his friend, the same Mr. Blackman, who he said was missing. I had to tell him that this person was dead, although I supplied no details. We took him into the basement where he identified the body. And I believe that he will visit you shortly with information about his family so that the body may be sent back to the United States. Once that is done, and I hope quickly, all the details will be completed and there will be no further disruptions or false rumors to frighten tourists."

"I'll be very happy to talk to the young man when he arrives, but I wonder if you aren't being hasty, Señor. Could it be that you are more interested in reassuring tourists than actually solving a murder? And what about the Americans who were at the sauna? Aren't you even interested in them? His friend, for example?"

"Please, Señora, you completely misunderstand me. It's just that everything seems completely clear and uncomplicated: a simple robbery gone wrong. So, please: you should pay attention to your duties—just as I am doing to mine." His careful, blunt words only added to the anger and contempt in his voice. Amanda was tempted to reply, but before she could say anything, he added, "And I have instructed the young American not to leave Puerto Vallarta just yet. Just a precaution. We may need him to identify the killer if he can."

"Or perhaps something else?" she added, surprised at his haste.

"No, Señora. He is not a suspect. You will not interfere."

The line went dead. This unpleasant man, she thought

as she put the receiver down, was giving her instructions. Well, she would wait for the victim's friend to appear and then she might well decide to interfere.

A little after one in the afternoon, as Amanda spread out the meager lunch she had brought from home, Nando came to the door of her office and, after knocking, opened it halfway. "There's someone to see you," he said softly, "and I think he is an American."

"Send him in."

Amanda stood and walked around the edge of her desk as a young man edged hesitantly through the doorway. He was wearing torn jeans and a white T-shirt with *Los Muertos Beach* splashed across the front and the design of a skull in black immediately underneath. The worried look on his face barely distorted his striking features: long blond hair completely shaved on one side, deep blue eyes, and skin the color of tarnished bronze.

"I'm Archie West," he said. "I've just come from the police station where I identified Jeremy's body. It was so terrible to see him there in that horrible basement lying under a sheet. That officer—someone named "Gonzaga"?—told me what had happened or what he thought had happened. I don't know what to do. He said to come here; that you'd help me." He was clearly on the verge of breaking down.

"It's Officer Gonzalez, Mr. West. Just sit down, please."

She was tempted to put her hand on his shoulder, to comfort him, but wondered if he would shrink away at such overt sympathy.

"I'm very sorry about Mr. Blackman—that was his name, right?" She was about to sit on the empty chair next to him but then thought it best to be more formal, so she resumed her seat behind the desk, pushing her lunch aside.

"Yes. I was very worried when he hadn't come back to the hotel last night, so I asked the management if they had seen him, and they sent me to the police station. That's where I identified his body. It was terrible. Really awful. I've never seen a dead person before. Lying on that table in the horrid room. And him... he..." His voice broke as he choked back a sob.

"I'm sorry," she repeated. And then it puzzled her as she thought about it: "Something I don't understand. Why didn't you report him missing a day ago? He obviously didn't come back to your hotel at night. Weren't you sharing a room?"

"I don't know, Ms...?"

"Pennyworth. Amanda Pennyworth."

"We were at the sauna together. I thought maybe he went home with someone."

"I don't mean to pry, but didn't that disturb you?"

"Well, yes, of course it did. I was upset. We're together... You know what I mean *together*. But sometimes... well, you know, you just go off with some other guy. Wouldn't have meant anything. Just happens sometimes. But I didn't think... I never imagined that he had been murdered. God! It's so awful. What a terrible place this is! So dangerous! I had no idea. Never would have come here!" He buried his face in his hands and began to sob quietly.

"I'm sorry," he continued after a moment, looking up and wiping his eyes with his bare arm. "Really sorry, but you know..."

"I understand," Amanda said automatically. "But I

really need to ask you some questions. About his family. I need to contact them. They'll want to take the body back to the United States. Do you have any information about where they might be and how I can contact them?"

"His mother and father are divorced."

"And...?"

"His Dad lives up the coast near Portland. I've never been there, but Jeremy always talked about the town he grew up in: Multnomah Village. He hated it; stupid little place with a stupid name, he always said. But I think his father still lives there, maybe even in the same house. Don't know his job or if he's retired. But it shouldn't be hard to find him. Jeremy always talked about how mean and small the town was: like a dysfunctional family, he said. As for his mother, she's moved away to San Juan Capistrano south of LA. I don't have the address, but we visited her a couple of times. She sells houses. And I think she kept the name Blackman. You could find her easy enough."

He looked exhausted and frightened as if giving the information had made the reality of his friend's death even more real and shocking.

"Why would anyone do this?" he asked. "The cop said it was a robbery. But why would anyone kill him for a few pesos? I think that's all he had. I don't get it."

"I don't understand any better than you do, Mr. West."

"Archie, please."

"Okay, Archie. But I do agree it's best that you stick around town until his parents come. I'll try to contact them."

"That's fine, I guess. Anyway, the cops said I shouldn't leave just yet. So I'm going to change my airline ticket. We were supposed to go home tomorrow. But I don't want to meet up with his father. They weren't speaking. Mom's okay, I guess, if you like that sort."

"'That sort'?"

"You know. Baked brown skin from too much sun. Lots of gold jewelry. And tough as nails. Real estate broker. Really thin. I think she's made lots of money. Anyway..." He looked guilty as if repeating these descriptions, probably borrowed from his friend, made him seem unkind, even nasty. "I don't mean to..."

"It's okay, Archie. I understand. Why don't you wait in the reception area just in case I need you while I try to locate his parents? Or better, get yourself something to eat and come back in an hour or so. I hope I'll have some information for you then. And when you pass by my assistant's desk, please give him all your contact information here: hotel, address, cellphone etc."

"Okay, ma'am."

He stood up and walked out the door stopping to speak to Nando.

Amanda looked down at the telephone and then said softly to herself: "Right... ma'am, is it?" But then she thought bitterly, what was she expecting, *mademoiselle*?

After a reluctant minute or so, she picked up the receiver and asked Nando to call Officer Benson in Los Angeles. Almost immediately, the call went through.

"Officer Benson, this is Amanda Pennyworth in Puerto Vallarta again. I have what I hope is enough information for you to locate Jeremy Blackman's parents. They're divorced. Father lives in Multnomah Village up near Portland—it's a little place apparently—and the mother, same last name, is a real estate broker in San Juan

Capistrano. Shouldn't be hard to find either one of them."

"I think you're right. I'll call you back when I have more information. And thanks."

"Thank you!"

Amanda hung up and then walked out to the reception area.

"Why don't you go out for some lunch, Nando. I'll stay here. The Los Angeles Police will probably call."

"Okay."

"Did Mr. West leave his number and address?"

"Yes, it's on this sheet," he said, handing her the top page from a tablet on his desk. "I also put a copy in my files."

"Good," she said and returned to her office. Ignoring her lunch, she sat down and swiveled her chair around so she could look out the window at the city and the backdrop of mountains. The scene was usually soothing with the pastel colors of the sunlit houses set against the dark forest that covered the steep peaks. There was one patch of woods that always caught her eye—a large grove of palm trees growing wild about halfway up the nearest hill. It appeared a much brighter green than the rest, its restless fronds shimmering in the breeze and intense light. Today, however, she just stared at the scene without really seeing it.

"This is making me nervous," she said out loud. "And I'm also talking to myself."

For the next half hour, she concentrated on a petition from an American businessman who had complained of difficulty getting permission to build a new warehouse on the outskirts of the city near the airport. But instead of calling one of her contacts in government or notifying the economic officer at the Guadalajara Consulate right away, she decided to wait for Officer Benson. She hardly noticed when Nando returned and only then when he buzzed her on the intercom.

"Your call from the States, Señora," he said, switching over the line.

"Yes, Amanda Pennyworth here."

"It's Officer Benson. I found two telephone contacts for you, the father and mother. Please write them down. And if there is anything else I can do, let me know. Good luck!"

"Yes, and thanks." She hung up after recording the numbers. No hope that anyone else could undertake what she had to do immediately: call the parents and tell them. And as for good luck? That had already turned bad.

She stood up and stretched, aware suddenly of how stiff she had become locked in a position of anticipation. Walking out into the reception area, she gave Nando the two numbers she had written down.

"Will you call these numbers for me, please, Nando? You don't mind waiting a few more minutes to leave; I know you asked to go early today. Telephone the mother first. And when I finish talking, I'll take the second call."

She wanted to apologize again, but she knew she would just be repeating herself. Instead, she turned around and headed back into the office, waiting for the first call to come through. It was better, she thought, that each of them would hear Nando's voice first, telephoning from Mexico. It would be a modicum of warning that something had happened. The rest was her burden, even though she had no intention of indicating that the boy was murdered or under what circumstances. Enough of a shock just to report his death!

"Your party, a Mrs. Blackman, Señora," Nando announced a minute later.

The person at the other end sounded irritated and rushed: "I don't know who this is I'm talking to or what you might want, but I hope it's important; it had better be. I had to step out of a closing."

"This is Amanda Pennyworth, American Consul in Puerto Vallarta. It's about your son, Jeremy."

"Yes. I have a son by that name. What's the problem? Not drugs, I hope. Everyone down there is on drugs from what I read in the paper. What did he do? Drink too much?"

"I'm afraid it's much more serious." She paused and then resumed. "I'm afraid that your son is dead."

"Dead? No. I think not! He's in perfect health! You must have the wrong party."

"There's no doubt about it," Amanda said firmly. "I'm very sorry to tell you, but he has definitely passed away. His body was identified by his friend Archie West, who's also here in Puerto Vallarta. I'm sure you'll want to come to Mexico as soon as possible to retrieve the body. I believe that the coroner and the police will release him to you for whatever arrangements you decide to make. I'll also be telephoning Mr. Blackman."

There was silence at the other end. And then, the woman resumed: "I'll have to get back to you. I'm in the middle of something very important right now." She hung up abruptly.

Amanda was shocked by her indifference, unless it was just a defense against the horrible news that her son had died.

A few minutes later, the intercom buzzed again and

Nando indicated that he had the father on the line.

She waited a moment and then began: "This is Amanda Pennyworth from the American Consulate in Puerto Vallarta, Mexico. I'm calling about your son, Jeremy."

There was no response.

"I'm very sorry to inform you that he has passed away. I think you will probably want to come to Puerto Vallarta to make arrangements to return the body to the United States."

"So that's where he went. Never tells me a thing or says a word to me. His mother thinks she can take care of everything. She'll do what she wants no matter what I say, anyway. Did you inform her? First? Yeah, I suppose you did."

"Yes, I did, sir, but in all honesty, don't you want to see your son?"

"Are you telling me what I should or shouldn't want? Damned government intruding in my life. I haven't had anything to say to him for years. Ever since he..."

"As you wish, sir, but..."

"Okay. Okay. It would give her too much satisfaction if I didn't show up. I'll be there as soon as I can get a flight. Puerto Vallarta, you say? Where's that?"

"It's on the Mexican coast south of Baja California. There's a fair-sized airport here; I'm sure you won't have any trouble getting a flight. Perhaps you want to come to my office after you arrive, and I'll take you and your ex-wife to police headquarters."

"So he was in trouble. I'm not surprised, given his lifestyle. That's what comes of—"

"I'll expect you here, then," Amanda interrupted. "Hang on and I'll have my assistant give you the address and my number."

"Fine."

Amanda switched him back to Nando and sat for a moment stunned at what she had heard... and not heard. What sort of parents were these? How would they react when they learned how and where Jeremy had died? Could they be any more indifferent or self-centered? She had certainly expected better.

It was well into late afternoon and as the window behind her darkened, it seemed to suck the light from the room, Amanda sat in the semi-obscurity at her desk, waiting to hear from either parent about their arrival plans. Although it was after six, she decided to linger a few more minutes, staring at the silent telephone, as if she could compel it to ring. But there was only silence, so she finally picked up the large bag that served as a purse and briefcase, shoved a few papers into it that she might or might not attend to at home, and walked out of the office into the dimly lit reception area. As she did, the phone on Nando's desk buzzed, and she reached over to pick it up.

The voice at the other end didn't wait for her to answer but began immediately: "This is the American Consulate, right? Nora Blackman here. I'm arriving tomorrow at noon on American Airlines. Please arrange to have someone at the airport to pick me up. I'll give you the flight number..."

"I'm afraid we can't do that, Mrs. Blackman," Amanda stopped her. "But you can take a taxi to the office. I can give you the address but any driver will know where we are."

"I would think under the circumstances..."

"Sorry, but we don't offer limousine service. Just walk straight out of the airport. Don't stop until you get outside and don't take an offer of a ride until you exit. Just plow through all the confusion. There will be a line of taxis waiting."

"And wouldn't you know it, my *ex* actually telephoned me this afternoon. To say he's arriving around the same time. Haven't heard from him for over a year and now this. Same baloney, though!"

"Then I'll expect you tomorrow. And please let me tell you how sorry I am about your son."

"Yes," she said and hung up. And then Amanda realized that Mrs. Blackman hadn't bothered to ask how he died.

Amanda spent a restless night, worrying about how to handle the situation that faced her the next day—challenging because of the circumstances, and doubly so because of the impossible personalities she now knew she would have to confront. She had no idea whether she would be called upon to be grievance counselor or referee between two brawling divorcees or both. Besides that, there were the circumstances of Jeremy's death that she had to describe, not just the seedy place, which was bad enough, but the manner of his murder and then the robbery. Sometimes in dreams, she found an answer, waking up fresh with determination and a solution that her unconscious mind had discovered. More than once she had marched straight from bed in the morning to the unfinished crossword puzzle lying on the table next to the couch, and filled in all the words that had stumped her. But not tonight, and not this morning! Everything remained a problematic blur.

After picking at her breakfast of overcooked eggs and burnt toast—she couldn't concentrate—she traveled to the Consulate by taxi and arrived just as Nando was admitting several clients. She greeted them and walked into her office, leaving the door ajar. She was grateful for what promised to be a busy morning of small problems to distract her from the looming confrontation with the Blackmans. And the time passed much as she anticipated: two Americans who had lost (or misplaced) their passports—half the time they would be discovered in some unexpected corner of a hotel room; a visa application from a student who had been admitted to Rice University in Texas; and the return visit of a businessman who was struggling through the impenetrable layers of Mexican bureaucracy to open a franchise business.

Nora Blackman was the first to arrive, around noon, announced by a faint yapping, which caused Amanda to get up from her desk and peer out the office door window into the reception area.

What she saw was not so much an arrival but a grand entrance, the dog appeared first, its paws flailing and skidding on the tile floor and then its owner gripping the taut end of a leash following behind. Amanda opened the door and watched as Nando half rose out of his seat. Two waiting Mexican clients stared with amazement at the woman who marched to the center of the reception area and then stopped, looking around until she saw Amanda.

"You must be the Consular Officer I spoke to," she said. "We'll need some privacy. In your office I suppose?"

Amanda looked at her and nodded, retreating inside. Nora Blackman followed and sat down on one of the two chairs in front of the desk. She patted her lap and the dog jumped up snuggling her breast and licking at her face.

"Okay, Betsy, Calm down. We're here finally. Be a good girl."

She was everything that Amanda had expected from Archie West's brief description: skin the color of desert sand, dark blond hair and brown eyes, and an expensive-looking green business suit. As she gestured, several gold bracelets ran halfway down to the wrists of her skinny hands. Her long hot-pink nails suggested an expensive salon.

But the dog. Amanda couldn't help but ask: "Did you bring that dog on the airplane?" She recognized it as a Bichon Frise, fluffy and white as a miniature lamb.

"Of course I did. It's my comfort dog. You don't expect me to travel without her, do you? And I had such a terrible time at the airport. My emotional support animal registration had expired—you have to renew the damn thing every year, for God's sake. What a racket! Typical of the government. As if I would need some sort of license. Not that I mind the expense. It's just the bother. Anyway, I told the TSA guy who stopped me that I was coming to pick up the body of my dead son and they had better let me through or else."

Amanda thought that she would not have argued the point very long. "I'm glad you could make it," she began. "It must be terrible for you."

"Has he showed up yet? This'll be our first family reunion since the divorce."

Amanda must have looked shocked because Mrs. Blackman went on quickly: "I'm sorry. I don't mean to be so blunt, but my *ex* and I don't get along. To say the least.

And being upset like this makes me blurt things out."

"I understand."

After a long hesitation, she continued: "Can you explain what happened?"

"I'd prefer to tell you both at the same time. As soon as your ex-husband arrives, we can go to the police station. I telephoned Officer Gonzalez earlier to say that he should expect us sometime late this afternoon."

"So what am I supposed to do, just wait around for him?"

"That's probably best, yes. I can get you a coffee, and you could sit in the reception area if you prefer."

"I think I'll stay here if you don't mind. Betsy doesn't like foreigners. She can be very protective of me."

"A coffee then?"

"Maybe you could send out; I don't suppose there's a Starbucks around. I'll take a double latte, French vanilla, extra sugar."

"All right. I'll ask Nando to go. And I'll have to leave you in here by yourself. Someone has to sit outside in the reception while he's gone."

Amanda stood up, walked around the desk and out of the office. She felt a vague sense of relief, if only momentary, because she knew the terrible part of the day had just begun, and if Mrs. Blackman was any indication...

After he left, she sat at Nando's desk and relaxed, shutting her eyes but then opened them quickly because she suddenly imagined a scene in the chilly basement of the police station with two hostile and frantic parents who despised each other and the dog snarling around the ankles of Officer Gonzalez.

The outer door swung open wide and she expected

Nando to walk in, but instead, a tall, middle-aged American man plowed through carrying an overstuffed shoulder bag. He looked around and dropped it on a chair next to a Mexican woman. Wiping his dripping forehead with a crumpled handkerchief, he walked over and sat down abruptly on the chair in front of the desk in front of Amanda.

"I'm Jeremy's Blackman's father, Edward Blackman. Took the first plane I could get out of Portland; had to change in San Diego. Damn, it's hot here!" And then looking as if he had finally noticed her, he said, "Will you tell the man in charge that I've arrived. He's expecting me."

"That would be me. I'm the Consular Officer," Amanda replied.

"Oh, sorry. Thought I had been talking to a secretary or something earlier. One man show here?"

"That's okay. My assistant is out for the moment. And your ex-wife is waiting in my office."

"Then let me stay here for a moment," he exclaimed. "Not quite ready to confront her yet."

As he stood up and moved away from the desk, Amanda took a moment to study his face. It was noteworthy for its lack of distinction: eyes a washed out blue, a small nose and mouth, smooth pale skin and gray hair cut in military style. Usually, she associated a face and a name with some sort of animal—the better to remember both. But in this instance, nothing came to mind. His voice, however, was memorable: sharp, without resonance, and pronounced with an edge, the ends of his words sliced off by impatience. She wondered if this revealed cruelty or just jitters.

"Okay," he said, jerking his shoulders back: "I'm ready to face her now."

Amanda led him to the door of her office, opened it for him, and followed him in, leaving it ajar so she could keep an eye on the reception area. Mrs. Blackman made no effort to stand up; her only reaction was to clutch her dog closely.

"I see you're still carrying around one of those damned substitute animals, Nora," he said, looking at his ex-wife.

"It's an emotional support animal, Ed," she corrected.

"Please sit down, Mr. Blackman," Amanda said as she slid around to her chair. "I think I ought to tell you a few things before we go to the police station—at least as far as I know them. I'm sure that the coroner and the police can supply more details."

She had thought about this carefully. While she would have to absorb the shock of forewarning them, she thought that learning everything in the frigid atmosphere of the basement morgue at the police station would be unbearable.

"Here's what I know. Your son came to Puerto Vallarta with his friend, a Mr. Archie West. I've spoken to him and he says you know him, Mrs. Blackman. Anyway, the two of them went to a local sauna three days ago. Archie left early, leaving Jeremy behind and only reported him missing the next day when he didn't come back to their hotel. But his body had been discovered earlier when the establishment closed. He had been robbed and murdered. That's all I know so far, except that the police are convinced it was just a robbery. Nothing more."

"Nothing more?" whined Mr. Blackman. "What do you mean a sauna? What kind of place is that?"

"You know perfectly well what it was," his wife said, "Even if you won't admit it to yourself. Your son is gay. So it must have been a gay sauna."

"*Your* son, you mean!"

"Come on, Ed. Stop denying responsibility for once."

"If you hadn't coddled him; like that damned dog you're making love to."

"It's nobody's fault. Certainly not mine! Who cares about things like that? Let's just get through this as quickly as we can. Then you can go back to being the angry hermit of the north."

Amanda felt like holding up her hand to halt this bout, but instead, she asked them both: "Do you know of any reason why someone would want to kill him? I mean aside from robbery?"

"What sort of question is that? What do you suspect?" Mr. Blackman asked.

"I don't mean anything special. It just seems a bit odd to me to kill someone for a few dollars. I just thought..."

"I certainly don't know of any reason, and it's Mexico, isn't it? What do you expect? Isn't that explanation enough?" Mrs. Blackman answered. "Unless you are thinking that his friend did it. Is that what you're implying?"

"I'm not suggesting anything. I just think it's very strange."

"Is it so surprising," asked Mr. Blackman, shaking his head, "given that...?"

At that moment Nando returned to the outer office carrying a paper coffee container and looked in her direction, but Amanda shook her head slightly; he paused and then sat down at his desk.

CHAPTER 4

The three of them plus Betsy, who stopped jumping around once the trip began, sat in the back seat of the yellow and black cab as it bounced along the cobblestone streets of the old city toward the police station.

"My God!" Mrs. Blackman exclaimed. "It's so rough my fillings are going to fall out."

"Dentures don't have fillings," her ex-husband said softly.

"Funny, very funny! Always the jokester when it's at someone else's expense. You don't realize how much you hurt people... or perhaps you do. You can be so ugly sometimes, Ed! You see what he's like!" She turned to Amanda who was sitting on her left by the door, and was about to continue, when the car braked abruptly and then swung into the police compound, stopping in front of the suspended pole blocking the entry gate.

Amanda rolled down her window and called out to the policeman visible just inside a small three-sided shelter.

"We're here to see Officer Gonzalez," she called out. "He's expecting us. I'm Amanda Pennyworth, the US Consul to Puerto Vallarta, and these are the parents of Jeremy Blackman."

The man walked slowly over to the car and put his head in, looking at each of them as if there was something suspicious he might discover with a cursory glance.

"What about that dog?" he asked, pointing to Betsy. "No dog. Can't let him in. This ain't no veterinary hospital."

Mrs. Blackman didn't understand at first but then bristled when she realized what he meant. She was about to answer, when Amanda laid her hand on her sleeve and said: "He can stay in the taxi. You can pay the driver to remain with him." She then informed the policeman.

"All right. Just pull inside and park. But that animal stays in the car."

The guard stepped back and raised the barrier. The taxi pulled into the compound and stopped. Before stepping out of the car, Mrs. Blackman instructed the driver: "Please watch her. She gets very nervous. And if you have to walk her, you can use this leash." She handed him a blue spool with a collar hook on the end of it.

The driver looked puzzled, so Amanda leaned into the window as she was leaving and translated her words, adding: "We will try to hurry, but I'll make sure they pay you well for waiting."

Once inside, Amanda and the Blackman couple stood in the reception area waiting for Officer Gonzalez to appear.

Amanda looked at the two figures fidgeting nervously and shivering despite the oppressive heat in the hallway.

For the first time since they arrived, she felt deeply sorry for this miserable couple. She had been so distracted by their angry exchanges—did they disguise the despair they felt by arguing?—that she hadn't had the energy or a moment to sympathize. And yet, however they might blame each other, she thought, this was a truly terrible situation and it occurred to her (she didn't know) that Jeremy might be an only son—the product of a union, that, however ill-matched, had created another human being who was perhaps the only trace left over from whatever affection had once brought them together. If they had ever loved each other this was truly a sad punctuation to the failure of their marriage. She was on the verge of asking if they had any other children but then thought the better of it. No matter the answer, the question would probably just intensify their grief.

Finally, the doors to the inner offices swung open and Officer Gonzalez strutted out. As always, his appearance commanded attention: a crisp khaki uniform, belted with a wide girth of black leather around his waist, and pants tucked into high leather boots. He greeted the American couple in his strongly accented but acceptable English.

"You are Mr. Jeremy Blackman's parents? I am very sorry for you. Please come back to my office." He opened the door from which he had just emerged and motioned for them to enter.

"You may stay here, Señora Pennyworth. There's no need for you."

"If you don't object, I will come anyway. There may be details that I can help with. And perhaps translate something difficult to understand."

Gonzalez said nothing but nodded, and she brushed by

him and into the large open space with its several mismatched desks arranged in imperfect rows. Several officers, standing around what appeared to be a coffee machine watched the group intently as they passed through.

When they reached the far end with Officer Gonzalez leading the way, he opened a door and ushered them into a small, stuffy room. There was a large desk with a single paper file lying at the center, and several chairs in a semi-circle around it. A dusty window behind it looked out onto the parking lot of the compound. A tired looking Mexican flag hung limp from a brass stand.

"Please sit," he said, pointing to the chairs as he walked around the desk. He remained standing and opened the file, glancing down at it and then back at each of them. Amanda thought for a moment that this tactic was meant to establish his complete control, and restrain however the parents (and she) might react to what he had to say. This was clearly an embarrassing situation for him and for the Mexican police, and his tactic, this pretense of masculine competence, was something she had seen many times before. And knew how effective it could be.

"I am sure this is a very unfortunate situation for you— Mr. and Mrs. Blackman, is it?—but I can assure you that we are doing everything possible to catch the killer of your son. In fact, I expect an arrest momentarily."

"Then you know what happened?" Mrs. Blackman asked. "You are certain?"

"Quite certain. Yes, it had to be a robbery. We know who was at that 'establishment' at the time... or we will soon. We have their identities and there is DNA evidence. I won't explain it, but it is convincing and substantial."

"How did he die?" Mr. Blackman asked.

"Please don't, officer," Mrs. Blackman interrupted. "I don't think I can bear hearing the details. It's enough that you know. And we can take him back with us to the United States?"

"As soon as we release the body, yes. And then it's up to the Consulate to arrange for however you wish to do it."

"Wait a minute," Mr. Blackman interjected. "I, for one, *want* to know more of the details. And I want to see him."

"He has already been identified by his friend. It's not necessary for you. And it could save you the agony."

"I don't care. I insist. To say goodbye. And to know what happened. You've scarcely told us anything. As for you, Nora, you can't just turn your head away like you always do. For once in your life face up to reality! It's our son we're talking about. Not some stray flea bag you picked up at the animal shelter."

"Betsy's not a... Oh, damn you!." She looked at him and then turned to Gonzalez. Amanda could see that she was blushing... from embarrassment or anger.

"All right. Have it your way... Officer, you can tell us how he died. If only to make my ex-husband shut up."

Gonzalez paused for a moment, perhaps surprised at the hostility of this couple: "I can take you to the basement where you can see the body, if you wish. And as to the cause of death, it was by strangulation. We figure prior to the robbery. We are quite sure in fact."

"Did he suffer? Would it have been quick?" Mrs. Blackman asked, as a stricken look flashed across her face, turning her complexion a livid white.

"We are certain of that. There were no signs of a struggle. Either he had been asleep or unconscious at the time."

"How could that be?" asked Mr. Blackman.

"It seems he had consumed a large amount of alcohol. Maybe he felt nothing at all."

Mrs. Blackman put her hands to her mouth in the futile attempt to suppress a sob. "Oh my God!" she exclaimed. "Oh my God!"

"If you'd rather not view the body," Amanda said quickly, "Why not stay here with me. Your ex-husband could go... if he still feels he needs to."

"No, I have to see him. He's not going alone. I need to see him too."

Officer Gonzalez cleared his throat, picked up the telephone, and dialed quickly. He mumbled something indistinct and then walked around to the door, holding it open for the couple to pass through. They did so slowly, so slowly that as Amanda watched, she thought that their hesitant pace looked like the scene from a bad dream where your feet are glued to the ground with long strands of some sticky reluctance clinging to every step.

"Not you... I'm sorry, Señora," Gonzalez said as Amanda moved to follow them.

"I'm going for the same reason as before," she said, slipping past him. "They will want me there, I'm sure. And I promise not to say anything."

He just shook his head with exaggerated disgust, walked past the waiting Blackmans, and led the way down the hallway to the stairwell with metal steps down into the basement where the morgue and autopsy room was located. The steel rungs rang a jumbled cacophony of sounds as they descended.

At the bottom, he continued on down the hallway that

was lit with hanging fluorescent fixtures that swayed slightly as their motion disturbed the air, casting distorted shadows on the walls. Toward the end of the corridor, he stopped in front of a metal door with a half-window. Again, Gonzalez led the way and pushed inside. At one end of the room, Amanda could see Señora Sanchez perched on a stool in front of a high table that held a computer. In the middle of the wall, to her right, was a row of three doors. Amanda was immediately reminded of the columbarium she had once seen at Arlington Cemetery in Washington, DC, except here there was a handle on each front and no name or loving inscription. She shuddered at the cold of the room and the dismal thought that these niches held anonymous bodies waiting in cold storage for burial or dissection.

When she slid off her seat, Gonzalez introduced her: "This is Señora Sanchez, the city patologo. She can tell you more about the murder and, if you still want, you can see the body."

"My deepest sympathy," she said as the couple approached hesitantly. "You will want to make sure this is your son, even though his friend identified the body."

"How did he die?" asked Mrs. Blackman. "Was it quick? I can't bear the thought that he suffered."

"I can't be certain, but I think he probably didn't. He might have been unconscious when it happened. There was considerable alcohol in his blood and he may have overstayed in the steam room. That can make a kind of delirium. Either way, he was probably not fully awake."

"But what happened?"

"I have determined that he died of strangulation. Someone either very strong or maybe in a rage."

"Could you collect DNA from the killer?" Mr. Blackman interrupted.

"There were traces of DNA in the body, yes. And they were intact so we can identify that person."

"I don't understand; you said *in*," he continued, "Not on the body but inside?"

"Yes, he had engaged in intercourse."

"So is that person the killer?"

Gonzalez answered. "We don't know yet, but that is a promising lead."

"How about DNA samples from around the throat?" Amanda broke in.

Señora Sanchez glowered at her. "Of course we thought of that, but the steam and heat in the sauna corrupted any traces left on the skin. He was probably inside for an extended time after he died. And anyway, when his body was moved by the staff at the sauna, everything was disturbed. So all we have is what we have."

"Then you don't know anything, do you?" Amanda asked.

"We will investigate; do not try to tell us what to do, Señora," Gonzalez said hastily. Turning to the parents, he continued. "You can depend on us."

"I want to see him," said Mrs. Blackman, who had been standing with obvious impatience, listening to this exchange. "Now!"

Without another word, Señora Sanchez walked over to the wall, grasped one of the handles, and pulled out a sliding gurney. On it lay the body of Jeremy Blackman half covered with a sheet.

Even from a respectful distance, Amanda could see the greenish tint of his skin and the rough collar of stitches where the coroner had cut into his chest.

Suddenly, Mrs. Blackman let out a low moan and collapsed into her ex-husband's arms. He held her tightly.

"I'm sorry," she said, and then recovering, pushed free. "Let go of me! Don't touch me!" I didn't mean to be... so weak." She shoved him again and then blurted out: "Please, I need to leave now. But if you are wondering, yes, that's my son. That's him... whatever happened?" Looking at her ex-husband's confused face. "How did we let this happen?"

Amanda watched the two as they walked together out of the mortuary room. She thought she could discern an insensible bond between them as they moved together, some unseen energy that passed around them, encircling them in a circumference of grief. And it was the first time either of them used the word *we*. Would this bizarre moment of intimacy last, she wondered? Could it? She doubted it.

And Gonzalez? Amanda caught a strange look on his face as he led them back up the stairs and into the office again. Was it disgust? Anger? Bewilderment? Perhaps he just didn't like Americans... or more likely he might be wondering how this strange couple had ever produced a son.

"Please sit down," he directed. And then addressing Amanda, he continued: "When we have finished here, you can proceed with moving the body to a funeral home, and then the family can decide what to do."

"Yes, of course, officer," she said. "We've handled such cases before and have an arrangement with two very reliable companies. It will be up to Mr. and Mrs. Blackman to decide what they want to do, then." She thought, however, that they were probably not yet ready to make the difficult decision of whether to ship the body back to the United States—and if so, where? She anticipated an argument even over that. Or if they decided to cremate him and take the ashes back on the airplane? Would they divide him half and half, each with an urn on the mantle? These were grizzly issues to resolve, and she wanted to leave the police headquarters as soon as possible. Any hasty decisions made here would probably be regretted.

"Are you ready to release the body?" asked Mr. Blackman, meekly. "Are you finished with it?"

"Almost. Yes, I think Señora Sanchez is done with the autopsy," said Gonzalez. "You can take possession once you have made arrangements."

"But how will we know when you have caught the murderer? I just couldn't feel an end to it until I know," Mrs. Blackman said sternly. "I want to be informed. You shouldn't think that once we've gone back to the US that you can ignore us."

It was clear to Amanda that she had recovered from her lapse into emotion. She was once again a woman with determination baked in like enamel.

"Please feel free to remain in Mexico," Gonzalez replied hastily. "But in any case, whatever you decide, I will inform the Consulate when we have caught the culprit, and they will communicate with you. It's all your choice."

"All right," she said, standing and turning toward the door. "Come on, Ed. I need some fresh air—even if it is ninety-five degrees outside." Without waiting for a response, she marched through the open plan area, ignoring the stares of the few policemen seated at their desks, and out the front door, her ex-husband and Amanda following.

Settling back into the cab, Mrs. Blackman held her dog tightly and mumbled a few words of baby talk into its ear. As the taxi began to move out of the compound, she suddenly announced, "I've decided I have to see the place."

"What place?" Mr. Blackman asked, turning around to face her from the front seat where he was sitting.

"Where he was murdered of course. I want to see it."

Amanda wondered if this was a good idea but said nothing.

"Are you sure?" her ex-husband asked.

"Would I say so if I weren't?" she continued. And then said to Amanda: "Tell the driver where to go."

"I don't know the address, but I'm sure he will know where it is, if you really want to."

"Yes."

Amanda leaned forward behind the taxi driver and asked: "Can you stop at the Olympiad Sauna before you take us back to the Consulate?"

The driver turned halfway around in his seat to stare at her. A look of surprise on his face quickly turned to amusement, as if he had expected another odd destination from these strange Americans: "Yes, of course, Señora. I know where it is."

He drove out of the gate, passing by the guardhouse and onto the cobblestone street in front, then turned south into the Zona Romantica. Beyond several narrow junctions, he turned left, past an open-air restaurant where the thumping rhythm of recorded music sounded loud even inside the car. About mid-block, he stopped and double-parked.

"It's right there; that open door," he said, pointing to

an inconspicuous dark entryway. Above it, a discreet sign announced the name.

Mrs. Blackman handed her dog to Amanda and slid out of the door.

"You're not going in, I hope," called her ex-husband through the window that he had hurriedly lowered.

"Don't tell me what I can do and what I can't, Ed. You certainly wouldn't have the guts." Crossing the street, she stood motionless, looking up into the obscurity as if she was expecting someone to emerge. And then she plunged inside, climbing up the obscurely lit staircase until she found herself in a small entrance. In front of her was a door. She reached to twist the handle but it was frozen. And then she turned to the grill set in the wall to her left and next to it, a protruding button. She pressed it and a moment later a young man appeared behind the barrier.

He looked at her curiously and said, "Lo siento, Señora, pero no entrada." He started to move away.

"Just a minute, you!" she cried out. "Let me in. I want to see."

"You cannot come in, Señora," he said in heavily accented English. "No mujeres."

"Get me the manager immediately," she said.

The boy looked at her curiously again and then disappeared. She could hear voices and then another, slightly older man appeared.

"I am Antonio," he said. "Who are you? What is it you want?"

"I'm the mother of the American who was murdered here. I want to see."

"What? *What* do you wish to see? We do not allow visitors."

"Let me in immediately," she said. "Or I will make terrible trouble for you. Now!"

Antonio stared at her and then she heard the sound of a buzzer. She turned and pushed open the door. When she walked inside, she could scarcely see because of the dim red lighting. The sound of music came from somewhere, music that she felt more than heard.

When her eyes became accustomed to the obscurity, she could see a bar immediately in front of her and a man standing behind it.

"You cannot stay," he said, "Just look and please leave. I am sorry about your son, but there is nothing for you here."

"I'll leave when I'm satisfied," she said, stepping farther into the bar area.

There was a man seated together at the far end. He appeared to be naked, at least from what she could see because he was sitting behind the bar. As she glanced around, she could see two men across the room sitting on a sofa of some sort. Spotting her, one of them quickly grabbed a towel and placed it across his lap. The other just stared back at her with no reaction at all.

"Where did you find him? I want to see it."

"No, Señora. You cannot come any farther. You have seen all that you will see. I will not allow it! You are disturbing our invitados, our clientes. Please leave now."

She stood without moving, the rhythm of the music seemed to grow louder and she could see more of the room and a staircase leading down.

"Is that where?" she pointed.

"Yes. He was found in the steam room. Now go. You must go."

She didn't reply but stood quietly trying to imagine her son walking around naked but for a towel, ignoring the leering glances... No, she couldn't imagine it!

"All right," she said finally. "Let me out."

"You must come around the end of the bar. That is the exit." He pointed.

She moved quickly, looking straight ahead and not at the man she had to pass by. Once out in the foyer, she climbed down the stairs and outside.

Standing for a moment at the entrance she turned around and looked once more and then crossed the street. She opened the car door and sat down inside.

"Did you go in?" Amanda asked.

"Yes. I just had to see; Ed wouldn't have had the guts. But I wanted to know," she said, reaching into her handbag and pulling out a handkerchief to wipe her eyes. "It's the only way I can make sense of this. To believe it really happened... All right. Let's get out of here. Tell the man, Ms. Pennyworth, and give me back my dog. I've seen enough. And now I want this to be over."

The driver understood without being told and turned back north at the next block and headed toward the Consulate. When they arrived, Mr. Blackman handed him a fistful of crumpled dollar bills.

"I have no idea what their paper dinero is worth," he exclaimed. "But I'll bet it's enough. I haven't the energy to be a money-changer today. He'll have to be satisfied."

"That's more than enough," Amanda assured him. She led them back into the reception room of the Consulate, greeting Nando as they passed by his desk.

"I'll be in my office with the Blackmans for a while," she announced. "If there's anything important, just let me know."

"Yes, Señora. I have everything under control."

She knew he did.

Inside her office, once the couple was seated, Amanda buzzed Nando to bring in some coffee, and then she settled into her chair behind the desk.

"I'm afraid this has been an exhausting experience for you both. I'm terribly sorry. But unfortunately, you still have to decide what to do with your son. I have the names of local funeral homes that we have worked with before. If you decide to ship the body back to the United States, it can be complicated and expensive, but it's certainly possible, and I wouldn't try to dissuade you. It's up to you."

"I want to talk to the boyfriend," Mrs. Blackman interrupted. "I'm just not satisfied yet. I need to speak to him. Do you have his address or phone number?"

"Yes, he left it with us. And I'm sure he's still around. The police told him not to leave the city."

"Why don't you telephone him now? Get him to come here."

"All right." As she was about to buzz Nando, he entered the office with three mugs of coffee on a tray.

"Thank you, Nando," she said. "And would you please telephone Mr. West? He's the young man who left you his coordinates yesterday. I'll take the call as soon as you can put him through."

After several minutes of silence—Amanda was grateful just to be alone with her thoughts—the phone module on her desk buzzed and she picked up the receiver. Nando announced that Archie West was on the line.

"Archie, this is Consular Officer Pennyworth. I have Mr. and Mrs. Blackman in my office. They would like very much to see you and speak with you."

She was happy that she alone could hear his answer: "Oh my God! No! Absolutely not! I couldn't bear that! Knowing what I know about them and how terrible they made Jeremy's life. Especially that father of his! No. I don't want to meet with them. Or talk to them... ever!"

Amanda ignored this and continued: "Good, and no, that's not too late. Why don't you take a cab to the Consulate right now. Where are you?"

There was a moment's silence: "I'm at our hotel in the Zona."

"All right. We'll expect you in about a half hour." Amanda imagined that he nodded yes, and she hung up.

"He'll be here," she said, and then noticed how defeated and tired both of them looked.

"Are you sure you're up for this?"

"Yes," mumbled Mrs. Blackman. "I want to know what happened."

"But he won't know. Or maybe just won't tell us," objected Mr. Blackman.

"He knows more than you think, Ed. And weren't you the one who was so curious about details just a while ago?"

Amanda realized that she had to break one of the fast rules of the Consulate—realized she had to solve a problem even before it occurred to the Blackmans—that they needed somewhere to stay. She would have to find them lodgings and the State Department never offered that service. But this once, she decided to help.

Picking up the phone, she buzzed Nando again: "Another task, I'm afraid," she cautioned, saying this in Spanish. "The Blackmans need accommodations for tonight and probably for at least three or four days more. Can you find something nearby? Somewhere that allows pets."

She put the phone down and looked up again at the dispirited couple. Mrs. Blackman was absently petting her comfort dog, while staring blankly past Amanda out the window, although it was doubtful she could distinguish anything in the afternoon glare. Mr. Blackman was watching her, or seemed to be, Amanda thought, and on the verge of saying something. But he remained silent. It was excruciating to see them in this momentary truce across the no-man's land of their hostile relationship. As a distraction, Amanda opened up a file that was sitting on her desk and tried to concentrate on it, but she found herself reading the same opening paragraph twice. She knew she wasn't good at this. She wanted to be sympathetic but in the back of her mind she was afraid that they would scorn any effort at understanding. Compassion training was something the Service never got around to. Closing the file, she looked up just as Nando knocked on the office door and entered. Mr. Blackman stirred expectantly.

"I found a hotel that will accept pets. It's the Splendida, not far from here and easy access to the Malecon. I've booked a room looking out onto the bay."

"Thank you, Nando. Just write down the details and leave them on your desk. Did you say they might check in late?"

"Yes, Señora."

The sound of the door closing as he backed out seemed to waken Mrs. Blackman from her distracted reverie and she started to ask a question that rose up at the end into an angry crescendo: "Did he say a room? You got us *a* room? *One* room? Do you mean I have to share it with *him*? What did he find us? The Honeymoon Suite?"

"Don't get so worked up, Nora," Mr. Blackman exclaimed and then gave her a twisted smile: "We spent years sharing the same space without sharing anything else. Why should tonight be any different? You're an expert at the cold shoulder. Even when you're in a room, you can make it seem like no one's there..."

"Okay," she replied. "Just this once. For Jeremy's sake."

"He's in no shape to appreciate it."

"And what's that thing your helper just mentioned: the Meracon?" he continued.

"The Malecon. It's the boardwalk along the ocean. Very pleasant at night," Amanda added.

"So we can stroll along hand in hand like it's our second honeymoon?"

"Shut the fuck up, Ed!"

Amanda felt she had to intervene, although the multiple roles of mediator, chief consoler, and tour operator were wearing very thin, and she knew she would have to strain to maintain a friendly and sympathetic front: "I could ask Nando to change the reservation or find you some other place. Although it's getting late..." She realized she should have asked for separate rooms. No reason for Nando to know they were no longer a couple.

"No. Keep the damned room. I'm past caring," Mrs. Blackman replied. "I'm so tired and Betsy needs a walk. Maybe if I go outside for a minute, I'll feel better. I'm sick of breathing your office air!" She stood up resolutely, smoothed the wrinkles from the skirt of her suit, and walked stiffly out of the office carrying the dog under one arm, its leash trailing down. She passed through the reception area without glancing at Nando and exited the front door.

"You see what it's like?" Mr. Blackman said.

Amanda just looked up at him and said nothing. She had no intention of allowing herself to be tempted into his deep pit of emotion and regret. And yet she felt immense sympathy for both of them and for their spoiled and fraught relationship whose only fragile link had been momentarily restored by the brutal murder of their son.

For the next ten minutes, Mr. Blackman questioned Amanda about her career with the State Department and her background. Much as she disliked talking about herself—and to a stranger, no less—something compelled her to grant him access to a carefully edited version of her history. Not that there was much to tell, however: the last long stint in Indonesia—she didn't mention the casual romance she had established there with the economics officer. And before that, three years wandering the fluorescent halls of the Harry S. Truman Building in Washington, DC. "If you could learn your way between the various conference rooms and could recognize where you were in each corridor," the joke went, "you were ready to carry water for the Ambassador in a war zone." And now there was the assignment to Puerto Vallarta. Something of a plum, although being by herself carried all the weight of responsibility. Solitary, she thought, was a better word for it, although she didn't say it.

After that, she continued, she would have to accept deployment to some sort of hazard zone—Iraq, Afghanistan, or China, maybe, if she wanted a promotion. The Service was even-handed, she explained, in distributing danger.

And then she stopped. She had the distinct feeling he wasn't really interested or paying attention, just nodding occasionally and making small-talk noises waiting for his ex-wife to return.

When Mrs. Blackman entered ten minutes later carrying Betsy, it was almost six. The window behind Amanda's desk, like a solar clock, had darkened, and made her wonder what had happened to Archie West. He was long overdue and she was ravenous, but the thought of continuing to dinner in the misery of their company, made her so nervous that she had to stand and walk out of the office and into the reception area. As she did, Archie West finally appeared. He entered hurriedly, obviously out of breath.

"Sorry I'm late. I walked. I should say I wandered. Didn't realize the time or where I was, until..."

Amanda was sure that his circuitous path had been guided by hesitation and doubt. She didn't blame him. If he was lost, it had to be intentional because Puerto Vallarta only occupied a narrow strip of land, laid out in a grid, and pressed between the sounding ocean and the dark foothills of the Sierra Madre.

Amanda reached out her hand and waved it toward the door to her office. "The Blackmans are waiting inside. They've had a terrible shock, as I'm sure you have. We just viewed the body of your friend and spoke to the coroner and the police. As hard as it was for me, I can imagine how you must feel. Still, they want to talk to you if you're up to it."

"I don't have a choice, do I?"

"No, not really. So prepare yourself."

She escorted him into the silent office. Only the dog seemed curious about the newcomer, wagging her tail and jumping up enthusiastically. Mrs. Blackman acknowledged Archie with a slight nod, but her ex-husband sat looking down at his hands and then balled his right hand into an angry fist and smacked it into the palm of his left.

Archie winced at the sound and backed up slightly toward the door, while Amanda took her seat behind the desk. The glare of the lamp she switched on cast a shadow on his face, making him look unnaturally pale and worn. Studying him for a moment, Amanda thought she could imagine how he would appear in twenty years when age and weight had rounded out the sharp, handsome outlines of his features—when the élan of youth had been spent in too many relationships, dissipated in tawdry encounters and hopeless affairs. She stopped herself. What in the world did she know of gay life? Why was she thinking in stereotypes rather than focusing on the sad boy in her office who had just lost a close friend—his lover. Who was she to judge? And maybe she was just thinking about herself.

Such thoughts made her feel old and out of touch. She wondered if he could sense everyone's confusion and tension in the room.

Mr. Blackman suddenly stood up, not to shake hands with Archie but tower above him and look down as he interrogated this witness whom he obviously blamed for his son's death.

"You need to tell us exactly what happened. It's the least you can do, after..."

"I'm very sorry, Mr. and Mrs. Blackman. I feel terrible. Jeremy and I... well, we were together, and I still can't believe he's dead. It was so cruel. Why would anyone...?"

"That's what we want to know, and I'm sure you can tell us," interrupted Mr. Blackman, raising his voice.

"You needn't shout, Ed," broke in his ex-wife. "The poor boy has lost his friend."

"But I lost a *son!*"

"Not that you really cared very much. I don't think you even liked him. When was the last time you uttered a decent syllable to him?"

"Shut up, Nora. I'll do the talking for once... So what happened? Why are you here in Mexico and whatever were you doing in that dump?"

Archie looked at Amanda as if he couldn't face Mr. Blackman. "We always wanted to take a vacation in Puerto Vallarta," he began. "Planned for weeks and got a great hotel room for not much money. I guess it was all Jeremy's idea, but I was certainly happy to come along."

"Just a minute," interrupted Mr. Blackman. "You say you were together. Were you living together? I didn't know about that."

"Well, practically, yes. We thought about finding a new place but hadn't got round to it yet. I have a lease on my apartment that doesn't run out for six months, but it's too small for two people."

"Go on, Archie," said Mrs. Blackman, placing her dog on the floor. "Don't let him interrupt you. Just tell us what happened."

"Well, we've been here five days now and went on a couple of day trips—you know, snorkeling and once to an adventure tour where you can ride a zip line over a gorge with a stream. You know what I mean."

"So why the hell did you go to that disgusting bathhouse, anyway."

"Ed!"

"It was Jeremy's idea. I didn't want to go. I don't like

places like that very much. Full of weird types; you know, businessmen on their lunch hour; guys you wouldn't look at twice anywhere else. Bodies that look a lot better with a suit on. Sometimes a pretty desperate place."

"So it's dangerous?" asked Mrs. Blackman.

"No, I don't mean that at all. Mostly sad. Just full of guys looking for something and not finding it."

"And Jeremy wanted to go there? I don't believe you. He was the last person I'd call desperate."

"Well, he said it might be fun. And as I explained, I didn't want to go."

"Were you afraid he'd find someone else. Throw you over for a quick fuck? Is that it?" Mr. Blackman said. "Now I'm beginning to understand everything."

"What?"

"And that gave you a very strong motive to kill him. Did you strangle my son out of jealousy?"

Archie stood silently for a moment as tears welled up in his eyes. "What do you think I am?"

"I know exactly what you are. Just tell me; did you kill him... out of rage?"

"No, I couldn't. Wouldn't. I loved him. If he had sex with someone else, I would have forgiven him. It wouldn't matter."

"That's hard for me to believe," Mr. Blackman said. "I know what I might do."

"Oh come on, Ed. Not everyone's a jealous monster like you. Give this boy a break. He didn't kill Jeremy. I believe him," Mrs. Blackman disagreed, suddenly sounding sympathetic.

Blackman glared at his ex-wife and then resumed: "Try to be honest with me, Archie, did you argue about it?

Fight over it? Did you see him with someone else?"

Archie's face suddenly became pale and he stuttered his answer: "I guess we did. I think we did argue. Nothing serious. And yes, I saw him with someone else. But I'd never, *never*... It didn't mean anything." He couldn't stop himself from crying as he sat down abruptly on the edge of the desk.

Amanda decided she had to intervene. "I think we shouldn't be questioning Archie like this. He's told us a great deal. And I'm sure the police asked him and if they are satisfied, perhaps we should be too. And anyway, why would Archie rob his best friend?"

"To cover up the murder, of course," Mr. Blackman replied with a satisfied smirk.

"No doubt that's what you would have done, Ed; always looking for an alibi!" Mrs. Blackman exclaimed, picking up her dog. "I think I'd like to leave now. I'm very hungry and tired and sad and this is getting us nowhere closer to knowing the identity of the murderer... Thank you, Archie, for being so candid about what you know... Come on, Ed. Let's find that hotel and have dinner and then go to bed." And to Amanda, she added: "We'll stop by tomorrow morning to talk to you about the funeral home and the arrangements we have to make... Okay, Ed? Enough!"

Scooping up Betsy, she walked briskly out the door, allowing it close behind her. And after a minute, her ex-husband, his bluster expended like a collapsed jib sail in a momentary calm, followed in her wake.

Archie started to stand and then collapsed again into one of the chairs: "I'm sorry. So sorry!"

"Sorry for what?" asked Amanda. "I'm not sure how

I'd react to losing my best friend and then, well, have someone accuse me of murder and robbery. Why don't you go back to your hotel now. You said that the police want you to stay for several more days. I won't tell you to make the best of it; there's no best possible. But if there's to be some sort of service for Jeremy back in the States, I'll try to get the Blackmans to include you."

"But shouldn't I be the one to take care of him? I mean we were partners and he only saw his mother occasionally, his father not ever. Couldn't stand him."

"I'm afraid under the circumstances, confused as they are, that his parents can dictate what happens next."

"That's so unfair. They were so uncaring and now this: snatching his body away... like they're in denial of who he was alive; forgetting how they treated him. Or so wrapped up in hating each other, they just ignored him."

"But legally..." She began and then hesitated. She could think of no words of consolation and waving the flag of legal obligations would only make him feel worse. "Go back to your hotel now. I'll let you know what happens. Please, Archie."

He pulled himself up slowly and Amanda could see that he was reluctant to leave, as if she was somehow the last viable tie to his friend and walking out of the office would signal the finality of his loss. Or maybe there was something he was on the verge of telling her.

"Thanks," he mumbled, although Amanda understood that she deserved no thanks and that he was actually offering none.

Alone in her office, she realized that she was exhausted, her emotions wrenched by the grip of this tragedy and her patience tested and drained by the bickering of Jeremy's parents. Not that she was entirely new to such tension. But her own parents, even at their worst, were only sullen and never cruel. She needed to leave today behind her. And so she did what often restored her energy: she picked up her briefcase, and then thought better of it, leaving it on the desk, and nodded as she walked briskly past Nando who was just straightening his work space for the evening, and exited the Consulate making her way to the boardwalk and the ocean.

Whenever she felt sad or spent, she craved life, anonymous life, and the accidental encounter with people who she could imagine to possess no cares; who would ask her for nothing. It renewed her spirits to watch the casual way Mexican families walked together, arms linked. Generations moving in rhythm: grandchildren holding hands with their grandmothers; everyone keeping the slow pace of a grandfather hobbling on a cane. Commerce, exchange, and hustle were everywhere. Tragedy never seemed to touch the joyful crowds sauntering along the Malecon. And their indifference to her sometimes made her recognize her alienation from a world that she only observed as an outsider. That was the essence of being a foreigner—the foreign half of the Foreign Service. But to be alone with herself was a terrible companion.

At such moments as these, she hoped that all her feelings of loneliness could be erased by the sound of waves crashing below on the seawall, signaling the possibility of infinite renewal; there was never a melancholy hint in the music spilling out of the bars or the lights from restaurants pooling on the dark pavement. Now and again she might stop to observe someone pausing to look casually at a tray of cheap jewelry, ready to bargain for something they didn't really want or need. Or children tugging at their parents as they stared rapt as the servers at the Italian gelato counter plunged their hands into its deep tubs to scoop out cones of multi-colored flavors. Walking through this ever-changing scene, observing the kaleidoscope of light and dark faces, she could almost feel the anxiety of the day dissipating in the wonder and curiosity of what she was observing. But tonight, none of this magic worked; she couldn't divert her thoughts from the awful day.

About halfway to her apartment in the Zona, she stopped for a coffee at Buonissimo, the Italian café that she often frequented. She sat in the tiny set-aside outdoor terrace, looking out over the boardwalk and the darkened bay. To the north were the twinkling lights of the marina area, where the Blackmans must now be in their hotel room. As she sipped the strong, syrupy espresso, she thought how lucky she was to be away from their rancor. If only... if only Romero were here... if only he hadn't been transferred to Oaxaca. She needed his steady hand to deal with this tragedy, certainly not Captain Gonzalez, who was so obvious in his distrust of her. But most of all, she just needed him. Perhaps when she was back in the apartment, she could call him, explain the circumstances of her predicament, but she knew that would only be an excuse to hear his voice and indulge in the memories of their time together before his reassignment. Better to wait until they could be together again, some long weekend, some vacation, something planned, something distant from this tragedy and her solitude.

She stood up and resumed her slow walk home. It was time to stop feeling sorry for herself.

CHAPTER 5

Captain Gonzalez sat by himself in his office. He waved away the acrid spiral of smoke from the smoldering cigarette wedged into the ashtray and grimaced. It had been three full days since the murder of Jeremy Blackman. At least, he thought, he had dealt with the parents—no more interference from them. And he had warned off that bothersome American Consular woman. It puzzled him what Romero had seen in her. To him, she was just another desperate, aging American woman who needed a good man to knock some sense into her. Well, he wasn't volunteering! Not him by a long shot! Just let her stay out of his way.

The trouble with the case, he thought, as he glanced down at the papers in front of him, was the damned bureaucracy in Guadalajara, Mexico City, and the United States or wherever the various records were kept. He had turned in several ID numbers gathered at the sauna, and they had to be checked against multiple lists: the National

Identity Card records, the Military Card, driver's licenses, and the school identity card (if they were under eighteen) or whatever piece of official paper someone had waved around to gain entry into the sauna. He was pretty sure the culprit was Mexican. Absolutely sure. Soon, he would have their names and addresses, and he wanted them brought in as quickly as possible. When he interviewed the men whose names turned up, he was certain he would catch the killer. But he needed to act quickly in case they left town.

But then there was the DNA evidence. Where the hell was that? Safely stored away, he hoped. It was simply a question of matching what Señora Sanchez had collected from the body to samples from the men he would interview and then be done with it; he'd have a killer in his grip. And he saw no reason to bother any of the Americans who might have spent the afternoon at the Olympiad. It was a clear case of robbery gone wrong and he always said he could squeeze a confession out of an agave leaf if he had to. It bothered him, however, that the Chief of his division had told him to track down the Americans who had been present, anyway... just to be sure. He was confident he was right, but he had telephoned the US Embassy in Mexico City with the driver's license and passport numbers of the Americans. Good luck with that! He would need it.

He picked up the telephone and called his assistant, Sergeant Perez.

"Gonzalez here. Any news on the names of suspects in the Olympiad murder?"

"Yes. Three profiles came in last night. Still waiting on the fourth."

"Waiting? Fuck!" Gonzalez shouted. "And just what

were you waiting around for? Someone to stop by and confess? Were you even planning to tell me?"

"Of course, Comandante. I just thought you would want everything all at once."

"Well, stop thinking and bring me what you have, now!" He slammed the phone down and snuffed out the cigarette. He needed to stop smoking; his wife was always going on about it, but when he was nervous or bored, he inevitably lit one up, took a few puffs, and then threw it down in disgust, letting it burn itself out into a sour ash.

A minute later, Sergeant Perez knocked at the door and entered immediately.

"Here they are. They all had military cards and so were easy to trace. Had to search the hotel records too, but for once that paid off. So we have three addresses. The fourth one may have been underage and so we are checking local school enrollments. It's a bit harder that way."

"I thought you had to be over eighteen to go to a place like that. Do they let children in now?"

"I looked up the rules on their website and, yes, you have to be eighteen. But I guess they allowed him in anyway."

"We should shut the damned place down for that reason alone. But I know the city would object. Just a mistake, they'll claim. And anyway, where would the tourists go? Have to keep the dollars coming in... Cancels all morality... Okay. Let's see what you've got."

Perez handed his superior a sheet with three names and addresses on it; two had phone contact numbers.

"You can see that all three are in Puerto Vallarta, at least I hope so. One is staying at a hotel; he's from Mexico City. The other two are locals."

"Good. We'll pay a visit right now to Señor Vargas before he leaves town. Do you recognize the name of the hotel?"

"Yes, sir, it's in the Zona."

"Of course it is. Let's go. And stop off to see Señora Sanchez and get a test kit for DNA. She'll know what she needs. Just in case I decide to use it. Right now. Then meet me out front."

Gonzalez stood up, grabbed his jacket hanging on the wall underneath the picture of the President of the Republic, and followed Perez out of the office. Waiting on the front steps of the building, in the shade of the overhang, he was already sweating. He pulled a large, wrinkled handkerchief out of the vest pocket of his uniform and wiped his face.

"Okay, I'm here," said his assistant as he pushed through the front door. Señora Sanchez gave me this box. She said we'd know what to do."

"Yeah. Come on then. You drive and I'll look up the address of the hotel as we go."

They walked to the small black and white Panda car. Gonzalez hated these small vehicles and he impulsively kicked the front tire as he opened the door. It wasn't because they were unreliable or too small for his large frame but because they were undignified. Nothing like the giant fleets of SUVs or Ford Rangers that the American police drove—red lights sweeping around in threatening circles, sirens blasting like a posse of hot rods. And all he had was a dim blue blinking light and the intermittent beep of a tin horn. The Americans really knew how to intimidate.

Opening his cellphone, he looked up the name of the

hotel and found it immediately.

"It's on Francisco Madero away from the ocean. Five hundred block."

Perez drove onto the bridge from Old Town into the Zona over the River Cuale and almost immediately turned left up a bumpy, cobblestone street. He stopped and parked in front of a small hotel, and both men got out.

The entrance was cut into a high wall with a large square of brown and red tiles inserted into the sidewalk in front. A young woman was moving a mop around it in a lazy, circular motion. She glanced at them as they squeezed by her but did not interrupt the rhythm of her chore.

Inside, they could see a sign-in desk on the right and then in front of them a small open courtyard. A fountain surrounded by pots of stunted palms gurgled. The sound of its splash seemed to freshen the hot, stagnant air. Above and around it were two stories of galleries with alternating doors and windows. A staircase on the left led up to the second floor.

Gonzalez stopped at the desk and punched a small bell sitting on the ledge. After a few seconds, a woman appeared from inside the office. When she saw the police officers, she hesitated, touched her hair to capture a stray lock, and then edged forward.

"Can I help you, please?"

"Yes, you can," Gonzalez said abruptly. "We're looking for this man. A Señor Pedro Vargas. Registered here, I understand."

"Yes," she said, "I think he is a guest here. Let me look for sure."

She pulled a large ledger book from a shelf under the counter, placed it on top, and opened it. Thumbing through several pages, she found the name and put her finger under the entry.

"Yes, he is here. Room 225."

"Is he in?"

"I wouldn't know that. Perhaps. I haven't seen him yet today. But our guests can take their keys with them when they leave, so I can't be sure. Do you want me to call his room?"

"No. Don't do that!" Gonzalez said firmly. "We'll find him." Turning to Perez, he continued: "Let's go." And he led the way to the stairs and up one flight to the second landing, taking two steps at a time.

Together, they walked around the outer sides of the courtyard and then stopped at the door of Room 225. On the knob hung a small card with thick black letters that read: "No Moleste." Gonzalez knocked and the noise of his knuckles on the flimsy wooden door echoed sharply around the walls of the courtyard.

"Vargas, are you in there? Open up. It's the police," he called out.

There was a brief delay; the lock made a faint click, and the door opened part way. What they could see inside was mostly darkness and the faint outlines of a disheveled bed. Only the face of a young man was really visible in the faint light. Gonzalez wondered if he had been sleeping or maybe doused the lights before opening the door.

"Yes, sir," he said, opening the door a bit wider.

Gonzalez shoved it hard, forcing the man backwards. He reached around the wall and switched on the overhead lamp. The unshaded light confirmed his first impression of the room. The double bed was unmade and there were clothes and a towel strewn on the floor. Vargas was dressed in shorts and a tight green T-shirt with *Señor Frog*, the name of the local nightclub, written across the top above the logo of a dancing toad. Gonzalez shook his head when he saw this souvenir. No one he knew had ever been in the huge, loud bar by that name on the Malecon. Only tourists. If even.

"Okay, Vargas. I guess you know why we're here."

"I have no idea. Why?" he stammered.

"Robbery and murder at the gay sauna."

"What? Why me? What's happened?"

Gonzalez grabbed a handful of the man's T-shirt and pulled him close and off balance. He knew it often worked wonders to assume that a suspect was guilty, to give him no chance to think up a story, an alibi, or an excuse. Around the station, he was known for his quick judgments and ability to extract confessions. Among some of the officers it had earned him the nickname of "Muerde," (the Biter). He never laughed at the pun on "Muerte," (death) and especially not "Mierda," knowing that he inspired fear and to him that was a lot more effective than respect. If that gave them the shits, so be it!

"I don't know what you're talking about," Vargas babbled. "What murder? What sauna?"

"So you want to deny that you were at the Olympiad a few days ago... when we have proof that you entered; we have your ID number? How do you think we found you? And stop lying to me. I have no patience!"

Gonzalez shoved the boy backwards so hard that he fell onto the bed.

"You were there and you murdered the American. We have DNA evidence to prove it."

Vargas seemed so stunned that he couldn't answer for

a moment. Finally, sitting up, he managed to blurt out: "Okay. I was there and yes, I think there were some Americans, at least they weren't Mexican, or I guess not. I heard them speaking English. But I didn't even talk to any of them. They weren't interested in me."

"We'll see about that. Maybe you killed him because he rejected you. Who knows why you did it? Anyway, you're going to come with us to the station right now; we'll give you a DNA test there. It never lies. And we'll be keeping you until the results come in. Get your shoes on."

"But what about my things here, my room?"

"I'll tell the manager to pack everything up and send it over to us. You'll be our guest for quite a while, I imagine. Not exactly the luxurious accommodations you're used to, however," he said, looking around the room.

Listening to this exchange, Perez wondered why Gonzalez didn't take the sample here and now. He had brought along the test kit. It would have been simple. But perhaps he feared the boy would leave town and wanted to keep him close. He didn't always approve of his superior's aggressive tactics, but he had to agree that he sometimes knew what he was doing.

When he was ready, Vargas walked out the door, giving a hasty look back at the room he was abandoning, and then joined the policemen who had stepped outside to wait.

"Search the room thoroughly," Gonzalez said to Perez. "That means everywhere. Take everything apart. Look for money, jewelry, the missing sauna key, anything, and then report back to me."

He gripped the boy's arm tightly, almost dragging him down stairs, leaving Perez behind. They stopped while he gave instructions to the woman who had stepped out from behind the counter to get a better look at what was causing the commotion.

"When my officer leaves, gather his clothes together," Gonzalez said with a sideways glance. "We'll send someone over later to pick them up. He won't be coming back."

Back at the station, Gonzalez turned the terrified prisoner over to the duty officer, directing him to lock him in one of the cells in the basement. After they had disappeared through the double doors, to go down the corridor and then below, Gonzalez thought to himself: I'll leave him alone for a couple of hours—let him marinate in his own fears. Soften him up. If he's guilty, he'll confess soon enough.

Picking up the telephone at the front desk where he was still standing, Gonzalez dialed three quick internal numbers.

"Señora Sanchez," he said when she answered. "I've brought in a suspect for the Blackman murder. We've put him in a cell. You can go and take a DNA sample now. We'll be holding him until the results are in."

Without waiting for a response, he put the receiver down and then walked back to his office, satisfied that he was well on his way to solving the case.

Several hours later, Sergeant Perez knocked at his office door.

Stepping inside, he tossed a wallet onto the desk and then eased himself into a chair facing Gonzalez.

"That's about it. I looked everywhere, under the mattresses, every corner of the room. Moved things that probably hadn't been shifted in a year. Seemed like it anyway from all the dust. But only this was worth bringing in. I left all his clothes on the bed. No secret compartments in his luggage. I ripped it apart. Nothing in the lining. And when you look, you'll notice that he had just one credit card: Santander Bank and about 300 pesos and some coins, his Military Card and National ID. That's about all, plus some old receipts he must have forgotten to throw away. Could be he's a promising suspect, no evidence he had much money and it's a cheap hotel, so maybe that's a motive for robbery, but he wasn't hiding anything in the room."

"Yeah..." replied Gonzalez. "Well, I'm just beginning with him. Let him worry a bit longer and then we'll see what we shake out of him. But in the meantime, we've got two other Mexican suspects to track down. "Let's pay a surprise visit to the next person on our list."

"How about the kid? Perez said. "When I stopped at my desk, someone had put his address out."

"Okay. Good. It'll be the kid first, then. Yes. He'll tell us everything, and maybe he's the murderer. Who knows? I wonder if his family knows about him." Gonzalez made an exaggerated kissing sound and then repeated it quickly, smacking his lips audibly as if he had just tasted a triumph.

Perez was startled for a moment and then forced a laugh: "I'm sure he'll want to talk to us alone. He probably doesn't want anyone to know where he was."

"Or *what* he is! You have the address. Let's go there now."

Gonzalez stood up and was half way out the door before Perez could follow. Together they climbed into the Panda car again and drove to the center of Old Town.

"Park here, away from the address," Gonzalez ordered,

when they approached their destination. "And you go up to the door and knock. I don't want him running away at the sight of me. Plenty of time to scare him. That comes later once we've got him back at the station."

Perez flinched at this comment about his appearance; Gonzalez was suggesting that he was less than forceful or masculine looking. But he let it pass and opened the car door, stepping out onto the street and then to the sidewalk. The tiny house was wedged between two larger structures and sat behind a crumbling white stucco wall. Three blue tiles embedded next to the wooden door displayed the number: 560. He pulled on the bell that dangled from a frayed leather cord above the latch and waited. After a moment he could hear footsteps flopping on the ceramic floor inside the entrance. The door opened and Perez quickly shoved one foot on the sill. The woman standing in front of him looked at him sternly when she noticed his uniform. She was short with severe black hair and a nondescript outfit. The only striking thing about her were her shoes—or rather, her pink furry slipper scuffs. She was carrying a mop.

"Señora Herrera?"

"Who wants to know?"

"The police. And I want an answer now."

"She's not here. I'm just finishing up. And I don't know anything."

"I haven't asked anything," Perez replied, thinking that her defiance was an automatic defense. "I'm looking for the son."

"They got three sons and a daughter."

"Felix," he said, marveling at her obstinacy.

"Yes, there's one with that name."

"Is he here? If he is, would you please fetch him? And now! I need to talk to him. Just a little chat," he added, quite sure that she would only warn the boy that a policeman was looking for him.

Without another word, she turned and disappeared. Perez stepped inside, leaving the door open behind him. The small entrance way opened on the right into a sunny living room. The floor still glistened, damp where the maid had recently mopped it. Heavy wood furniture had been moved out of place, but he could imagine its usual arrangement, around a low table and in front of a large television set. Through a tiled archway in back, he could see what looked like a dining area, and, beyond it, he supposed, a kitchen alcove. On his left was a steep staircase leading up to the bedrooms. He shifted from one foot to the other impatiently waiting for the boy to appear. This was one of the discomforts of his job. He had a recurring hesitation about invading the lives of others, barging into their intimate spaces, and seeing how they lived and imagining what it would be like to be in their skin as a suspicious and uninvited stranger invaded their private circumstances—looking with prying eyes that transformed every ordinary and normal object into a possible clue or piece of evidence. He never dared confide such thoughts to Gonzalez or any of his other colleagues at the station. They would write him down as a dreamer or worse.

Finally, he heard muffled voices at the top of the stairs and then the sound of footsteps. He walked out of the living room and waited at the bottom of the steps as a young man slowly descended alone. The maid remained out of sight but Perez was certain she would be listening.

The boy was very young looking, with a shocking mane of long blond hair, bleached almost colorless, that contrasted with his dark skin. He was wearing tight jeans and a white T-shirt embossed with the picture of the pop singer Juan Gabriel. (Perez immediately identified the face: everyone had their suspicions about that one!) When Felix reached the bottom, Perez could see that he was about his own height, slightly built and holding himself in an almost studied, feminine way. He also looked his age, which had to be sixteen or seventeen—clearly not old enough to be a customer at the Olympiad. For a moment, the detective wondered if he had been accompanied by some older man who vouched for his age or gave some convincing reason (or bribe?) to get him in.

"You are Felix Herrera," Perez asked for the sake of formality.

"Yes, sir."

"You will come with me now. We have identified you as someone who was present at the Olympiad Sauna the day an American man was murdered. We have questions for you—at the police station—and we will be taking a DNA sample. You don't deny that you were there, do you?"

"No, sir," he stammered. "But I know nothing of this. I will answer whatever you want. But I did not know anything about some man who is murdered." Perez was surprised at his calm and he wondered for a moment if keeping the secret of this young man's sexual inclination had made him a practiced liar.

Clutching his arm, Perez walked around the boy, put a foot on the first step of the staircase, and leaned forward, projecting his voice up.

"Señora. I am sending someone to search the house.

Please inform the family. Do you hear me?"

"Yes, I will tell them," came the disembodied voice.

"And tell them that they may visit their son at the police station, but we will not release him until we are satisfied. Do you understand?"

"Yes," she replied, walking into view on the top landing and staring down. "Yes."

Perez pulled the boy's arm and guided him out the front door and toward the police car. Gonzalez was leaning against it smoking a cigarette. He flicked it on the ground and looked at Felix with disgust.

"Get in," he ordered. "In the back seat. Perez, you drive. What took you so long?"

They got into the car but Perez didn't answer, thinking that this was not a question but just a sign of impatience. After all, it had only been a few minutes and they were lucky that the boy had been home.

Without turning to face him, he told Gonzalez that the maid was aware they would be sending a team to search the boy's room and the rest of the house.

As they drove, Gonzalez looked straight ahead and said nothing, but Perez could almost smell the anger and tension of his superior's body—something emanating from his dislike of the suspect sitting behind him.

When they reached the police compound, Perez stopped in front of the entrance so Gonzalez could take his charge inside. Then he parked the car and followed. By the time he reached the small dark interview room in the basement, Felix was seated across a table from Gonzalez, looking very small and suddenly frightened.

"Go get his file," Gonzalez ordered without turning around. Perez knew that no file existed yet but understood this was a standard tactic of intimidation, so he retraced his steps and went back upstairs to the large open-plan area where he had his desk. Opening a drawer, he pulled out an unused folder and dug out several used sheets of paper from the waste basket to place inside. He then returned downstairs and shoved it across the table. Gonzalez opened it so that Felix would be able to see scrawled words and typed lines, but he wouldn't be able to read anything upside down. He would fear or imagine that the police had already gathered substantial information about him. Once again this was a trick that Perez had learned from his superior to frighten a suspect into telling the truth—and to be cautious about contradicting what he thought the police already knew about him.

When he sat down across from Herrera, Perez saw that Gonzalez had turned the adjustable table lamp on and aimed it at such a level that it would shine in the suspect's eyes unless he raised his head. He almost felt sorry for the boy who must be sinking under waves of guilt—imagined or real—no matter what he had done.

Gonzalez began, opening the dossier and glancing at it as if it contained a list of questions he needed to ask: "You were at the Olympiad Sauna three days ago."

"Yes, sir," Felix mumbled.

Gonzalez slammed his open palm on the metal table. "Louder. Act like a man!"

Felix opened and then shut his mouth as if he wanted to protest.

"And you are underage. Did you go alone?"

"No, sir. I was with a friend."

"His name."

"I'm sorry, I didn't know his name. I mean, it must

have been something like Miguel. Maybe."

"So you picked him up. You're a prostitute then?"

Felix looked horrified: "No, sir. We just passed each other on the Malecon. You know. We talked. Bought me a coffee. And then he suggested that we go to the sauna. I told him that I wasn't eighteen and couldn't, but he paid the guy at the window extra. And we went in."

"Did you see the American? Did you have sex with him too?"

"No! No! Yes, I mean, I think there were foreigners there. And maybe they were speaking English. Not much talking going on," he said, gaining confidence.

"Do your parents know about you? That you're a rent boy?"

"I'm not! I told you! It was just this one time and he was very nice... insisted. Don't tell my parents that! Please! I have enough difficulties with them."

"So they do know," Perez broke in.

The boy said nothing, but Gonzalez was clearly not satisfied.

"Get Señora Sanchez in here, Perez. For a DNA test." And then addressing the boy as the other detective left the room: "We are going to search your belongings and your house. We'll turn everything upside down, open every drawer; look in and under everything. If there is any evidence in your room it will speak to us. Every secret you have will be uncovered. Do you understand that? So it is best for you to tell me now."

The boy gulped and shook his head slowly. Gonzalez could see that he was fighting back tears.

"I've told you the truth. I don't know anything about Americans or about dead people... Leave me alone!"

"And if we do find anything, it will go badly for you. You understand that don't you," Gonzalez continued. "So let's go over your story again."

Felix looked at his accuser, obviously struggling to control himself. He began quietly: "All right: I met that man Miguel walking on the Malecon. Yes, I admit, I was out looking for someone, for some fun, and I could see that he liked me. You can tell at a glance. The eyes tell you everything, and he was obviously interested. I usually don't go for older guys, but I thought, 'Why not?' and so I let him pick me up. He invited me for a coffee and we talked. He told me all about himself, but I didn't listen because people never tell you the truth and I didn't care much anyway. He said it was his day off from work. He didn't tell me his last name and I lied about mine. Invented something. You know how it is."

"I don't know anything," Gonzalez interrupted. "That's why you're telling me."

"As I said, we went to a café on the Malecon and stayed about a half hour and I could see he wanted to... get together, you know. He asked me if I had a place to go and I said no. So he suggested the sauna, but I told him I was too young to get in there. And he said he could fix that. So we walked back into the Zona and to the Olympiad. It made me nervous to go to that place. I have friends who've been. Told me all about it, but not me, yet. Then we went inside and he paid the man to let me in. We got a room."

"And then you had sex, right?"

"Sort of..."

"What?"

"I mean, I decided I didn't really want to. I don't know. I guess he was too old, and the whole place was making me nervous."

"Was he upset?"

"Not really. He said he understood. And we got dressed and left."

Gonzalez looked at him sharply. "I don't believe you. Yes, I think you might have gone with that man. But I think you stayed. Did you ask him for money? Is that what happened? And he refused?"

"No, no!"

"So you stayed and looked for someone younger, more... appealing to you and you found the American. We'll know if you had sex with him."

"No, that's not true! I left."

"But the man you picked up stayed on, right? You didn't see him leave, did you?"

"Not exactly, but I'm sure he did. I was embarrassed. I didn't want to see him anymore."

The door to the interview room opened and Señora Sanchez stepped in. Without any greeting, she walked around the table to where Felix was sitting and opened the DNA kit, extracting a swab and a long plastic tube.

"This is very easy," she said to him. "Just open your mouth and I'll take a sample. Painless."

"Except for the consequences," Gonzalez added. "When it proves you're guilty."

Felix opened his mouth and Señora Sanchez swiped the inside of his cheeks with the swab and put it in the receptacle.

"I'll have some results for you in about a day," she said, packing up the kit and walking out of the room. Before she could leave, however, Perez poked his head inside.

"We're going to search the boy's room now. I'll let you

know as soon as I find anything."

"Fine," said Gonzalez, standing up. "Come with me, son. We'll be keeping you here until we know more."

"But my parents!"

"Sergeant Perez can tell them where you are if the maid hasn't already."

Perez and another officer drove back to the Herrera house and this time were greeted angrily by Señora Herrera, who stood in the middle of the doorway, her bulk blocking their entrance.

"Where is my son? What have you accused him of doing?" she shouted as soon as she saw their uniforms.

"You need to be calm, Señora," Perez answered. "He is at the police station answering questions."

"About what? He has done nothing!"

Perez ignored her outburst: "We are here to search his room, so if you will please stand aside, we can do our job and then depart."

She hesitated and then edged a few feet to the left, allowing them to walk single-file into the hallway. When she tried to follow them upstairs, Perez turned back and cautioned her: "Please Señora, stay where you are; let us do our job."

"How do I know that you won't steal from us?" she called.

Perez just scowled and continued up into the boy's room.

"You look in the desk and take the bed apart," he said to the other officer. "I'll search the closet."

Working steadily for ten minutes or so, the two men turned everything in the small room upside down. The desk drawers lay on the ground with their contents scattered about. The mattress had been upended, exposing the dusty frame of the bed. All of the boy's clothing lay across the chair or in a pile in the center of the room, pants pockets turned inside out.

"I've found something; almost missed it," Perez said suddenly. Standing on his tip toes he had retrieved a small cardboard box jammed into the far end of a shelf in the closet. Pulling it out, he placed it on the desk and opened it. The top layer was full of cut-out pictures from magazines: movie stars, singers, and celebrities. Then there were two tattered photo magazines of nude men. And beneath this tawdry erotic debris lay his secret: a gold ring and a small roll of pesos held together with a rubber band.

"Well," he said to the other officer, "whatever all this means, we've found his treasure. Let's go back to the station. I think the boy will have to explain this."

Walking downstairs, Perez was confronted again by Señora Herrera, now standing in front of the door, blocking their exit. When she saw he was carrying the box, she stammered in anger: "So you *are* taking something. Let me see what that is."

"I'm very sorry, Señora, but this is evidence, and we cannot show you."

He and the officer brushed past her and outside as quickly as possible. He had no desire to argue with the woman. And Gonzalez would be very pleased at their discovery. Felix's mother followed them part of the way and then stopped at the entrance, hands on her hips, shaking her head.

Back at the police headquarters, Perez immediately informed his superior of his discovery and Felix was once again summoned from a cell in the basement to the interview room where he sat across the table from the two officers.

This time, Perez took the lead, spreading the contents of the cardboard box in front of him. The boy blanched and opened his mouth to talk, but the officer raised his hand, halting any protests or denials.

"I don't want to hear any inventions, any more lies, or excuses. Just answer the questions as I ask them. It's time for the truth."

Felix visibly shrank into his chair, putting his hands together. The gesture made Perez think of prayer—and perhaps, he thought, the boy was silently uttering some invocation of divine succor—from the saint that protected the guilty... that is if Judas was a canonizado.

Pointing to the cut-outs and magazines, he began: "No one cares about your collection of pin-ups. You are welcome to dream about all the men you want. It's when you rob and murder them, however, that the police become interested." He shifted his glance to the pesos. "These must be the bills you stole from the American, aren't they? Why don't you tell us about it—you robbed him, didn't you? And then killed him."

Perez was careful not to say how the American had died, and he seriously doubted that the boy was strong enough—and certainly not aggressive enough to strangle someone. But he was convinced he knew a great deal more than he was saying.

Felix looked aghast and seemed unable to speak. He just shook his head.

"You have to answer," broke in Gonzalez who glared at Perez as if his colleague was treading on the boy's story too lightly, too carefully, too gingerly.

"All right," the boy sobbed. "I'll tell you about it. It's my money."

"Where did you get it?"

"I've been saving it for months. I work sometimes as a cleaner in the stores along the Malecon. That is my pay."

"And this ring," the policeman said, holding it up. Where did you get that?"

"I... I found it."

"You are lying again," Gonzalez intervened, half rising out of his chair. "The money is from prostitution. And you stole the ring from the victim at the sauna, didn't you?"

"No... Yes! Okay, I'll tell you. I found the ring at the back of a drawer in one of the jewelry stores where I work. They never missed it. Probably didn't even remember they had it. But I don't do sex for money. Never! I wouldn't."

"But this seems like a lot of Pesos for pushing a broom around," Perez interrupted, removing the rubber band and counting the bills audibly. "Almost 10,000... tell me frankly where did it come from? You robbed the American, didn't you?"

"No! Okay. I saved most of it, but that man I was with gave me 2000 pesos."

"Just like that? And for nothing?"

"No. I told him my story and I guess he felt sorry for me. Said he would help me."

"And what story is that?"

Felix gulped and then began quietly. "It's because of my parents. They hate me and I got to get away. I've been saving. You know when my father found out about me—I don't know how—maybe he just guessed. But he beat me up. Just that once but I thought I was going to die. Even then I was so ashamed; I guess I felt I deserved it. And afterwards everything changed between us. He just didn't admit I was there anymore. It was like being a fantasma in my own house and he could see right through me. He stopped calling me by my name. Do you know what that's like? Not to have a name anymore? Not to be a person?

"And then my mother was even worse. Just the opposite. She certainly knew I was there 'cause she took to watching me all the time. I could see her looking at me, trying to figure out something. Finally, one day she drags me to the church and tells the priest everything. She said I'd never dare confess my sins but she would tell him since I was a coward to do so. She spoke just a few more words and then walked out, leaving me alone with him. It was awful. He made me kneel down and pray... but he told me every word to say, what to ask God for. Do you think I hadn't already asked God to change me? What good would this do, but he held me down and kept repeating that I was sinful and filthy in the eyes of Jesus. That I was doing things so unforgivable that Jesus would turn his face away in disgust. It was horrible. I didn't know what to do."

Gonzalez stopped him. "Why are you telling us this little fairy story? We need to know the truth and this is some sort of fantasy you're recounting, isn't it?"

"But you wanted to know about the money. And it's because of them. I've been saving to move away. I'll go to Guadalajara, maybe, when I have enough saved, or even Mexico City. Get a job. I can't stay here with them. Don't you see? They don't want me anymore. I didn't do anything."

Neither Perez nor Gonzalez said a word but looked at each other. Perez was the first to speak: "We'll take you back to the cell where you were. As soon as Señora Sanchez checks your DNA, we'll know if you are telling the truth."

He stood up and motioned for the boy to follow him. When he looked back at Gonzalez, who remained seated, he nodded slightly. The boy's story made sense to him. It was just terrible enough to explain everything. And he felt sorry for him with such terrible parents. But evidence is evidence and if he had sex with the American, they would soon know.

Once Felix had been shut away, Perez returned to speak to Gonzalez who had gone back upstairs. Entering his office, he said, "I'm not sure, but I think I believe some of that story. If he had told us right away, I wouldn't have, but there's something about dragging it out of him that makes me believe it's true. We knew he was hiding something; didn't want to tell us, and we wouldn't have known except for the hidden pesos."

"I'm not sure that's all," Gonzalez said. "Anyway, take someone with you and go talk to that man Miguel something. He's on your list, isn't he?"

"Yeah, we traced him. He lives up in that big apartment complex at the end of Rio Calle. I'll go now. Could be he's still home for his Cena unless he takes his lunch downtown somewhere."

CHAPTER 6

Amanda woke that morning as brilliant sun streamers shimmered around the room, dancing over the tops and edges and out from the bottoms of the curtains that stirred and billowed in the cool breeze. She peeled off the sheet but lay still for a minute, listening to the sounds that floated up from the quarter: the hiss of distant traffic, the sharp, raucous greeting of one crow to another, and the sudden clatter of a metal pan from the kitchen across the back garden. No matter what the day promised or threatened, she loved these delicious few moments when she could imagine that all of the life around her was rousing, fresh and untroubled by the memory of yesterday's problems and obligations. Those would rush to greet her soon enough when the responsibilities of the day crowded into this instant of empty drifting.

She loved to linger in this time of emerging from sleep, when the dreams that often came just on the edge of consciousness were most vivid, as if they might speak some portent of the future... or explain some puzzle. And she never tired of anticipating the first cup of coffee, strong, sweet, with foamed milk on top or the frozen croissant she popped into the oven. It amazed her that she had found a great bakery, very near her apartment that specialized in dark breads, baguettes, and other foreign confections.

But today she had to get up, shower, and dress. No delay this morning.

Her first appointment of the day—not that it had been formally agreed—but she was sure it would be the Blackmans arriving back at the Consulate early. There were arrangements to be made at the funeral home for their son; decisions to be taken; and formalities to be initiated if they decided to return the body to the United States. And she wanted to check with the police station to see if there had been any progress in solving the case. She wondered. There was something strange about this beyond the tragedy of it, something implausible that she couldn't quite put her finger on. Something beyond expected. Of course, murder by its nature was always a burst of excess, although there might be instances when it could seem plausible, even necessary.

But she feared that the detectives on this case were not curious enough to consider anything more than a robbery gone wrong. They would probably be satisfied if they could accuse someone, anyone, if they could find one trace of evidence and then be done with it, without trying to understand why. Not that she was an expert—not by any means. But motivations and explanations—the emotional facts of life, not its crude slap-you-in-the-face realities— had always intrigued her. Maybe, she thought, this accounted for her fascination with mystery stories, although she dismissed the (boring) procedural novels where the reader just watched while the investigator examined each new piece of evidence, one fact at a time, like fitting the pieces of a jigsaw puzzle. Nor did she really enjoy such classics as Sherlock Holmes where the surprise solution was far-fetched and based on the detective's uncanny deductive powers. There was something unpleasantly passive about the expectations in reading such stories.

No, she preferred the Belgian Georges Simenon whose Inspector Maigret often discovered the identity of a killer early on but remained unsatisfied until he had uncovered the motive, the tipping point of the crime. Perhaps this fascination is what made her opt for a double degree in literature and psychology and then finally a career in the Foreign Service where every day brought new problems and a stream of people to meet and understand. It was a lot easier than worrying about herself and her future: pausing to consider what in the world she was doing bumping around the globe from one assignment to the next: rootless and rushing toward whatever. A promotion? That's what everyone in the Service talked about—obsessively almost whenever they met up—jealously watching for the next careful step up the ladder. But was that a life? Or just running from it?

She arrived at the Consulate shortly before 9:00, earlier than Nando for a change. Opening the door into the reception area, she switched on the overhead lights and adjusted the air conditioning. Before going into her office, she glanced at his desk. It was always neat, with twin coffee cups bristling with sharpened pencils and ballpoint pens, a computer terminal and adjacent mouse, and a neatly stacked pile of papers needing his attention. Behind his chair on the low bookshelf were several books—an English-Spanish dictionary as well as a small library devoted to Puerto Vallarta. In an open space in the middle sat a family portrait of Nando, his wife Isabel, and their two children. At either corner of the wall stood the furled flags of the United States and Mexico, and over the desk, the seal of the United States—the eagle gripping thirteen arrows in one talon and an olive branch in the other. It could be almost anywhere, she thought.

Since Nando had been the last to leave the previous night, she knew she would find a tidy batch of papers ready for her signature. Entering her office, she sat down at her desk and looked at the slim stack of papers. She switched on her computer and immediately found an official communication from the Embassy in Mexico City. No surprises there! It was marked "personal," an email from the Ambassador (no doubt written by his secretary) asking for a progress report on the investigation into Jeremy Blackman's murder. Reading between the lines, it seemed clear to her that either Mr. or Mrs. Blackman had been in touch with the Embassy asking (demanding, probably) them to intervene. It worried her that they had gone over her head to apply pressure. But she understood, even sympathized. It would make things more difficult, but she had dealt with Embassy interference before and had several contacts there who could help quench any fires (or doubts) about her competence. And anyway, she wasn't responsible for the investigation. It was entirely a police matter.

Nando and the Blackmans arrived simultaneously, and without waiting to be announced, the American couple marched straight into her office (without the dog). She stood to greet them.

She immediately noticed a dramatic change in both of them. Nora Blackman was sans comfort dog. She looked haggard and drawn and had the aura of desperation. All the bravado of the previous day had been dissolved by emotion, and she looked empty and pleading, as if she finally realized and truly felt what had happened. Even her dress was disheveled, a far cry from the tidy business suit she had worn the day before. She stood twisting her hands as if she could wipe away her grief.

Ed Blackman was also visibly subdued. He had discarded his suit—and his formality—in favor of slacks and a white shirt. His face also showed deep lines of anguish that Amanda had not noticed before.

"Please sit down," she said, gesturing. "Can I get you coffee? Anything to eat? Nando can go out."

"No," replied Mr. Blackman, taking his seat clumsily and then leaning forward, staring at the floor. She thought for a moment that he was afraid to look at her for fear of more bad news. "I think we've both had enough coffee in the last twenty-four hours to satisfy any caffeine addict. No, but thank you," he said finally and looked at his ex-wife.

She took this as a cue and began to speak: "We're wondering what you've heard. Have the police found the killer?"

"I don't know anything yet. But I plan to call the station this morning and speak to Captain Gonzalez. Remember? You met him."

After an uneasy moment of silence. Amanda finally asked: "Have you decided what to do about... Jeremy? You need to make some sort of arrangements"—she hated that awful euphemism!—"And whatever you decide, I'm here to help."

"We don't know yet," Blackman interrupted. "We couldn't. How can you—I mean—how can you just fly to another country to pick up the body of your son, go through the bureaucracy to get the body home, and then bury him somewhere—we'd even fight over that wouldn't we, Nora?—or should we take a paper bag with his ashes back in a suitcase? What would we do then: divide them up fifty-fifty? Two ounces of his life for her; two ounces for me? And she scatters hers off the Santa Monica Pier and I keep mine in a jar on the mantel?"

"Ed! You monster! Stop!"

"Last night," he continued, "We had dinner at the hotel; the first time we've been together in more than ten years. Oh, we used to see each other when we handed him off, like on a prisoner exchange, yeah, but... No wonder he got so screwed up."

"That's not why he was gay and you know it," Mrs. Blackman said loudly, a hint of antagonism and command returning to her voice.

Blackman glanced at her angrily but continued: "Well it got him murdered, didn't it?! And you know, last night, it made me sick to see those tourists at dinner, chattering away, completely ignorant of what had happened to us. Couldn't eat a bite. Do you know what that's like, to hear laughter all around you when you're bleeding inside? Who gave them the right?"

Amanda was astounded by this outburst. At their first meeting, he had seemed so much in control that she wondered if this was belated emotion and pain about the loss of his son or whether he was always bitter and sarcastic.

"You're not helping, Ed," Mrs. Blackman interrupted.

"And I suppose it'll be harder to take his body home because he was murdered. Just one more ream of papers to fill out, I suppose; more formalities and stamps to collect; more officials to bribe."

"Stop it, you bastard," she cried out. "This isn't about you and your inconvenience! And you're making things so much worse; just like you always do! You're so hostile. Get ahold of yourself!"

Blackman looked at her intently this time and his face suddenly changed: "I'm sorry. I'm sorry. It's just..."

Amanda waited for this awful moment to pass because she didn't trust what she might say. Emotion could be catching, like some pathogen floating in the air, and she did not wish to come down with anger, to catch their contagion.

"You don't have to decide this minute," she said. "Perhaps we can visit one of the local funeral homes. I can recommend one that we've used on occasion. They can explain the various options. And I can certainly help with the paperwork; whatever you decide, there are certain things you have to do. And yes, we will need to get a release from the police." She paused: "Why don't you sit outside in the reception. I'll call Captain Gonzalez to find out how the investigation is proceeding. I'm sure you want to know."

Without a word, they got up and slunk out of the office; Mr. Blackman closed the door behind them. As she watched, Amanda was struck by how two people could occupy the same space and yet seem entirely alone with no gesture to acknowledge the physical presence of the other; the way an intimate couple could become perfect strangers; the way almost every failed relationship of hers had ended up in looks without a hint of recognition. Perhaps, she thought, that was just the way things were.

She picked up the phone and buzzed Nando: "Would you get Officer Gonzalez for me?"

She took the next few minutes to check her email but found nothing of immediate importance beyond the communique from the Embassy. Finally, the intercom sounded and Nando put her call through.

"Captain Gonzalez, this is Amanda Pennyworth at the American Consulate calling. I have the Blackman couple in my office and they are deciding what to do with the body of their son. I'll let you know as soon as I can. Will he be released soon?"

"Yes, Señora. I am certain that Señora Sanchez has finished."

"Then can you tell me if there is any progress in finding the killer. They are very anxious to know."

"There is always progress, Señora, but I cannot tell you exactly what we have discovered. But we will certainly catch him."

"About that..." she ventured. "I'm wondering if you are looking at the Americans who were at the sauna. Surely, it's possible one of them is implicated."

"You are welcome to wonder, Señora, but I do not need advice about how to conduct my investigation. Leave it to the experts. We will catch him and I will inform you when we do."

"It's just that..."

"Please, Consular Officer," he said, softening his voice.

"I realize your concern, but I am sure that we are doing all that is necessary."

This change in tone gave Amanda a sudden rush of suspicion; he had tried being blunt and dismissive and now he was trying charm. It made her distrust him even more.

"Of course; you must be right; I have no doubts about the competence of the police," she replied graciously. Two could play *this* game, she thought, and then put down the phone.

She sat quietly for a moment and then stood up to walk out into the reception area. The Blackmans were sitting quietly along the row of seats against the far wall, two chairs separating them.

"I've just talked to Officer Gonzalez," she announced. "He reports that they are making progress. But no specific details."

"In other words, they have nothing," Mr. Blackman said.

"I'm not sure it means that," Amanda replied. "But in any case, perhaps I should contact the funeral home? We can go now if you like."

"Yes," Mrs. Blackman said, standing abruptly. "We need to face this, Ed. Get the facts and then we can make a decision. So tell them we are coming."

Amanda turned to Nando and asked him to inform their approved funeraria, the Hermanos Guzman estab-lishment, that she would be visiting in a few minutes with a couple who needed their services: "And have them make an English speaker available," she added.

That done, Amanda led the couple out of the Consulate and hailed one of the taxis that was parked in front of the building.

"It's just a short ride," she assured them.

The building itself, when they approached, looked nothing at all like the made-over mansions or elongated ranch houses of typical American funeral homes. In her limited experience, at least, there was always an aura of dignity, even subdued elegance about such places in the United States. with their attached (generic, fits-all-faiths) chapels, manicured lawns, large parking lots, and covered entrance ways—as if the dead required shelter from the rain or a luxurious send-off into the Wherever.

Here, however, the building made the angle where two busy cobblestone streets met in Old Town Puerto Vallarta. It was a large white and orange gingerbread structure with a third-story tower, vaguely reminiscent of a church steeple positioned over the front corner. The windows and doorway frames as well as struts running from the second floor up to a metal roof on the third were painted chrysanthemum orange, the color she knew to be associated with death in Mexico and the commemorations of the Dia de los Muertos.

As they descended from the taxi in front, Amanda quickly explained, when she saw their astonished look, that this cheerful color scheme was traditional and portrayed an unusual, but not a disrespectful attitude; just a different custom.

Inside the funeral home the atmosphere was markedly different: cool, quiet, and somber, with a thick rug and a reception desk, several arm chairs and a sofa in an area with a low table arranged as a conversation cove. They were met by a middle-aged man dressed in a dark business suit.

"I am Señor Alverez," he announced as he bowed slightly to greet them. "And Señora Pennyworth, I believe: welcome again," he said with a studied smile. His English was accented but precise, as if he had learned phrases from a textbook.

From a previous meeting, Amanda recalled the same tone that was both welcoming and withdrawn, and not too friendly—after all the business of death demanded a respectful distance together with the impression of competence. She could almost admire his ability to translate the impatience and desperation of sorrow into a discreet financial transaction, leaving unspoken and undescribed every detail but the most essential ones: every gesture and word a euphemism.

"This is Mr. and Mrs. Blackman," Amanda began. "They need to know the options about bringing their deceased son back to the United States."

"Yes, of course," Alverez said, moving slightly toward the couple, although he made no effort to shake hands. He motioned for them to sit around the table. When they were settled—Mrs. Blackman perched nervously on the edge of her chair as if she were a bird that might take flight at any moment—he said, "As you will see, there are several catalogues that picture categories of coffins as well as cremation urns. Once you have decided how you wish to convey your son home, I can show you the actual containers that are available. Please take your time."

His soothing voice must have convinced Mrs. Blackman to relax slightly because she edged back onto the seat. "But we haven't decided anything yet," she announced. "And I'm not sure what to do."

"How about if I make a suggestion, and then you can

argue for the opposite and then we'll know where we both stand," her ex-husband said suddenly.

"Or the other way 'round, Ed. I'm sure you'll want to take charge."

Amanda was tempted to intervene. She detested being an audience to their drama. It was like being trapped in a theatre where the same bad first act kept playing over and over—never to a resolution. But she said nothing and looked at Alverez who maintained a perfectly calm demeanor. She thought he must have heard it all before: the grief that sluiced into the dry conduits of ancient feuds, releasing a flood of resentments.

As if on cue, both of the Blackmans picked up a catalogue and began thumbing through, glancing hurriedly at the pictures of the caskets and the design of funeral urns.

"I feel sick doing this," Mrs. Blackman said, tossing down her brochure. "I can't stand the thought of shopping for some container to hold my son's remains. I just don't believe he's dead... I'm sorry, Ed, that I blew up at you a minute ago. It's so hard. My brain just can't keep all my emotions in separate places."

"It's okay," her ex-husband replied. "I feel the same as you. But we have to make some decisions."

Alverez nodded slightly, but let them continue.

"I think he should be cremated," Mrs. Blackman said quickly. "What's the point of a casket and a grave? It won't bring him back or explain what happened to him. What do you say, Ed? Simplicity?"

"Just to make sure, I'd like to look at some coffins. I'm inclined to agree, but..."

"I don't think I could face comparison shopping for

caskets. But go ahead if you're curious."

"If you wish," Mr. Alverez said, standing, "I can show you several actual models but I also have a variety of very tasteful urns on display."

"All right," said Mrs. Blackman, giving her husband a dismissive look: "Would you come with us, Amanda? I may need someone to lean on."

It wasn't what she had bargained for, but Amanda nodded, and the four of them entered a large room through a back door in the reception area. The lighting was subdued, but bright enough to highlight three rows of coffins of different wood finishes mounted on trestles. Along the side and back wall were niches containing urns.

Amanda remembered the first time she had dealt with repatriating a body to the US and how it had jarred her: evoking the terror she felt as a young girl during an outing to the Field Museum in Chicago and a visit to their renowned hall of Egyptian mummies, with their open caskets and corpses wrapped in tattered and blackened swaddling. She had nightmares for weeks afterwards. It was the first time she had been brave enough to argue with her mother: Why had she exposed her to what had brought such terror? She had demanded to know, but her mother had just ignored her. And here, in this semi-lit showroom, this air-conditioned catacomb, the shapes of caskets brought it all back again, but without the sharpness that had haunted her childish imagination.

If she blanched slightly, no one noticed it. In fact, both of the Blackmans appeared more curious than anything, walking around the caskets, peering at the white silk linings of two or three with lids propped open.

Responding to their interest, and, Amanda thought,

keen to conclude a deal, Alverez said with a hint of the salesman's enthusiasm: "All of these have more or less the same interior: cushioned silk, although, of course, the quality varies according to the price. And, if you wish, we can modify any model you choose." His expressionless mask was slipping, and Amanda thought she could see the huckster's eager countenance behind it.

"Ed," Mrs. Blackman said, abruptly turning away. "You decide. I'm completely drained. Just make some decision so we can get out of here."

"Okay, Nora. I guess your choice of an urn is best. We can decide what to do with the ashes later. I'll agree to anything. Why don't you and Amanda go back to the Consulate. I'll take care of the details here. It's enough."

"That's wonderful, Ed. Yes, I want to leave. Whatever you want."

She walked quickly out of the room not even waiting for Amanda.

Still standing with Mr. Blackman and Alverez, Amanda hesitated: "Before I leave, Señor Alverez, would you please remember to send on all the paperwork I will need along with Mr. Blackman when he is finished here. I can take care of my part. And one more thing. You'll have to obtain the boy's body from the police station. I'll notify them."

She turned and left, denying herself the satisfaction of seeing the surprised look on the man's face, although she was sure the location of the body shattered his placid mask.

Back at the Consulate, Mrs. Blackman and Amanda sat in her office.

"You can see what he was like now, can't you?" Mrs.

Blackman asked as she peered across the desk at Amanda.

"I'm not sure what you mean?"

"Mercurial? Is that the word? In any case, that's the polite word for him. I prefer to think of him as fickle or unreliable. You never knew which Ed would say good morning: the mean, sarcastic blow-hard, Mr. Know-Everything-in-Advance or Mr. Flighty, the spine-less chump who would give in to your latest whim."

"Damn, I miss my dog!" she said suddenly. "Would you please have her brought over from the hotel? I'm really upset without her."

Amanda almost laughed out loud at the request: "I'm afraid I can't do that, Nora. But you could telephone the hotel yourself and try to arrange it. In the meantime, I need to talk to the police. Perhaps it's best if you wait outside. You can call from Nando's desk."

Mrs. Blackman stood up—reluctance obvious in her demeanor—because she suspected she had been dismissed and it irked her when any conversation ended without some little triumph, like missing the realtor's commission she collected from a successful transaction.

Amanda watched as she closed the door, just slightly too firmly, and thought: "That's a couple who deserve each other." She picked up the phone, asked Nando to find Captain Gonzalez for her, and then waited.

"Amanda Pennyworth, here," she replied when the call came through. Without waiting for him to respond, she continued: "I have two requests: I will send over the paperwork for you to release the body of Jeremy Blackman to the Guzman Funeral Home. Señor Alverez will contact you for details. That is, if you are finished with your examination. Further, could you tell me if you've made any more progress on solving the murder? Mr. and Mrs. Blackman are very anxious to know something before they return to the United States. I have assured them that you are making progress, but any new information would be helpful."

For a moment, she only heard the ambient noise of a busy office from his end. Amanda guessed that the policeman was considering how much he should reveal before he answered.

"We are satisfied," he began. "We can release the body now. And as for progress in finding the killer, we are, of course, closing in on him. It's just a matter of time before we will have him. You may assure the parents."

Amanda could almost feel the nudge in his voice urging her to back away. But she needed to know: "Have you talked to the Americans who were at the sauna. One of them, his boyfriend, came to the Consulate and we talked. I'm sure he knows something. Maybe the others..."

"Please, Señora. You asked that before. Let the police finish their work without interference. You would only contaminate our investigation. And I can promise you that the Americans had nothing to do with it."

"Well, if you say so," Amanda replied and hung up. But she wasn't confident at all. And she didn't like hearing the word "finish" as if the police had already made up their minds to accuse someone. It was going to be difficult to persuade the Blackmans that the police would solve the case when her skepticism would undoubtedly show through her reluctant words of assurance. As a diplomat, the expression of false confidence always gave her the greatest difficulty: to convince a person of a truth she herself didn't belief in. But that was, after all, half—maybe more—of the job.

She glanced down at the pile of papers that Nando had placed on her desk while she was preoccupied with the Blackmans. Their demands were taking her away from her other obligations and, she thought, tonight she would have to remain in the office late until she caught up. But what she really wanted was a leisurely meal on the beach, sitting in the soft air of the evening, feeling its hot breath envelope her, and listening to the passionate ocean jam its fists into the sea wall in frustrated anger along the bay. What she wouldn't do for a strawberry margarita right now!

This moment of selfish contemplation ended abruptly with a knock on her door. Nando poked his head inside and announced that Archie West had arrived and wanted to talk to her.

"Send him in," she replied reluctantly.

"Yes, Mr. West," she said, standing as soon as he appeared. "What can I do for you?"

"I want to know what's happening," he said, as he slid uninvited onto a chair in front of her. "I have a right to know."

"Perhaps you do." But she offered nothing.

He sat for a minute, waiting for her, and then began: "And there's something I didn't tell you and maybe you need to know. Jeremy and I were planning to be married. We bought a couple of rings here in Puerto Vallarta. Found a cheap place. See," he said as he thrust left his hand across the desk. "We've been wearing them. I know you're not supposed to before the ceremony and all, bad luck... but it was just for practice. He said he wanted to know what it felt like. You know. Other people looking at us; guessing."

Amanda reacted swiftly: "Did you tell the police?"

"Why would I tell them anything? They weren't interested in what I had to say."

"But it's evidence... if he was wearing his ring in the sauna. Perhaps they found it."

"I don't know that. Maybe he took it off. Anyway, that's not why I'm here. I want to be part of this... whatever his parents decide. If there will be a funeral or some sort of memorial service."

"I suppose you can ask Mrs. Blackman. I'm sure you noticed her outside when you came in."

He said nothing, and Amanda picked up the telephone. "Get Captain Gonzalez immediately, Nando. I'll hold."

When he answered, she began. "I'm sorry to intrude, Señor, but I have some important information for you, and it can't wait."

"Señora?"

"I have Archie West in my office, you know, the boyfriend of the deceased. Well, he just informed me that Jeremy Blackman may have been wearing a gold wedding band or maybe had one in his possession. Did you find it?"

There was a momentary silence: "Thank you for telling me, Señora Pennyworth. That is important information. It will help us find the killer. And please, if anything else happens that we should know, call me immediately." He hung up before Amanda could ask anything further. But she was pleased. Maybe they would listen to her now and investigate the Americans.

At the police compound Captain Gonzalez leaned back in his chair; a very satisfied look spread over his face. As soon as Perez came back from interviewing one of the other locals, they would confront Herrera again. He had never believed the story about stealing the ring from his workplace. Yes, he was a thief and a liar, and now they had all the evidence they needed to tie him to the victim. No doubt he was also a murderer. Perez could still interview the others, just to eliminate them; best to do it right away. But he was sure now.

CHAPTER 7

Perez stopped his police car at the gatehouse to the apartment complex and then, after waiting a moment, rolled down the window and peered inside. The guard certainly knew he was there, but made no motion to get up from his seat where he seemed in the thrall to something on his cellphone. The policeman was accustomed to this sort of belligerent inattention, the dawdling refusal to acknowledge his presence—just one of the small ways that ordinary citizens registered their aversion to authority. He tapped his horn and the guard glanced up with an exaggerated and feigned look of surprise on his face. He got up slowly, opened the door, and approached the car.

"Yes, Señor? May I be of service?" he asked, knowing full well that Perez wanted entrance to the grounds.

"Will you please raise the gate?"

"Is there some problem?" the guard asked.

"There will be if you don't allow me to pass through right now," Perez replied in a tone that indicated he had

had enough of this game.

"Of course, officer. Immediately, Señor." The guard walked with deliberate slow steps to the edge of the moveable barrier, pressed a release and it raised up slowly, but only enough so that the car would not scrape the bottom, but not so high that it could proceed quickly.

Once inside, Perez parked, got out of his car, and looked around at the sprawling development. It was a modern building, or rather a series of connected buildings on several levels making a semi-circle of wings linked by elevated walkways, and set in a carefully tended garden of palm trees and expanses of emerald-green lawn, splashed with bright flower beds. He could hear the faint noise of traffic coming from the highway separating the apartments from the green arms of the forested ravine that rose up behind the complex.

"Dinero," he said to himself, as he mounted a staircase that led to what looked like some sort of office. He was sure there would be a *conserje* or a rental agent or someone present because an establishment this exclusive always had an army of employees, workmen, gardeners, and maids who would materialize suddenly as if they knew you were about to appear.

He opened the door of the office and a young woman, seated behind a desk stood up to greet him.

"Welcome, Señor," she bubbled almost too enthusiastically. "May I help you?"

"Yes, you may. I am looking for the apartment of Señor Torres, Miguel Torres. I believe he lives here."

"Yes, officer. He is well known to us and a long-time resident—that is, almost as long as the building has been here."

"And his apartment number?"

"Let me look." She sat down and typed something into her desktop computer. "The south wing, number 425. Just step outside and take the walkway to the left. It's at the far end and on the fourth floor." She hesitated as if ready to ask what Perez knew she wanted to know: Why? Why was a policeman asking for him?

"Thank you, Señora," he said, turning to leave. "I'm certain I can find it."

"And if you need any more information?" she asked. "We're always ready to help."

"No need. But thank you."

He paced along the catwalk, passing by two structures until he reached the far end. He found himself on the third floor and took the staircase up one flight and then entered a long, cool hallway. Apartment 425 was in the middle of the corridor. He raised the brass head of the door knocker and let it thud against the metal housing. He heard nothing from inside but shortly the door opened; a man stood in the frame. He was of medium height and well-built, with striations of silver deposited in his carefully manicured, black hair. He had a short mustache that traced the contour of his upper lip. Dressed in shorts, barefoot, and a T-shirt, his age was not readily apparent. You could guess, but it would depend on the angle and the light, Perez thought.

"You are Señor Miguel Torres?"

"Yes, officer. How may I be of assistance?"

"May I come in? I have several questions to ask you. Informally, I should add—at least... for now." Perez watched the man's face carefully to see if there was a reaction. He often added something vaguely threatening when he confronted a suspect, to throw him off-guard.

"Of course. Come in and sit." Torres seemed perfectly at ease, but Perez wondered if this was an act.

Together they passed into a large living room with a floor-to-ceiling window looking out onto a small deck, and beyond that to a dazzling view of the town, its white stucco structures spread out on a narrow apron below and extending to the ocean in the distance. The door leading outside was part-way open and a breeze stirred through it. On the walls, to either side of the room, were several large, colorful paintings. Off to the left, Perez could see into a dining area with a large, dark table set with twin silver candelabras. The walls were painted a deep purple, but the room was brightened because of several large built-in mirrors. A statue stood in the corner, about a meter and a half tall, a copy of something Roman or Greek, depicting a naked man with drapery discreetly slung over his shoulder and gripped in his left hand.

Gesturing for Perez to sit down, Torres said quickly: "I think I know why you are here. And I'm very happy to cooperate."

Perez settled into a large, leather armchair and looked carefully at Torres before responding. Nothing made him more suspicious than a suspect who volunteered complete candor without being asked. His experience told him that a part of the truth was always locked away in a strongbox of lies and evasions. If details were too easy to uncover, then he was certain there would be more hidden away somewhere.

"I expect you want to ask me about the murder at the Olympiad," Torres continued. "Yes, of course I know about it. There was a mention in the newspaper. But, beyond that, I can't tell you anything else. I was there, as you must have discovered. But what else can I say?"

"Please, Señor Torres. I will ask questions. I am not interested in hearing a story."

Torres looked surprised for a moment, and then managed to rearrange his expression into a vague smile: "Of course, officer. Certainly. As you wish."

Perez also smiled, not to put the man at ease, but because he thought he had him exactly where he wanted: Torres was upset, suspicious, and perhaps too practiced in his answers. Perhaps he had anticipated a visit and prepared himself. Perez thought he could often sense when a suspect was circling around the truth. But he would have to guard against letting his growing distaste for this man show through his questions. He had a brief moment to wonder why he had developed an immediate dislike. Was it his lifestyle? That he was gay? Or more likely the ease and nonchalance of someone comfortable with the surroundings of money.

"I need for you to describe what you were doing at the Olympiad."

"I went in the afternoon. I don't make it a habit, but I met someone on the Malecon. You know how it is."

Perez said nothing; he knew from the boy they had interviewed how the encounter went. But he let the man continue.

"What was this person's name?"

"I think it was Felix. At least he said so. But you know, names aren't important or always honest. So I didn't pay much attention... anyway, we met and stopped for a coffee."

"Do you make it a habit to pick up underage boys?"

"I don't see how that's relevant, officer."

"It's very relevant because the victim of the murder is also a young man. Is that the sort you prefer? Perhaps he refused you and you attacked him."

"Absolutely not! That's absurd. I wouldn't. Do you think I'm desperate?"

"I have no idea; are you?" Perez interrupted.

Torres was obviously displeased, but continued: "Anyway, after we talked for a while, I suggested to the boy that we go to the sauna. I prefer not to bring anyone back here that I don't know well. There's always a danger of robbery. And there are my neighbors to consider." He stopped for a moment and looked around the room. "We live in glass houses here."

Perez said nothing, hoping that his silence would pry some interesting detail out of Torres.

"We went in together. I paid for his entry. And then after a time, I left. I really don't like places like that. Dirty... He stayed behind. That's all I know."

"And that's all. Nothing else happened? Did you see any Americans?"

"There are always Americans at such places. But I didn't notice anyone in particular."

Perez waited.

"Except now that I remember, I think maybe I heard someone arguing. At least a moment or two of raised voices. You know the music was pretty loud and constant and I can't be entirely sure. But I thought it might be English. I wasn't listening."

"Did you have sex with anyone else? Or talk to anyone?"

Torres glared at him: "Certainly not! I wasn't there

very long. I didn't even..."

"And that's all? You had sex with an underage boy and then you left—just like that?"

Torres winced, and looked away. Perez couldn't tell if it was guilt or embarrassment or both.

"Don't deny it. We have proof that you convinced the assistant at the door: bribed him... It doesn't look good for you when you lie. Now let me know anything else. Any detail."

"There's nothing, Señor. I just left. Why would I kill an American? Or anyone?"

"I will be taking a DNA sample from you to see if it matches what we have. Then we will know what you did. And if you don't tell me everything, it will go very badly for you when we find out. We always do."

Torres looked distraught. He half rose up from his chair and then fell back. "All right. There is something else. I didn't want to tell you. Didn't think it was relevant."

Perez waited.

"I'm sorry to say that I paid the boy."

"Which boy? The American?"

"No, of course not! I told you, I didn't have anything to do with him. No, it was the boy I came with. He asked me for money and I gave him 2000 pesos. It wasn't much. The money didn't mean anything. I felt sorry for him."

"Then why didn't you tell me straight away? Why hide it?"

"I don't know. Maybe I was ashamed to have to pay. And we didn't even..." He ran his right hand through his hair and turned slightly sideways.

Perez had the distinct impression this was a gesture he often performed in front of a mirror.

"And did you give him anything else? Are you telling me the whole truth now?"

"What else do you mean? Of course not! I've told you everything. I had nothing to do with any murder."

Perez paused and then decided to pursue another possibility: "Do you think the boy, Felix, could have done it?"

"No, I don't. He may have been out for money. I didn't suspect that at the time, and it makes me shudder to think he might have been all along... That's all I know. I have nothing more to tell you."

"Then you will have no objection to a DNA test. I have a kit in my pocket and we can do it right now."

Torres hesitated: "You're treating me like a criminal. I'm not sure."

"If you refuse, we will *certainly* think that. And you can accompany me to the police station straight away. They will clarify for you what you can and can't do."

"All right. Yes. Go ahead then. I have nothing to hide."

Perez thought to reply that this man probably had a great deal to hide, but he held back. Instead, he stood up and reached inside his uniform breast pocket and extracted a long plastic tube. Opening it, he pulled out a swab and approached Torres, who had a look of panic on his face.

"Just a collection from inside your mouth. Open please."

Torres did as asked. And when Perez had finished, he put away the kit and walked toward the door. Turning around, he said: "Don't think of leaving town."

He took one last look at Torres who had sunk into his chair with the blank stare of dismay distorting his handsome face.

Perez closed the door behind him and retraced his steps across the catwalk and down to the parking area. He was fairly convinced that Torres had nothing to do with the murder, but sometimes new evidence could reverse his convictions. Maybe the DNA sample would reveal something. But he was now even more suspicious of the boy Felix who was still in custody. There was no plausible explanation for the ring they had found in his possession and he did not believe for a minute that he had found it lying around in some store where he worked. That explanation had to be false and it made him look very bad. But could such a slight person commit such a brutal murder? Would rage make him powerful enough? And why, he wondered. Robbery just didn't seem a convincing motive especially since the boy had been paid for his presence by Torres.

As he drove back to the station, down along the twisting road along the river that led to the center of town, he considered where they were on solving the murder. Gonzalez was convinced that it was a simple robbery gone wrong and was sure that one of the Mexican men had killed Blackman and taken his money. And maybe that ring they found... since the victim had been wearing one. Implausible as it might seem, Felix had to be the one. It certainly did look that way. And perhaps they would know more when all the DNA evidence had been collected. But he wasn't convinced... and there were the Americans that the woman from the Consulate had been anxious to interview. Perhaps she was right. But he admitted to himself that he was confused. He had stepped into a world that he knew little about and he wondered about the men he had interviewed, what they thought; even how they dreamed.

Was this life that he was suddenly becoming aware of a simple parody of his own: attraction, courtship, marriage... children? No, it couldn't be the same. But then what were the rules that guided friendships, love, and especially, casual encounters? And anger and betrayal? Did they want to be women? Like women, but not the same? He had never thought much about it because he didn't care. Of course, when he was young, he had known boys in school who seemed effeminate, and there were one or two obvious classmates that everyone teased. But so far the men he had interviewed didn't seem like this at all. What impressed him was how ordinary they seemed, different from each other, of course, but he couldn't have picked them out passing along the Malecon. So how did they know each other? What signals passed between them? The way they looked or walked? But maybe there wasn't some secret code and that was why places like the Olympiad existed? That was a mystery he didn't need to solve. He shook his head and concentrated on driving.

Once inside police headquarters, he went straight to Señora Sanchez's office. Peering through the glass in the upper half of the door, he saw that she was not present, so he went to the room that served as a laboratory and mortuary. He found her sitting on a high stool next to an elevated work table filled with test tubes and apparatus he couldn't identify.

"I've brought another DNA sample, he said, placing the kit in front of her."

She looked up from the ledger book she had been reading: "No results yet from the samples you gave me. So

I can't tell you anything."

"When will we know, Señora?"

"Soon, I hope. It depends on the laboratory in Guadalajara. Is there some rush?"

"I'm sorry. It's just that we think we have a suspect and Captain Gonzalez will be displeased if there's a delay. He's always in a hurry."

"It's not for his pleasure that I do my work here," she said curtly, looking back at her file, as if too busy to continue. "On your way out, please leave the sample there on my work table."

He shrugged and walked out of the laboratory and back upstairs. He found the Captain sitting back in his desk chair, hands behind his head, looking very satisfied. Before he could speak, Gonzalez silenced him with a hand gesture.

"I am certain now that Herrera is the murderer. That Señora from the American Consulate just telephoned with new information. The ring—that ring that you found in the closet with the pesos—was stolen, yes. But not from the store like he said, but from the finger of the dead boy. It was a wedding ring. The two Americans were going to be married." He put his hands down on the desk and looked carefully at Perez, his look of aversion becoming a satisfied smirk.

Perez remained standing and began to speak, but before he could say anything, Gonzalez commanded: "Sit down, sit down. Are you planning to run away? You have interviewed another suspect and taken another sample, yes?"

"Yes, I have. I've just come from talking to Señora Sanchez in the lab. I'm afraid I have bad news—I mean, no news yet. The samples from Vargas and Herrera have yet to be analyzed as well as Torres, of course."

Gonzalez swore under his breath. And then brightened: "But we have the ring. That proves something doesn't it? I think we must talk to Herrera immediately. And after that, if he doesn't break, I want you to interview our fourth suspect. Do it this afternoon! I shouldn't hold these two suspects much longer; their families have already been here twice. Maybe the new sample; maybe the last person we interview; maybe the boy will confess. I hate the way this case keeps getting more and more complicated when I know there is a simple explanation at hand."

He stood up. "So let's go talk to Herrera again. And don't be so soft with him this time."

They left the office and descended the staircase to the basement, their boots ringing on the rough metal surface of the steps. Gonzalez spoke to one of the guards as they passed along the corridor by the small cell area and then opened the door to the interview room. They remained standing, waiting for the boy to be ushered in. Even with the door open, the room remained close and damp. There was a large vent in the ceiling but if there was breeze flowing out of it, Perez could not feel any air stirring. The accumulated heat and humidity had caused the cinderblock walls to sweat. And there was a pungent odor, as if the motionless atmosphere held a residue of lies and evasions that had emanated from their investigations. Perez had always wondered if this repugnant environment was accidental—a fault in the construction—or intentionally designed to add physical discomfort to the verbal assault they would unleash on the fabrications of a suspect.

After a minute or so, the guard appeared, holding the

arm of Herrera, pushed him into the room, and then shoved him down roughly onto a metal chair standing by the table set in the middle. The two policemen sat opposite him.

Perez waited for Gonzalez to begin, but he said nothing, just looking at the boy who turned away in fright. This was another of the tactics his superior used to establish his command, to intimidate, and demonstrate his superiority. And then he reached into the breast pocket of his uniform and tossed the gold ring onto the table. Herrera flinched as if he had been struck.

"No more lies, boy. You will explain this ring and where you got it."

"I told you," he stammered. "I found it at my work. No one missed it. I admit that I took it." He looked as if even he no longer believed this unlikely story.

"But we now have other information about where this really came from. You need to give up your false explanations. We never believed you anyway."

Herrera said nothing but looked down at his hands. Perez wondered for a moment if the boy was unconsciously staring to see if they looked like the murder weapons—the hands that had strangled the American.

Gonzalez leaned over the table, picked up the ring and held it up to the boy's face.

"Look carefully at this," he commanded. "And tell us now. Where did you get it? And don't lie this time!"

Herrera suddenly began to sob and tried to speak, but the words seemed jumbled and disjointed from emotion.

Perez started to reach out and touch Herrera's arm, but the boy drew back in terror.

"I don't know where I got it, officer. That's the truth,"

he said finally.

"So you still lie. But we know. And we know that you killed the American to steal it. And we know that he was wearing this ring."

"No! No! I didn't! Okay. I took the ring!" he gulped. "He was already dead or maybe just too drunk to notice. Lying there in the steam room. I couldn't have killed him! I didn't! Never! Why would I?"

Gonzalez made no effort to hide the look of anger on his face: "So you admit you're a thief and a murderer, and then you took his key and went to his room and robbed him."

"No! No! I didn't! You can't make me admit that. I never would!"

"Then how did you know he was dead if you didn't kill him?"

"I touched him. Shook him once and he didn't move. I thought... I don't know why I took it. I just did. I felt it on his hand. I'm sorry. I'm sorry! But I didn't kill him!"

Perez looked intently at the boy trying to decide what was true after so many false explanations. His grimy face was streaked with ribbons of tears and he seemed not to know what to do with his nervous hands. He certainly looked guilty, no doubt, but of what? He wanted to know if he had had sex with the American. If they only had the right DNA sample they would know that too.

Gonzalez said nothing but stood up, walked around the table and grabbed the boy by his arm, jerking him half out of his chair.

"If you continue to lie to us, you'll regret it... Perez, take him back to his cell. And, if his parents bother us again, inform them that we have evidence against him and we will continue to hold him. They won't be allowed to see him." He spat on the floor, shoved the boy back down, and walked out of the room. Perez, stood up and guided Herrera back to the cell area telling the guard to lock him inside. He then walked back upstairs to the office. Gonzalez was sitting behind his desk, a look of satisfaction on his face.

"I think we have him," he said. "Most of the story at least. Maybe a few more hours downstairs will convince him to confess the rest of it... You know Perez, this case both bores and disgusts me. It feels like I have something dirty on my uniform, and I want to brush it away and be done with it."

Perez wondered for a moment if the prejudices of his superior were clouding his judgment, making him imagine certainties in the blinkered light of circumstantial evidence.

"Well there is something you should know. I found it this afternoon and it corroborates part of Herrera's statements. When I visited Señor Torres, he confessed giving the boy money."

Gonzalez looked very unhappy. "How do you know that was the truth? Perhaps they were conspiring together?"

"No, I don't think so. He didn't want to tell me. He was ashamed of paying for sex. I'm convinced he was telling me the truth. Of course, there will be the DNA sample. When we have that, we will know more. But I think I believe Torres and maybe even Herrera. It just doesn't seem plausible. You don't kill someone for a ring. And the money we found is now accounted for. Torres told me how much it was; it seems to fit."

Gonzalez waited for a minute and then said, angrily,

"You have one more suspect to interview; one more sample to take. Do it right now! This case is winding me up in knots and I want them untangled pronto. Get to it!"

Without a word, Perez turned and walked out of the office. He was sure that Gonzalez blamed him, but for what? He was merely doing his job; reporting what he knew from interviewing suspects. It wasn't his fault if the captain couldn't think of the words to fit all the evidence of a crossword puzzle, where they were constantly finding new clues to fit into open spaces.

Returning to his desk, he pulled out his case notes. He spent a half hour writing up impressions of his interview with Torres and then the partial confession of Herrera. When he had finished, he put the file away and looked up the name of the last Mexican to be interviewed: Juan Molina whose address was situated at the far southern end of the Zona Romantica. He walked outside and decided to take his own car. He wanted to surprise Molina and he worried that the sight of a police car pulling up outside his apartment or house might make him bolt.

The address was located above Los Muertos Beach off the Aveneda Amapas where the town narrowed and mounted up into hills that sprouted a number of luxury hotels. Molina, however, lived in a shabby two-story apartment building on one of the side streets, an older structure that affronted the new construction that was transforming the area into an exclusive neighborhood for tourists and expats. Perez parked his car several meters away from the front of the building and then walked up to the front of the wooden entrance leading into a courtyard that he could see through a separation between the edge of the door and a high wall. There were four names and four call buttons on a small panel and a speaker embedded in the stucco. He chose one arbitrarily—but not Molina's. The answer, which he could barely understand for the static of its transmission, asked his identity.

"Police," he replied. "I need to enter."

After a moment, the buzzer on the door lock sounded and he stepped inside. The square enclosure was paved in broken tiles, with tufts of grass growing up between edges where the mortar had disintegrated. A scruffy palm tree grew in one corner. On the right side was a staircase leading up to a second story gallery with two doors. The walls of the building were white but with several dark blemishes of uncertain age where cracks or areas of crumbling material had been repaired and long awaited paint. As Perez walked across this small entranceway, a door to his left opened and a woman emerged.

Perez greeted her quietly: "Gracias, Señora. I'm here to talk to Señor Molina. Can you indicate his apartment?"

She gave him a conspiratorial nod and then pointed to a door on the second story. He smiled a silent thank you and turned to go up the staircase. Up on the second floor, he knocked at the nearest door and waited. There was a vague commotion inside and Perez had the distinct impression that he was being observed. But no one answered. He knocked again and this time put his face close to the door and shouted: "Open up Molina. I'm sure you're in there. This is the police."

Finally, the latch moved silently and the door opened a crack. Perez could see that it was impeded by a brass chain.

"What do you want?" came the voice of a young man.

"Open the door, immediately. This is the police. I need to speak to you."

The door shut and Perez could hear the faint clink-clack of the chain swinging against the wood, and then it opened wider. Molina was standing in the entrance, dressed only in shorts and sandals.

"I was sleeping. What do you want?" he asked.

Perez pushed him aside, against the wall, and entered the dim hallway: "I need to talk to you."

"All right," Molina said, recovering his balance. "There's no need to do that! I have a right to be suspicious, don't I?"

"We shall see what rights you have," Perez said, walking into the small, untidy living room. "Sit down," he ordered.

Molina followed him cautiously, as hesitant as if this were the first time he had ever been in the room.

They sat and Perez looked around at the furnishings. They were sparse and shabby: two chairs, a small television set perched on a flimsy metal table, and a leather couch with a sizable rip down the side. There were two posters of guitar players on the walls. A window provided the only light. It struck him immediately that this was a person who well might have robbed the American. The poverty of the room spoke of a powerful motivation.

"What's this about?" Molina said, half stretching and yawning.

Perez wasn't sure if the boy had been sleeping, or if this was an act meant to convince.

"I assume that you have heard about the murder at the Olympiad," he began. "You were there, weren't you?"

"Suppose I was?"

"Yes, we have confirmed that. No need to deny it."

"I'm not denying anything... yet. But what do you want from me? I can't tell you anything."

Perez paused for a moment and looked at him carefully. He was thin and about medium height with dark skin and hair. His eyes were a vivid black, intense and moody. It gave him a striking appearance that Perez thought alternated between sinister and handsome.

"Did you have sex with the American? Did you rob him and kill him?"

Molina said nothing but smiled faintly and shook his head. "I don't like Americans. How could I rob him? You don't carry money walking around that place in nothing but a towel anyway."

"I don't know how you did it, but it's certainly possible. Maybe you took the key to his room, took his money."

Molina said nothing, so Perez continued a little louder than he needed: "I want you to get dressed and come to the police station with me, immediately. We'll take a DNA sample there and Captain Gonzalez will want to speak to you."

Molina said nothing but stood up slowly and walked out of the room. Perez followed him.

When Molina reached the small bedroom, he turned to Perez with a smirk and said: "Are you going to watch me get dressed?"

"So you don't try to escape or do anything funny."

Molina laughed and went to a small closet and pulled out a shirt and jeans. He then turned back and slipped off his shorts, standing naked in front of the policeman.

"I'm sure this is what you wanted to see," he exclaimed. "Take a good look. Would you like for me to turn around too? Maybe you'd like to look at my ass? I know about your type and all about your uniforms!"

"Shut up and get dressed," Perez said. "No more games. You're making a good deal of trouble for yourself. And I don't have much patience."

Molina walked slowly around the bed to a small shelf in the corner and picked up some underwear. He turned to see if Perez was still watching; then slipped on the shorts and went back and quickly put on his shirt and jeans. Once he had dressed completely, he announced: "I'm all yours, officer."

Perez ignored the taunt and seized his arm roughly and escorted him out of the apartment, jerking him down the stairs, across the courtyard and out onto the street.

He stopped: "I'm warning you just this once to be careful. You won't find anyone else at headquarters who will stand for your stupid jokes and insults. Unless you want that face you think is so handsome to be reorganized."

"I don't see a police car," Molina said looking down the street. "Maybe you're not even a cop. Just dressed up like one."

"I came in my own car. Parked just there in front of us. I thought if you saw some official vehicle, you might run. And no jokes."

"Yeah, I might have," Molina said. "You'll never know, will you?"

As they drove back down toward the center of Puerto Vallarta, Perez decided he had had enough of this cocky young man.

"We'll be sending a team to search your apartment. If there's anything there, we will find it. Never fails."

"I'm sure you'll find lots, but I had nothing to do with

some murder. I'm completely innocent."

Perez shook his head; no one is entirely innocent, he thought. Everyone has their secrets: things they wouldn't admit, perhaps even to themselves. In his experience, things hidden were the most dangerous and revealing of all. And it was his job to pick at the scars of such concealed objects until they bled out the truth.

Back at the station, Perez took Molina directly to the basement interview room, shoved him inside, and locked the door behind him as he went to look for Captain Gonzalez.

"I've got Molina in the basement," he informed his superior. He was about to describe him when he thought the better of it. Let Gonzalez find out for himself: no reason to get him worked up beforehand. Molina would be in enough trouble if he played the fool with someone who was so quick tempered and anxious to hang guilt on anyone's neck.

"Did you get a DNA sample?"

"No, not yet. Wanted you to know first. I'll get Señora Sanchez to stop by. And I'm sending out a couple of officers to search his apartment."

"What's your impression of him? Seem guilty?" Gonzalez asked.

"Not sure," Perez added, but didn't finish saying that he knew Gonzalez would quickly break this boy down. He had seen it many times before: an arrogant, self-important suspect stripped down to a confused core of excuses and contradictions. Even if he wasn't guilty, Gonzalez might make him confess.

On the way down, Perez detoured to the laboratory/ morgue.

"I've got one last suspect for you in the interview room... from the Blackman case," he told Señora Sanchez. "That should wrap it up."

He left, went upstairs to organize the search, and then rejoined Gonzalez who was just sitting down at the table opposite Molina. The boy smirked when he entered.

His boss began quietly, a strategy that Perez knew would explode from the subdued to a fury of questions and accusations. Molina looked confident and sat back in his chair looking from one policeman to the other, no doubt thinking it wouldn't go badly for him if he just kept cool.

"You were at the sauna. We have that information, so please don't deny it."

Molina nodded but said nothing.

"And," Gonzalez continued, "You were aware that there were Americans present. Did you speak to any of them?"

Molina shook his head.

Perez thought he should intervene: "You need to answer out loud, son. Shaking your head isn't enough. We might misinterpret and then you could be in serious difficulty."

"Okay, yes, I think there were Americans—at least a couple of guys speaking English. You think I'm an expert on nationalities or something?"

Gonzalez suddenly slammed his fist down on the table: "That's the last sarcastic answer I'm going to tolerate. Do you understand that? You're in very serious trouble here."

Molina was about the answer when the door opened and Señora Sanchez walked in carrying a DNA kit.

"I'm here to take a sample," she said, walking around the table to stand next to Molina: "Please open your mouth and I'll take a swab."

"What if I refuse? I know I have rights."

Gonzalez reached across the table and grabbed the boy's collar and jerked him out of his seat: "We can always take a sample from your bloody nose if you'd prefer." He shoved Molina back into his chair, which tipped back precariously.

"Okay, okay," he said. "Go ahead."

Señora Sanchez quickly took the sample, put the swab away, and left the room. Molina slouched down in his chair as if he could evade the two policemen staring at him.

"You know why we're collecting your sample, don't you?" Gonzalez continued. "We took DNA from the victim's body that will prove who the killer was. If you had anything to do with him, you'd better confess it now. I can't promise you any leniency. If you're a murderer, you'll pay for it. But I'm in a hurry and you don't want to know what I'll do to save time."

Molina suddenly looked terrified and shrank further. Perez immediately thought of a rodent timidly poking its nose out of a burrow and then cringing at the sight of something large, moving darkly. He knew that Gonzalez could cast the shadow of a predator when he thought his victim was trapped.

"I didn't do anything!" Molina cried.

"Get him out of here," Gonzalez ordered. "I've had enough lies for today. You'll stay with us for a while, young man, until the DNA tests are completed and we've searched your apartment. Then we'll be charging someone. Probably you."

He stood up to leave and Perez escorted the boy to an empty cell—the only one remaining—and told the guard on duty to lock him inside. As he was leaving, he thought he heard Molina whimpering, the hard shell of his insolence had cracked open with nothing but the soft stuff of fear inside.

CHAPTER 8

Even though it was more than a mile from her apartment, the next morning Amanda decided to walk to work along the Malecon. She often had her best thoughts listening to the rhythm of the sea breaking along the shore, sliding up the beach and farther on toward the middle of Old Town, pounding against the pile of rocks and the concrete embankment. Because it was early, the morning mist clung to the tops of the mountains to her right and ahead of her, the thick, humid air wrapped the high-rise hotels of the marina area in a feathery gauze. All along the boardwalk, the stores, souvenir shops, and cafés were beginning to open. Billboard signs with photographs of shrimp dishes, lobsters, and tacos, stowed inside for the evening, already stood outside restaurants. Their menus, spread open like children's picture books, were already placed on stands by each entrance. Sandwich boards advertised breakfast. Although she recognized some of them, and they certainly knew her by sight, a few of the waiters stepped out in front of her to invite her inside, as if she were just a passing tourist. She nodded, walked around them, and continued on past the opal shop, the leather store, and the T-shirt emporia where a young man was just then waltzing a manikin out onto the sidewalk.

The front entrance of almost every store was still wet from its morning washdown—a ritual that she had once imagined was meant to cleanse away yesterday's disappointments and clear a way of hope for the day's success. Peering inside the large pharmacy and souvenir shop she could see two saleswomen, one sweeping the floor and the other wiping down the glass countertops. In another hour, the whole of the boardwalk would be filled with vacationers strolling along, looking inside stores for nothing in particular and rarely buying anything this early. A man wearing a sombrero and sitting on the seawall had spread three brilliant multi-colored rugs beside him in a clash of primary colors. He looked at her with earnest expectation. Farther on, a woman had set up a tiny cross-leg table with a tray of costume jewelry. The odd jogger was already weaving around the statues and palm trees around the plaza in front of the white-washed Navy Museum. She observed a group of American women—it had to be Americans, she thought—who passed by her, fast-walking with the grimace of determination on their faces. An older man was being urged along by a trio of chihuahuas lunging forward against their leashes. The whole town, she thought, was stretching its limbs for the new day; commerce was wiping the sleep from its eyes.

Normally, to watch this quickening made her light-headed and confident, ready for whatever bureaucratic snarls she might face or unpleasant characters demanding her immediate attention. But how many times had she begun the morning recently with a light step and a positive attitude, only to confront a sluggish day of unending complications? That was the job; she knew what she had signed on for. By the time the office closed she was almost always exhausted and ready to unwind. What a wonderful metaphor that: to unwind! Some days it did seem that a web of difficulties had been woven around her, tied her thoughts up in knots that only a stiff drink or two and then dinner (if she bothered to make it at all) could loosen. Yet most mornings began again with a buoyant feeling, especially when she ambled along the Malecon. But today, for reasons she knew well, she had a strange feeling: Sadness? Perplexity? Anticipation? What was it that weighed her step, that made her look at all the stirrings around her without catching the contagion of their cheer and optimism? For her, the new day had already clouded over with apprehension.

She paused for a moment in front of the bronze statue of the mermaid and her child, a sculpture that always amused her and carried her imagination to the churning white caps from which she always imagined this figure to be emerging. But today, it seemed only a twisted piece of molded metal, lifeless and dull in the slanted morning sun; and the sea behind it paused to a calm dirty-blue reflecting pool. She turned away and continued on, trying to articulate what weighed on her spirit, what distorted her vision, like seeing the world blurred by tears. Was this the effect of loneliness? Overwork? Or the awful murder that she feared would never have a convincing solution?

Of course; that was it; she needn't invent some unresolved existential condition. The Ambassador in Mexico

City was bound to be concerned and she needed to send in a report today. The fact that he hadn't yet demanded more information was not an indication that when he did he would go softly on her. But she had delayed telling him what she only vaguely knew. No doubt he would fault her if no resolution was immediate because of pressure bearing on him from Washington and from the American press, which loved to blow up any story about the dangers of tourism in Mexico. Events like this could be quickly amplified in the arena of international squabbles and competition, twisted into evidence by some Congressman about the perils of immigration. In this instance, there might even be jeremiads in Sunday sermons about the evils of sexual deviance. She could imagine.

"Slow down!" she told herself. "One thing at a time." One worry was enough for the time being, and primary on the list was a conversation with the Blackmans planned for late afternoon, to resolve any paperwork issues about transporting their son's remains... and then see them off. Comfort dog included! She was the one who needed one!

For the first time that morning, she smiled. But at the back of all this anticipation, she knew she needed a vacation, some long sojourn back to the US: home perhaps to Chicago to see her parents; they had been insisting for a long time. But the thought of returning home was unnerving: to sleep in her old room with its mementos of the past preserved like museum pieces; to listen to her mother talk as if Amanda had just graduated college and was preparing to "settle down." Despite the fact that she herself had a career, her mother had suddenly become anxious about grandchildren. And when Amanda had announced her intention to apply for the Foreign Service, every objection they fired at her was a "what about?" What about this... what about that—down a list of their expectations for her. All those questions still remained unspoken between them. No, she couldn't face Chicago just now. Much better to go to Santa Monica where her old college roommate was always urging her to visit.

When she arrived at the Consulate Office, she immediately called police headquarters. If she had to talk to Captain Gonzalez so be it! Even if he chided her for interfering.

But instead of the Captain, Sergeant Perez came on the line after a relay from the main switchboard: "Sergeant Perez here," he answered.

"This is Amanda Pennyworth at the American Consulate. I'm inquiring about the Blackman murder case. Do you expect Captain Gonzalez soon?"

"I am assisting on that case, so perhaps I can help. But if you wish to speak to my superior. He is busy right now. I can have him call you."

"No, no" Amanda said, trying to disguise her relief. "If you know anything, perhaps you can tell me."

He hesitated, and then lowered his voice as if he was afraid of being overheard: "I shouldn't really tell you much, Señora, but I understand that you have been very helpful." He paused as if still unsure. "I can tell you that we have interviewed all of the Mexican men who were at the sauna around the time of the murder and we have taken DNA from all of them."

"So there was DNA on the body? Is that the reason for samples?"

"Yes. Evidence of intercourse."

"And you are quite certain that it was a Mexican?"

"Well, there is other evidence too. One of them has admitted to stealing the ring from the victim's finger."

"Can you tell me who it is?"

"I would prefer not to."

"But you think he is the killer?"

"Captain Gonzalez is convinced, yes."

"But you?"

"Not so sure."

"Do you think it would be wise to question the other Americans who were present—I mean in addition to Señor West, his boyfriend."

"I believe one is a tourist and perhaps if he is still in town, yes, I might pay him a visit. The others, I'm not sure—"

For some reason (she pondered about it later), she added quickly, "I could go with you. Perhaps to translate."

Perez did not hide the amusement in his voice at this excuse: "Of course, why not? I can give you his name. Better, why don't you ask him to come to the Consulate? I will meet you there?"

"Okay. Let me have his number and I'll have my assistant phone him and then let you know."

"Perfecto."

"And the other Americans?"

"One at least is permanent here. We could wait. The other has an address in a condominium in the marina area, so I don't know."

After she hung up, Amanda wondered why Perez had wanted a meeting at the Consulate. Perhaps to put the American off guard or maybe he wanted to make this unofficial, so that, if the man complained, Gonzalez would not blame him. It was a peculiar strategy, but it might be for the best. And what a relief it was to talk with an officer who was prepared to accept her help.

She got up from her desk and walked out to talk to Nando who had just finished speaking to the last early morning visitor about a tourist visa.

"I have a number here of the hotel where a Señor Aaron Arlington is staying. He's an American tourist. Would you please telephone him? Be sure to mention that you are calling from the American Consulate. Then switch him over to me. If he asks why we want to talk to him, well, of course, you don't know, do you?"

"No... of course," Nando answered with a broad grin that showed he was enjoying the conspiracy.

She returned to her office and waited for the call. She hoped the man would still be in his room, early as it was. But it took several minutes and she had time to open her computer and glance at her email. As she had feared, there was a message from the Embassy marked FOR YOUR IMMEDIATE ATTENTION.

She ignored it, set the computer on "sleep," and then turned to look out the window behind her desk. The sun had just cleared the grip of the mountains behind the city and it shone brightly on the white-washed houses, choosing to wash them in pink through the kaleidoscope of moist morning air. In the garden of the house behind her building two tall palm trees swayed slightly in a breeze, their fronds wavering in the flickering glow. She imagined she could hear them rustle as they grazed against each other. She was feeling better, more optimistic and cheered by the sight of this vibrant square of light cut into the wall of her office like a video postcard or an advertisement for some vacation paradise. She swung her chair around when she heard the phone buzz and returned her thoughts to murder.

"It's your party," Nando said when she picked up the receiver. "They had to find him at breakfast."

There was a click and she spoke immediately: "Mr. Arlington, this is Amanda Pennyworth from the American Consulate here in Puerto Vallarta. I'm wondering if you could stop by the office today. I have some things to discuss with you?"

"What's the matter?"

"I'd rather not discuss this over the telephone if you don't mind. But it's very important. I am here all morning at your convenience."

"We were planning to take a trip to the back country today. Visit to the John Houston, you know, the movie director: his finca and ranch. Did you know he spent years here?"

"Yes. That's a lovely trip," Amanda said. "But if you came right now you would surely have time. It's not that far."

He hesitated, obviously curious and perhaps even apprehensive about this summons: "I suppose I could. If you give me the address. Yes, I could."

"In an hour then." She hung up after repeating the address twice. She immediately contacted Sergeant Perez and he assured her would join her as quickly as he could.

"Now, the Ambassador," she said out loud after replacing the receiver.

The email was exactly as expected: hastily written questions demanding immediate answers. She thought that he must be responding to pressure from the State Department in Washington; perhaps even feeling guilty that he was, so far, out of the loop: "What is being done about the murdered American? Have the parents been notified? Are the police being cooperative? Do they have any suspects?"

Amanda could have responded to his last question with a generic answer: "Yes, of course; there are always suspects." Whether or not they perpetrated any crime was another matter entirely. He must know that the Mexican police were remarkably efficient in this one respect: they usually arrested someone and almost always found that person guilty, whether they actually were or not. Of course, in the case of a murdered American, they might be somewhat more diligent, but the outcome would probably be the same. She decided not to say anything more and wrote a hasty reply.

Half an hour later, Nando rang her to say that Señor Arlington had arrived and was waiting to see her. She hesitated to ask him in, preferring to wait for Sergeant Perez.

"Let him wait for a few minutes. I'm expecting the police to appear any time. Get him some coffee or something, will you, Nando? I'd rather not talk to him just yet. You can tell him I'm busy for the next ten minutes."

Looking through the glass in the upper half of her office door she observed Arlington standing in front of Nando's desk, gesturing. He was older, perhaps in his sixties—she couldn't tell from this angle—with silver temples and a full head of dark hair. Perhaps he was six feet tall. He had made no concession to the tropical weather of Puerto Vallarta, wearing a long-sleeved white shirt and, when she stood up briefly to get a better view, dark pants. He looked like a businessman dressed for dinner on a Sunday after church.

Because Perez did not appear in the next few minutes, she opened the door of her office and called out to him.

He had taken a seat in the waiting area and stood up immediately and stepped forward. "I'm Aaron Arlington. What's this all about? I'm in a hurry."

Amanda waved him inside and pointed to one of the chairs in front of her desk. She decided to be formal and returned to sit behind to her desk. "I suspect you know why I contacted you."

"No, I can't imagine. Is there something wrong with my passport?"

She ignored his question but a sudden dislike of his feigned innocence, perhaps, made her more aggressive than she intended: "It's only because the Mexican police haven't gotten around to you yet. So in a way, it's a bit of a warning."

"Police? I'm baffled," he replied.

"I'll get straight to the point, Mr. Arlington. You were at the gay sauna on the day and at the time when an American boy was murdered. Surely you've have heard about it. The police have your name because we traced your ID. The hotel had your passport number. Surely you knew you couldn't hide."

He was very quiet for a moment, looking genuinely distraught.

"Okay. Yes, I admit it; I was there. But of course I know nothing about some murder. That's why I didn't come forward and... well, also because of my wife. She has no idea."

"No idea that you're a homosexual and that you frequent gay bath houses?"

Again, he sat silently. "Yes," he began again, finally. He seemed unable to disguise his shocked reaction to her frankness. "She's completely unaware. I don't go out much, but she would be horrified if she knew. I can just imagine what she would do. It would wreck everything: my marriage; my business. So I've had to keep it a secret. It's a miracle that we were at breakfast when you called. The waiter found me and I took the phone call at the desk, so she couldn't hear what I was saying."

"What excuse did you give her? Wouldn't she be suspicious when you suddenly left her at the hotel and rushed to the Consulate?"

"I made up a story about the Embassy trying to get in touch. I told her I had forgotten to leave my office the name of the hotel here. Important business to attend to that couldn't wait."

"And she believed that?"

"I suppose so. Why shouldn't she?"

Amanda looked at him and thought she could imagine his wife, accustomed to accepting the implausible excuses and unexplained absences of a double life. She must have learned to cooperate with the preposterous.

"Did she ask you how we found your hotel?"

"Didn't say a word."

Better not to ask than to receive yet another lie. This had to be a relationship, Amanda thought, built on the carefully laid bricks and mortar of indifference, a wall of dissimulation between the two that one probing question and honest answer could undermine and bring all crashing down.

"I hope you'll understand me," he continued. "It would ruin me if it got out. Can we keep my wife ignorant?"

Amanda was surprised at his choice of words but said only: "I can certainly try. There's probably no need for her to know."

"Then, I thank you," he said, standing. "If that's all... She'll probably be wondering."

"Please sit down, Mr. Arlington. You haven't even begun to describe your activities at the sauna. And Sergeant Perez of the Mexican police is due here at any minute. I'm sure he would like to hear what you have to say for yourself."

Amanda was sorry that she had to give Arlington forewarning to concoct some sort of story of careful half-truths. But there was nothing she could do—certainly not ask him anything that would give him clues that he could later spin for the police.

What was it about him that made her so suspicious, she wondered? Was it his very ordinariness, the regularity of his features, the distinguished, self-confident aura of success? Had she so often been confronted with situations in her work where people invented excuses or were hiding something, or acted as if they were, that if faced with someone who seemed to be telling the truth he seemed to be a practiced liar? It was a bad habit of hers to think the contrary of obvious. How many times had that gotten her into trouble before? She needed to be more cautious and a bit generous too.

The more she thought about it, the more she realized that behind her frank questions lay a nervous reaction to this man. She supposed that he reminded her of her father: an accomplished administrator in the sprawling Illinois University system, and a man risen to a position where challenges and contradictions could be passed down to committees or underlings to be resolved. From an early age, she had dared and then delighted in arguing with him, although most of the time she had to concede that he was right. But now that she stood alone with all the enormous and petty responsibilities of the Consulate, she recognized something of his officiousness in herself. And it didn't help to imagine Arlington as an adversary— and renewing longstanding issues with her father.

A knock on the door interrupted what Amanda realized had been a prolonged moment of uneasy silence.

"Sergeant Perez is here," Nando said, stepping aside to allow the policeman to enter.

After Amanda introduced the two men, she asked Arlington to repeat what he had told her.

Perez showed no reaction but asked almost apologetically, "Did you see or talk to the boy named Blackman."

"No," replied Arlington, looking intently at Perez as if responding to a challenge. "No."

Perez ignored the answer and continued, marking off a mental list: "Did you have sex with him?"

"No. I told you. Did you not hear me? I didn't talk to him or see him."

"Do you have any idea who might have killed him? Or why?"

"How would I know something like that? How did he die? Was it one of the other boys in that place?"

"I can't give you any details," Perez continued. "But if you saw or heard anything, it would help."

"I didn't see anything... except I think I heard an argument or at least raised voices."

"American?"

"As far as I could tell, yes. But I was minding my own

business."

Perez looked at him with obvious disapproval.

"And the reason you didn't volunteer this information to the police was because of your wife?"

"Yes and no. I didn't think it could be important. And, of course I didn't want her to know. I don't make going to such places a habit. And I'm imploring you not to question her. What could she possibly know?"

"Perhaps she could confirm the time you returned to the hotel that evening."

"No need, no need. I was back by six. We ordered drinks for the room at that time. You can check with the hotel staff; they'll confirm it."

For the first time, Amanda thought she saw something weak and dishonest in Arlington's face, the passage of dishonesty, a narrowing of his eyes. But he really did seem concerned that his wife would discover where he had been.

"Thank you, Señor Arlington," Perez said, finally. "I see no reason to question your wife. I'm satisfied."

"Then I'll go now," the American said, standing up abruptly and regaining his confidence. "I've been away too long. My wife will be worried." Reaching into his wallet, he withdrew a calling card and passed it to Perez, who glanced at it and handed it to Amanda. It was embossed with the logo of his law office and "Senior Partner" next to his name.

When he had left the room, Perez asked Amanda: "Do you believe him?"

"I didn't at first. I thought he was acting suspiciously. But now I think I understand why. So, yes... But where does that leave us?" Amanda almost corrected herself but let pass the suggestion that she was working with the police.

He seemed not to notice. "We have DNA samples of the four Mexicans present. Three of them are in custody, at least until they have to be released."

"There are two more Americans," she interrupted. "Perhaps we could talk to them together. I can leave for an hour or two, right now. Nando is so reliable!" She was taking a chance, but this policeman seemed completely different from Gonzalez. Maybe she would later regret her impulsiveness, but a hasty adventure was better than making excuses to the embassy.

"All right, Señora. I have the addresses. We can go now. If you want, we can try to visit both."

He didn't need to add that Captain Gonzalez would be furious to discover she was meddling in the investigation and that he was acting without orders. They both realized it.

The address of Anthony Duncan was in a cul de sac toward the south end of Puerto Vallarta in what looked like a cove hollowed out of the bottom of a large forested hill. The house was set back slightly. Over a high wall the second story peered out onto the street with two large windows, blinking back the brilliant late morning sun. There was a steep sidewalk in front with two steps cut into it. Perez parked the police car and he and Amanda climbed up and stood in front. Blue and white tiles buried in the stucco over the arched entrance announced "Casa Alegre." Through a hole in the wooden door on the outside and beneath this greeting hung a brass chain ending in a ring. Perez pulled it down sharply and a bell rang somewhere in the house behind. There was no response, only the distant sound of a dog barking. Amanda noticed what seemed to be a camera perched discreetly at the right side of the archway. No doubt, if anyone was home, they were deciding whether to answer, she thought.

They waited several seconds, and Amanda pulled the chain again.

"Put your badge up to the camera," she instructed. "If they're home, they'll answer this time."

He did. Eventually, they heard footsteps and the door swung open. A man, wearing only a white terrycloth bathrobe and sandals peered out at them. He was of medium height with brown hair streaked by the sun. What Amanda noticed most was his tan: a ripe brown, his legs, his face, and the open triangle of his robe: all the color of burnt ochre.

"Señor Duncan?" Perez asked.

"No. I'm Stephen Miller."

"Is he home then?"

"What's this about?"

"If he is home, we will speak to him now," Perez said. He pushed inside the entrance and into a small tiled courtyard, embraced on three sides by walls; at the far end the house rose up. Amanda followed. Scattered around the patio were large clay pots with flowers and trailing vines and in the corner, a tall gilded birdcage sat on a pedestal. The blue and yellow macaw inside hopped up on its highest perch and chattered with disapproval as they entered.

Perez stopped abruptly and asked again: "Answer me: Is he here, then?"

"Yes, I believe so," Miller answered. "If you will wait

here, I'll fetch him."

"Actually, we don't mind coming in," Amanda said. "I think we're disturbing your parrot."

"All right; this way." Miller gave them an irritated look, turned, and walked to a glass door to the right of the house at the back wall.

Once inside, he led them into a living room where the décor was very traditional with a dark red tile floor, and yellow walls; a lazy fan made vague ripples in the air. There were several large leather chairs and a sofa, but Miller made no suggestion that they should sit. He merely said: "Wait here. I'll be back." Amanda wondered if this was the sort of unfriendly greeting that Perez... or any policeman had to experience daily. Perhaps that explained the gruff manner of his superior.

After several minutes, they could hear the scampering nails of a dog which appeared first in the archway that led to the entrance hall. It was a tiny animal that barked once with a high-pitched squeak and then retreated. Followed by his housemate, Duncan entered next. He too was dressed casually, wearing shorts and a white cotton blouse with a panel of flowery embroidery down the front. He was close to six feet tall with a thin brush cut of dark hair. The lower part of his face was shadowed by a stubble beard. Like his partner, he was weather-stained from hours in the sun.

"What's this about, officer? And who is this woman?"

Amanda saw a look of exasperation pass over the policeman's face. He was clearly tired of the aggression of these two.

"Perhaps it would be best if your friend left the room. This is a personal matter. And this is Señora Pennyworth from the American Consulate."

"He stays," Duncan exclaimed. And then turning to Amanda, he added, with a tone of sarcasm: "So you're here to protect my rights? Good! I appreciate that."

She said nothing but sat down on the edge of one of the leather chairs. The others also seated themselves, and the dog, which had been waiting just outside, raced across the room and leaped into Duncan's lap.

"I assume you know why we are here," Perez began.

"Not a clue," Duncan replied too quickly.

"It's about the murder at the Olympiad... Are you sure you want your friend to hear this?"

"We don't have any secrets," he assured them, although Amanda thought that his partner made a sour face.

"Well, then... we have discovered that you were at the sauna the day that the American was murdered. What do you know about it?"

"Only what I read in the expat newspaper. And that's not much. Just that he was murdered; no details."

"But you were there. Did you encounter him?"

"What's that supposed to mean?" Duncan asked.

"Anything you can tell us. Did you notice him? Did you talk to him? Anything?"

"Sure, I noticed. He's... he was very cute. I said hello but he ignored me. I guess I wasn't his type. I saw him with another guy: young like him, but not so cute."

"And you didn't have sex with him; didn't follow him around? You have nothing to add?"

"If you think I'm lying or embarrassed to talk in front of Stephen, just reassure yourselves. We have an open relationship. We tell each other everything. Nobody gets jealous; nobody worries. You probably don't understand that. You're married, I see," he said indicating the ring Perez was wearing. "So you're probably used to sneaking around when you want a little excitement."

Perez ignored this insult; his eyes lit on the ring Duncan was wearing: "And maybe you can answer this: Did you notice if the boy was wearing a wedding band?"

"No, can't say I did, but it's awfully dark and I didn't get that close. I really can't help you officer." He lifted up his dog, smacked his lips in an air kiss, allowing it to lick his cheek and then settled it back into his lap, as if to say that the interview was over and the animal required his attention.

Amanda had been quiet, but now she broke in: "Did you see an older man, probably an American?"

"Yeah, I think so. Looked like a banker strutting around in a white towel; a bit out of place I thought: gray hair and all. Straight looking—although you can never tell. Takes all types."

"Did you speak to him?"

"Why would I? He was a lot older than me. Good looking, but really not for me." She noticed that Miller was watching Duncan intently. It suddenly struck her that he was being very measured in his choice of words—perhaps with his partner in mind.

"Do you have any more questions? I've told you everything I know."

Perez stood up: "I think not... for the time being. You will remain in Puerto Vallarta, of course. And should you think of anything, some small detail, something you saw, please contact me."

"How long will that be, officer? We were planning a

trip to Dallas. I have some business there."

Perez just looked at the two men and then reached into his wallet and withdrew a card, handing it to Duncan. "Until I say so."

Amanda also stood and she and Perez walked out of the living room, leaving the two roommates still seated. Once outside and in the small courtyard, Amanda asked: "Did you believe him?"

"Not entirely."

"Was he lying?"

"Yes, I think so, but perhaps not to us. I doubt he had anything to do with the Amcrican. But it seemed like most of what he said was for the benefit of Señor Miller."

"I agree. He was trying to make light of looking for sex. I doubt if he would have said anything at all about being there except for our visit. Did you see the look his partner gave him? I don't think he knew. And I wouldn't want to hear what they're saying to each other now. But no, I doubt if he's a killer."

"And the other American that we saw this morning, Señor Arlington?"

"A slippery character. Not telling the entire truth either, I'm sure. But maybe I just sensed his habit of lying. After all, if he's sneaking around having sex with men and hiding everything from his wife, if he's hiding in some closet full of disguises, then perhaps that's it. Maybe he's not even sure who he really is. Lying to himself. But it would be hard to pull off, don't you think? I mean someone would have to know eventually. Always the off chance."

"I have no idea, Señora. It's not my world. I know nothing of such things."

Amanda could have added that he wasn't trying very

hard to understand a world that was strange to him. He was content to sift through the evidence in a case where motivations made no sense. But perhaps his attitude was right. Maybe the sexual identity of everyone they interviewed, and even the location of the crime in a gay bathhouse, had nothing to do with its solution. Maybe the answer lay somewhere else. Or worse: Captain Gonzalez might be correct about the Herrera boy. She didn't want to admit it, but it was probably just a robbery gone fatally wrong. Still, she wasn't satisfied with that answer. It seemed too simple and, if anything, Amanda loved a mystery full of complications and dubious explanations. Why was she never satisfied with the obvious, she wondered? Perhaps that was the attitude that made her a star pupil in her literature courses in college, where analysis always sought to unmask the meaning behind the literal. But in thinking about a crime with so few clues, with the only ones pointing to a single suspect—the person who had admitted to stealing the ring—how well did her dissection of metaphors, parsing of similes, and deconstruction of arguments serve her?

Perez interrupted her thoughts as they approached his car.

"I'll take you back to the Consulate. I think that's all we can do now. Then just wait for the DNA results to come back."

"You don't think we should have taken samples from the Americans?"

"Yes, I do, but Captain Gonzalez told me... ordered me not to. He is determined that one of the men he has in custody, or the other man that I interviewed... one of the Mexicans is guilty. There's nothing I can do."

"But what about the other American, the one in the timeshare? Shouldn't we talk to him also?"

"I suppose so, Señora, although I don't believe we are learning much."

"Just to be sure, then? It's not so late and not far from the Consulate. Will Captain Gonzalez be angry?"

"Of course. He is always angry. But I'll call the station and tell them I had to return home for a few hours."

Amanda said nothing but she wondered if Perez made a habit of investigating solo away from his blustery chief.

Traffic back through the Zona and Old Town was light due to the prolonged lunch hour and they approached the marina area around 2 p.m. When she first arrived in Puerto Vallarta, Amanda had gone on several excursions that departed from the large port which gave its name to the zone, but she had rarely visited the complex that surrounded it. The huge hotels were visible from the highway, but set back behind high walls and formidable gates. Unlike the rest of Puerto Vallarta, this enclave was like a generic international resort with a sampling of high-rise architecture and well-known franchise names. It could have been Ft. Lauderdale or somewhere in the Bahamas.

To enter the area, they first had to pass by a gatehouse manned by a uniformed employee who waved them through when he recognized the police car. The curving road divided several times like an evolutionary tree with each turn-off leading to the entrance of a different and more spectacular hotel as they neared the ocean. It was impossible not to be impressed by their meticulously maintained grounds, Amanda thought, with the huge groves of coconut palms towering above their lush gardens. Along the center of the divided road there were plantings of agave cactus with their broad pale-green leaves that always reminded her of spikey tongues alternating with beds of bird-of-paradise flowers in full bloom. The low walls on either side were draped with mounds of crimson and lavender Bougainvillea.

The condominium they sought had a more modest appearance than its neighbors and a Spanish name: Casa Playa, an older building that might well have been one of the first ventures in the area. Perez drove up to the front and stopped under the canopied portico. As they got out, a man in a brown uniform emerged quickly from the glass front of the building.

"Please do not park there, Señor," he called, waving his hand. "You will be blocking the entrance."

Perez looked intently at him for a moment and then brushed past and then turned to say: "We have business with one of your residents, amigo. And the sooner we can speak to him, the sooner I will move the car."

"All right, sir," the man mumbled, following Amanda and the policeman. He halted once inside and Amanda and Perez continued on to a glassed-in office to the left. When she saw them, the woman sitting at her desk stood up and emerged from the doorway.

"May I help you, Señores?" she asked, obviously noting the policeman's uniform.

Perez pulled a small notebook from his breast pocket, flipped it open, and thumbed through the pages.

"Do you have a Francis Parker staying here? Perhaps as a permanent resident or a guest?"

The woman looked at him suspiciously and then she stiffened. Amanda was sure that her instructions were to shield residents from harassment and she looked the part: lacquered dark hair, a crisp white blouse, and a tailored blue skirt, the uniform of a perfectly costumed and officious employee who would reveal little about the occupants of the building—whose job was to observe everything and say nothing.

"May I ask: What is the purpose of your visit, Señor?"

"You may ask, if you want, yes," Perez said with a momentary smile. "And then you will tell me."

"And this woman?" she continued, ignoring his answer. "Is she also with the police?"

"Señora," Perez said loudly. "Enough! Please! Do you have a Francis Parker here or not!"

"Of course, Señor, at your service," she replied. "I believe so... yes. Let me be sure of the apartment number. If you will please wait."

Perez looked at Amanda and shook his head while the woman retreated to her office and sat for a moment at her desk to type something into the computer. Amanda was sure that this was an act, designed to indicate that they were trespassing on the privacy of the residents. The woman glanced at them, stood, and then re-emerged: "Take the elevator to the third floor. It's apartment number 306, to the left."

Perez looked around the room, spotted the elevator cove and walked toward it. He paused briefly and turned back: "Thank you, Señora."

"Are people always so hostile? Does it bother you?" Amanda asked as they stepped into the elevator.

"It's a game," he replied. "I take nothing seriously. I think people want to be sure they are not seen to be cooperating too freely with the police... in case someone should ask. They can always say: 'I had to tell; no choice...'"

Amanda laughed. "I think I might feel the same way."

Perez nodded and returned her smile, but bowing slightly as he followed her into the hallway of the third floor.

The apartment was located about halfway down a dimly lit corridor that smelled slightly of mildew and bleach. There was good reason to use tile flooring in this climate, Amanda thought, rather than a carpet, but at the same time, ceramics would create clatter and amplify any noise of footsteps and conversation. Not an easy choice, but they had compromised by placing a narrow rug along the center.

They stopped in front the doorway and Perez pressed the doorbell. They waited, but could hear nothing from inside. Perez held the button down again.

"He could be out, of course."

"Of course. He could be. Let me try again." This time he rang for almost ten seconds.

As they were about to turn away, the door opened slightly. Perez leaned back and pushed hard and the person inside jumped back abruptly allowing the door to swing open, smacking against the wall with a loud crack.

"You didn't have to do that!" he said angrily.

Perez entered the apartment and Amanda followed. Her first thought was that the receptionist had warned the occupant and that accounted for his reluctance to answer.

"Are you Francis Parker?" Perez said as he peered at the man standing in the foyer of the apartment. And not waiting for an answer, he continued: "I'm Sergeant Perez of the Tourist Police and this is Señora Pennyworth from the American Consulate... Perhaps it's best if we move inside. I have a number of questions for you."

"No hablo Español," the man replied.

"No problem," Amanda said. "I'll translate for you." And she explained the purpose of their visit as they moved into a large room. It was crowded with mix-matched furniture, decorated with several prints and cheap posters that Amanda recognized: a Picasso and a faded Monet reproduction. Only the glass wall at the far end where she could make out a swimming pool set in a garden of flowers and palm trees redeemed the clutter and bad taste.

"Please sit down," Parker said, perching on the edge of an overstuffed leather arm chair and indicating a sofa opposite.

Amanda settled down onto the couch and almost laughed when she realized how low it was, allowing Parker to tower over her. Perez chose to remain standing.

Looking carefully now at Parker, Amanda was struck by something incongruous and strange in his demeanor. His luxuriant auburn hair was brushed up in a pompadour with closely shaved sides. His face was pale with large blue eyes and a sensuous mouth. Although he sat with his legs spread apart, in a studied and aggressive position, Amanda couldn't help but notice his soft, round arms and something about the jaw. She was almost *sure* that Parker was a woman. She looked at Perez to see if he noticed anything but could detect no reaction at all.

"Señor," he began. "We're here to ask you some questions about the recent murder at the Olympiad Sauna. Don't bother to deny you were present that day. We got your passport number from the staff there."

"Of course," Parker said, his voice gruff and forced. "I certainly don't deny it. Awful place. I'll certainly not go again, especially if they murder the patrons there!"

Perez looked at him curiously, but continued: "Did you see or talk to anyone?"

"Of course I did. I met that nice boy—maybe that American. I don't know if he was the one who was murdered. I think there were two of them, but no names, of course. Obviously not in a place like that. No names."

"Did you have sex with him?"

Parker laughed and then covered his mouth. "I'm sorry," he continued. "No, I didn't have sex with him or anyone else."

"Did you see or hear anything suspicious?"

"Of course I did, Señor Policeman! Everything is suspicious and furtive in a sauna. Everyone's hiding who they really are, even from themselves—imagining they are attractive and then wondering about how big a cock or what nice ass might be hiding underneath someone's towel or what it would be like to..."

Amanda looked at Perez to see if he understood everything that Parker had said. If she had to translate, she would censor.

"But I certainly didn't kill anyone. Why in the world would I?" Parker asked, his voice sliding up the scale of gender.

Perez looked puzzled again. But he certainly seemed to understand what Parker was saying and continued: "Could you tell if the person you talked to was drunk?"

Parker stood up abruptly. "No, I don't think so. But I did hear some sort of argument and it was in English. Why don't you ask the other Americans who were there? I didn't do anything. And now if that's all, I'm rather busy."

"Just a minute," Perez said, holding up his hand. "Not

so fast. Would you be willing to give us a DNA sample?"

Amanda could see that he didn't have a kit and wondered why he asked.

"Of course I will. If you want I'll come to the police station tomorrow morning if you like or later today. I'm happy to cooperate. And now..."

Perez paused, glared at him, and then shrugged his shoulders. Amanda translated the last words just to be sure, and when she finished he motioned to her: "I think that's all for now. Will you be in town for a while? We might wish to interview you again."

"I'm staying to the end of the month. It's a timeshare. At your service, sir," He stood and walked toward the front door of the apartment.

Amanda and Perez left quickly, saying nothing as they went down the elevator, passed through the reception area and then to the police car parked at the entrance. But Perez made no motion to start the engine. Looking straight ahead, he said, quietly: "I don't understand what I just saw. Can you explain to me, please?"

"I wondered if you noticed," Amanda replied.

"Yes, I noticed something, but what did I notice?"

"That Francis Parker is a woman."

"Pretending to be a man? I don't understand."

"Surely you do; surely you know. There have to be lots of men and women in your country who feel that they were born with the wrong bodies: men who are women and vice versa. Is it so unusual?"

"I thought it was only Americans who were like that. Like stories my wife reads in the revistas. I've never seen Mexicans..."

"Come now, officer. Of course you have. And it's not

just in magazines. Maybe you just don't want to admit it to yourself?"

"I've never thought about it much. I suppose you are right. But why would he—or she—go to a sauna like that? I'm confused."

"I have no idea," Amanda replied, thinking that her job description had never included the task of explaining complex gender behavior to anyone.

"When I was at the university," she continued, "there were a few students who talked about making a transition to another gender. Everyone knew about it. I'm surprised that it isn't common knowledge here."

Perez looked at her for a moment and then smiled: "You know we are a very conservative country, Señora, at least we pretend to be. That means we ignore all the things that are obvious. So there are many things we never talk about, or if we do, it's always concerning foreigners. Things you read about in *People en Español*, or maybe you can see on an American telenovela; just not in one's own experience." He turned away, and started the engine. "But do you think he did anything? I mean robbed and murdered Blackman?"

"No. I'm fairly sure he didn't. And her DNA sample wouldn't reveal anything anyway, would it?"

"Why not?"

"Because you said it was to compare with semen found in the body, and he hardly..."

"Okay, yes, I understand."

"So now," Amanda said, "I'm even more puzzled about who the killer might be. No one seems to have had a motive—none of the Mexicans nor any of the Americans. And, frankly, to kill someone for a few pesos? It's frustrating to think about, and I'm horrified to imagine that someone is going to get away with murder." She stopped. "Do you suppose that the owner of the sauna or his employee could have done it? For whatever reason?"

"No. I'm absolutely sure not. That would make even less sense in a case where nothing else makes sense. Perhaps Gonzalez is right, then. That Mexican boy did it. And maybe we will know something when the DNA results come... Right now however, I will drive you back to the Consulate."

"Yes, I need to get back. The Blackmans are due late this afternoon."

"Sorry to hear that," he said as he pulled out of the driveway and onto the road back to the main highway.

When Amanda finally walked into the reception area of the Consulate, Nando stood up and said quietly: "Mr. and Mrs. Blackman are in your office waiting to talk to you."

Amanda looked puzzled. "Why did you let them in?"

"They insisted. Just barged in and told me they would wait for you there. I couldn't stop them. She said something about not wanting to sit outside with all those other people."

Amanda scowled: "Okay, Nando. It's no problem; I apologize for that. I'll deal with them."

She opened the door to her office and looked at the Blackmans sitting on either side of the room, the desk separating them: two people occupying the same space but miles apart in their emotions. Mrs. Blackman was cuddling her dog and her ex-husband was staring absently at the floor.

When Amanda entered, he glanced at her but did not

stand.

"Been on a banker's holiday?" Mrs. Blackman asked. "Your assistant said you would be right back. It's been hours waiting for you!"

"I'm sorry. Something came up that I had to attend to. How can I help you?"

"We've just come to find out what is happening with the investigation... before we leave."

"You've completed all the arrangements with the funeral home then? The paperwork is done?"

"Yes," said Mrs. Blackman. "I'll take the ashes back with me to Los Angeles. But really, can't you tell us anything? I mean what have you been doing all this time? Don't the police know who did it yet? Is it so difficult?"

Amanda sat down at her desk and looked intently at one and then the other. What she saw was a distressed couple, sitting as far away from each other as they could on opposite sides of her small office. She thought for a moment how terrible it would be not to be able to share feelings at so great a loss, a tragedy that gravely affected them both but was still not great enough to bridge over the torrent of anger that separated them.

"I don't know exactly what the police think. But I will certainly let you know if there are any developments. It's all I can do. I'm not in charge of investigating anything... just helping where I can. You do understand that, I hope."

"Obviously that's not an acceptable answer," Mr. Blackman said. "You bureaucrats! Always hiding behind forms and more forms to fill out, giving vague responses to questions when you actually know the answers, hiding behind misdirection and complication. Doing everything by the Book of Obfuscations. Do they give lessons on how to be elusive back in the State Department in DC? How to reassure a listener with meaningless prattle? Do you have any idea that when you speak, you never say anything? You're just pouring words like salt on our grief!"

Amanda was surprised at his vehemence, all of which now seemed directed at her. Yes, she had to admit she was hiding what she knew; even lying by omission. But if she revealed what she had learned, it would still amount to nothing conclusive: just more suspicions and dead ends. Even if she believed the police would find the killer... a killer... she wouldn't necessarily be convinced he was the one. So how could she honestly convey all of that complication to two people primed by their anger to doubt every word she uttered? Was it this atmosphere of mistrust or their hostility to each other that charged the air, needing only a spark to flare into another explosion of accusations?

"I can only add," she said, tempering her distress, "that the police have several suspects in custody. Please be assured that you will be the first to know what they find out. I have your addresses, but perhaps you could also give me your text and email contacts. I can send you a message or call you as soon as there is news. I promise."

She passed a blank paper and pen across the desk, and Mr. Blackman wrote down the numbers.

"Just a minute," Mr. Blackman said suddenly, as if he had remembered something very important. "What happens next? You said they have a suspect. And now what?"

"It's not like the US," Amanda said almost apologetically. The Mexican system of justice is very different."

"I'll bet it is!" said Mrs. Blackman.

Amanda ignored this and continued: "The whole

structure is changing to be more like the American practice, but not yet in Jalisco—that's the province here. The old way... comes from the nineteenth century... and leaves everything up to the judge. You don't get a jury trial and you don't have all the courtroom drama of the English system with lawyers bickering and cross-examining witnesses."

"So the judge just makes the decision: guilty or not?"

"Pretty much. The prosecutor and the defense present him with written arguments and then he decides whether there is sufficient evidence of a crime and culpability and then where guilt or innocence lies. No oral arguments allowed, although that seems to be changing."

"You sound like a damned textbook," Mr. Blackman said angrily. "What kind of justice is that?"

"It's their justice, not ours. You need to understand that. And yes, I've read up on trials here because sometimes Americans—tourists or expats—get caught up in the system and I've had to explain what happens and what doesn't happen any number of times. I really just thought you should know."

"And what if someone bribes a judge?"

"Well, I assume that happens sometimes. But in the US, juries aren't always perfect, are they? I can think of some famous cases of injustice. You can too, I'm sure."

"So what will happen? What do you think?" Mrs. Blackman asked. Amanda could see that her frustration was about to erupt in tears. "I just want what's right for my son. Is that possible?"

"I hope so," Amanda said, trying very hard to inject a tone of optimism in her voice. "And now, can I have your information, Mrs. Blackman?"

"You still have that old number and email address?" Mr. Blackman asked his ex-wife.

"Yes. Of course."

"Then I'll include it under mine and leave it with you. We each have a flight this evening, late-ish. But don't think this is the last you've heard from either of us," he warned.

He scribbled something else on a sheet of paper and passed it to Amanda. Mrs. Blackman stood up abruptly, still clutching her dog, and went out of the office, not looking back. Her ex-husband followed, picked up two suitcases that were leaning against Nando's desk, and departed without a word.

Amanda thought they acted like two bloodied boxers in a prize fight who suddenly gave off landing blows on each other to turn against the referee. How she hated becoming the object of their assault.

She worked steadily during the tail end of the afternoon, looking up only as she noticed the room darkening and then again when Nando peeked in to say he was leaving for the day. He gave her a curious look as he asked if he should switch on the lights.

"Sure, why not?" she replied casually, as if she hadn't considered it.

He left and Amanda watched him disappear through the front door of the office. No doubt he thought her strange, traipsing around the city with policemen... and maybe wondering if she too belonged to the tribe of Americans represented by the unpleasant and troubled Blackman couple and all the others who laid their difficulties on his desk at the Consulate. Well, she thought, she did represent them. And all the Americans who ever visited Puerto Vallarta with their misadventures, their arrogance and distrust of Mexico, and their worries and fears; they were her kindred. Her job defined her identity; her function was to share their problems. Too bad that Nando only saw the peevish and desperate side of her countrymen. She wouldn't be surprised if he sometimes thought of her as the same.

After twenty more minutes, she decided to leave. Tomorrow she would call Sergeant Perez again and find out what further progress was being made. And she knew she had to write to the Ambassador again; she had put that off far too long. But tonight, she just wanted a drink, maybe two... and then dinner at one of the outdoor restaurants next to Lazaro Cardenas Park near her apartment. As she thought about it, she had a sudden craving to consume something fiery, something to burn her mouth and make her eyes water; something to make her feel alive again. There was a small taco place near the square where she sometimes had dinner. She had never seen an American inside, although curious tourists sometimes peeked in until they saw that the clientele sitting in the smoky interior were entirely Mexican families, and then passed on. But she could relax there; chat with the owner; and forget about the murder mystery and all of the unpleasant and guilty people every one of whom seemed to have something to hide. Tonight she just wanted to breathe in the spicy atmosphere and sip a frozen drink.

CHAPTER 9

Sergeant Perez went immediately down to the basement of the police headquarters the next morning to see Señora Sanchez. She was sitting on the high stool next to her slated desk, glaring at the screen of her laptop when he entered. He always disliked the atmosphere: chilly, smelling of disinfectant and the lingering presence of dead souls, he thought—if they had an odor. How could anyone work in such a place?

"Good morning, Señora," he called out, trying to urge enthusiasm into his voice.

She just turned to him and nodded as he approached.

"Do you have any results yet from the DNA tests? I was hoping to take something to Captain Gonzalez this morning. We need to make progress on this murder and he's expecting to make a formal arrest shortly. Just to keep the Americans quiet."

She laughed, but Perez could see from her eyes that she was not amused.

"Yes, I do, and it is just as I expected."

"You knew? What?"

"Yes, in a way, I knew or I expected."

"So?"

"The laboratory at Guadalajara where I sent the specimens has bungled everything. They lost the original sample so there is nothing to compare."

"Then can we take a new sample from the body? Is it still here or at the funeral home?"

"No. The American parents decided on cremation, so all the physical evidence, if there ever really was anything conclusive, is gone up in smoke and ash."

Perez stiffened. "Captain Gonzalez will be furious. He wanted that information."

"But what would it prove anyway?" Sanchez asked quickly.

"I know how his mind works. Any kind of evidence for him is decisive. I'll have to tell him. Do you want to come with me and explain?"

"No, I'm happy to leave that to you. And I'm not responsible for the black moods of Gonzalez. I can't do anything more, except maybe to tell him, if he asks me, that this isn't the first time... or the last. But I think he knows that anyway."

Perez shrugged and walked quickly out of the laboratory and up the stairs to his superior's office. He took a deep breath, knocked on the door, and, when he heard a mumbled response, walked in.

Gonzalez was sitting at his desk, leaning back—his usual pose of nonchalance, hands behind his head—with a cigarette smoldering in an ashtray. The window that gave onto the parking lot beneath was half open, but there was no breeze and a ribbon of acrid smoke spiraled upward, dissipating just before it reached the ceiling.

"What's the news, Perez?" he asked.

"I'm afraid that the news is not good."

Gonzalez glared at him as he sat down, and Perez had the distinct feeling that he was intruding. His superior said nothing.

Perez continued: "Señora Sanchez just informed me that the DNA evidence has been lost or corrupted. She couldn't say how exactly, but the lab in Guadalajara can't give us any results."

Gonzalez opened his mouth and Perez was sure he was about to curse, and then, suddenly a smile broke out on his face. He picked up his cigarette and inhaled deeply.

"Doesn't matter at all."

"I'm sorry, Señor, Captain, I don't understand. I know you were counting on the DNA evidence."

"Well, I was, of course. But no one has to know."

"I don't understand."

"It's very simple. We will just interview each of the suspects again and tell them that their DNA matched what was found on the victim. You'll see. We'll get a confession that way. And then we'll have our murderer!"

"But can we do that?"

"With men of that sort, of course. We can do anything we want. Yes, damn it, then we'll know. Anyway, I'm sure it's that young man who stole the ring and keeps lying to us. We've got him now!"

Perez was momentarily shocked, but then not so surprised when he thought about it. He knew his superior as a man who thought of boundaries and rules as mere hesitations and only observed by the weak. Being careless about protocols and the niceties of procedure had made him a feared but respected policeman with an enviable record of solving crimes that accounted for many convictions, Perez thought, even some on the flimsiest of pretexts. He was a man who hated an open file, a box of useless evidence, or a suspect who vociferously claimed his innocence. Once he made up his mind, the guilty would be punished. And in this case, involving the murder of a foreigner—and an American just when relations between the United States and Mexico had entered yet another fragile passage—required immediate resolution, no matter anyone's actual guilt or innocence.

Perez shook his head, but Gonzalez appeared not to notice.

"We'll interview the suspects we have right now. I can't hold them much longer as it is. Come on," Gonzalez said, standing up and crushing his cigarette with an extra twist into the ashtray. "We need to get on with this. Let's squeeze our little sparrow 'til he sings."

He picked up the phone and dialed four digits. "Bring that boy, Herrera, to the interview room," he ordered. "If he asks why, tell him we've found new evidence, and then shut him up alone for a few minutes to wait for us. We'll be down shortly." He hung up the phone, looking very satisfied. Perez had to admit, his chief certainly knew how to intimidate a witness; it was said he could force a confession from a corpse.

Ten minutes later, they headed through the open work space and then back down the stairs to the interview room. Gonzalez greeted the guard who was standing nearby and then twisted the door handle, but didn't open it. Again, he said something indistinct to the guard and then suddenly flung the door open so that it banged against the wall. Herrera was sitting at the interview desk, looking pale, small, and very guilty—that is, Perez thought—if guilt was the same face as fear.

Perez remained standing by the open door; Gonzalez said nothing but sat down across from the boy, putting his hands on the table.

"We have information back from the laboratory in Guadalajara," he began, opening the file he had been carrying and pretending to read. "I'm afraid it's very bad news for you. Your DNA matches exactly that found all over the victim. So it's finally time to start telling us what really happened at the sauna. We already know that you stole the American's ring. You've been lying all along. And now we know that there are traces you left on the body."

Perez inhaled deeply. This was an even greater distortion than he imagined. None of the suspects knew that the DNA would only prove a sexual encounter and nothing had been said about its presence elsewhere. This prevarication was breathtaking!

He expected the boy to cry out and shout his innocence, but instead he seemed to collapse further, as if the bones in his body had bent under some great weight crushing him down into the metal chair. He said nothing, but his eyes were wide open with terror. He started to speak, but his voice broke.

"Why don't you tell us the truth," Perez said gently. "We have the evidence; there's nowhere to hide, son."

Gonzalez looked at his junior officer but said nothing.

Herrera gave Perez a pleading look, and then finally blurted out, between the sobs that suddenly shook his body: "Okay. Yes, I... I went to the American's room. I admit it."

"And," shot Gonzalez, "Also the steam room? You followed him there?"

"No," Herrera almost shouted. "No! We were just together... you know what I mean, in his room. We had sex. That's all."

"You're lying again," Gonzalez said, leaning over the table. "You admitted you took the ring in the steam room. Is that where you killed him?"

"No, never! Yes, okay, I admit I took the ring off his finger; I already told you that. But that was later and he was drunk or dead or whatever. How could I kill him? I don't know how to kill anyone! I'd never be able to."

"Maybe it was an accident?" Perez suggested. "Maybe he woke up when you were stealing the ring and you just defended yourself?"

Herrera gave him a strange look and then he answered with more confidence perhaps because he thought the policeman was providing him with an escape: "Yes, I suppose it could have been an accident. I don't know. But it wasn't me! When I saw him, he was just lying there; I said something to him, but he didn't move. That's when I decided to take the ring. I had seen it before. I'm really sorry. I shouldn't have. It was so stupid. I've never done anything like that before. But I thought I could sell it. And get away."

Perez was certain this would also be the last time the boy ventured into any sauna... even if he wasn't convicted of murder. Although he knew what Gonzalez thought, he wondered what a prosecutor or a judge might say with such flimsy evidence.

"I've heard enough," Gonzalez said abruptly, and Perez

could see the momentary optimism of the suspect wash away with a returning tide of fear. Both policemen got up and left the room, closing the door behind them. Outside, in the hallway, Gonzalez told the guard to escort the boy back to a cell. He then turned and headed back up the stairs to his office. Perez trailed behind.

"What do you think?" Perez asked, when his superior had settled behind his desk and lit another cigarette.

"I don't think; I know," Gonzalez snapped. "He's guilty."

"But the evidence is so weak. Could you convince a prosecutor? And a judge? And what about the other suspects. Aren't you going to confront them? And the Americans?"

"No, let them all go. And the Americans were never suspects, anyway. We've got our *asesino*." He pronounced the last word with obvious pleasure. "I'll get in touch with the prosecutor right away. You can leave."

As he walked down the hallway, Perez considered what had made Gonzalez so certain. Was it dislike for Herrera? His lies? Prejudice? Or just a desire to be done with the case, to wash the smell of something offensive off his hands. He also wondered if Herrera's parents would even hire a lawyer. The boy had explained that relations with his father were angry and hostile. Would the man defend his son or throw him unprotected into a system that was bound to judge the friendless harshly. Perez understood that it wasn't his job to sympathize with criminals, but this case bothered him. More so because he thought the American parents might make it even more difficult for the boy to receive justice once they knew of his arrest. He also realized that he shouldn't reveal any of his doubts to Señora Pennyworth at the Consulate. But he fully intended to anyway. She would want to know and she had been helpful up to now.

Back at his desk, he was about to telephone her but instead decided on a visit. He needed to get away and the investigation was now out of his hands since Gonzalez had made up his mind. And Perez didn't dare tell him of the interviews he had conducted with the American Consul. Nothing would change his mind now, and anyway, they hadn't discovered anything incriminating: strange, yes, but nothing conclusive. And everything about this case was strange.

Driving back toward the marina area and the Consulate, Perez stalled in the late afternoon traffic of ancient and rattletrap buses belching diesel smoke and impatient cars zig-zagging in the clogged highway. He hadn't noticed before and normally paid little attention to the weather, but as he had to stop in front of one red light after another, he could see the effects of drought on the median of short palm trees and flowers exhausted and limp and surrounded by clumps of dusty brown grass. It would probably begin to rain soon, and then every afternoon there would be showers that immediately evaporated into low clouds of steam, coating everything with a glistening sweat. He almost laughed because the image reminded him of the Olympiad Sauna and the men in its steam room: if you wanted a permanent rainy season; that's where it was! This case is haunting me, he said to himself.

Parking in front of the Consulate, he walked up the stairs to the entrance. He could see the assistant sitting at his desk and a Mexican family clustered around him, looking down at some sort of document. He entered and Nando motioned him to wait. He then picked up the phone, said something, and indicated that Señora Pennyworth would see him immediately.

She was sitting behind the desk, looking tired and worried when he entered.

"Please sit, Sergeant," she said, "I was just about to leave. So I'm hoping you're bringing good news. I could use some. I just finished another conversation with the Blackmans. They're on their way back to the US... to their separate homes with the ashes of their son." She did not add that she was relieved to see them go.

"News of a sort," he began. "But I'm not certain how good it is. And I shouldn't tell you, but I will. We're going to charge that boy, Herrera, with the murder. It's complicated, but he has confessed to having sex with the murdered man and we know he stole the ring. Gonzalez thinks that's enough evidence."

"And you? You aren't convinced are you?"

Perez knew that he had sounded vague and she had immediately sensed it.

"The other suspects will be released," he continued. "And the case will go forward to the prosecutor and the judge. It's out of our hands now."

"So it's decided, then. And you didn't even consider that one of the Americans did it. The boyfriend—we know that they argued, didn't they? It could have been him. He certainly had a reason to be angry. And the others? I think there's something wrong in not trying to find out."

"There's nothing to be done. Once Gonzalez makes up his mind... The case will surely go forward; and now it's the judge who will decide. I just wanted you to know. I think that's the end of it."

Amanda said nothing for a minute and then said, trying hard not to sound bitter: "I hope not. But nothing about this makes sense to me. Do you really think that boy could be the murderer? Tell me honestly?"

Perez answered quickly: "No, he may be guilty of many things, but he is no murderer. He is so young and small. I don't believe it."

"And you will just let it go... like that? Even with your doubts?"

"What can I do, Señora?"

"Nothing, I suppose. Nothing if it's decided." She could have added that perhaps her hands were not so bound up in regulations as his.

"If there's nothing else, Señora..."

"No, I guess not. Thank you for keeping me informed. I appreciate it."

Perez opened the door to the office and hesitated in the threshold, as if something was holding him back.

"I'll tell you what happens with the trial, if there is one, Señora. But, you understand..."

"Thank you, Sergeant," Amanda said. "I'm sorry your hands are tied. Not like—" she stopped because she had no intention of telling him that she was determined not to let the case just drop.

She stood up, took a half step around her desk, and then fought back the urge to shake his hand. After he left, she sat down again. Why had she thought to do that? Was it for reassurance; as a gesture of closure; a signal that everything was settled and fine? Some unconscious sign of affection? No. Not that, surely not: flirting with a married man! But nothing was settled, at least in her own mind and she felt responsible—to the victim's parents perhaps, but mostly to herself. She hated unraveled feelings, as if the pattern of truth was hidden somewhere in this frayed tapestry with its dangling loose ends. But what in the world could she do?

Picking up the phone she buzzed Nando: "Please see if you can locate that American, Archie West. I need to speak to him immediately. If he is still in Mexico. You have his number."

She put the phone down and waited. Ten minutes passed and finally Nando knocked at her door: "I found him," he said, leaning in. "He's on his way here but can't stay long. His plane for Los Angeles leaves later tonight."

"Good," Amanda replied. "Thank you, Nando."

Los Angeles, she thought. So much of what had happened in this mystery seemed to originate in that city. Growing up, Jeremy had been passed between his parents—one located near Los Angeles and his father who remained up north. But Mrs. Blackman had remained nearby. West and the victim both had apartments there in Venice or nearby. And that unpleasant American, Arlington something—she had forgotten his first name—had come from somewhere near LA with his wife to vacation in Puerto Vallarta, and he too had ended up in the sauna.

"No," she said out loud. It was only the smallest of coincidences. Even if almost half of the persons linked to this event had some tie to that city, it had to be accidental. Chance had brought them all together. And there was the proximity of California to Mexico, and how many daily flights? She might look that up some time. Although it would prove nothing.

Archie West appeared in the waiting room of the

Consulate a half hour later. He was pulling a small roller bag. Waved into Amanda's office immediately by Nando, he leaned his bag against the wall and heaved a knapsack off his shoulder onto one of the chairs in front of her desk. A metal canteen attached to the side clanged against the metal leg of the chair as he collapsed into the other seat.

"I'm really in a hurry," he said, "I've got a plane to catch."

"You'll have time, I think; we're very close to the airport," Amanda said. "There's just something I wanted to ask you before you left."

"And, in exchange, maybe you can tell me what the police are doing? If anything? Have they arrested anyone? They called and told me I could go. But I hate to leave not knowing. And his parents won't have anything to do with me. I tried Mrs. Blackman. Your assistant gave me her number. But she wouldn't say a word to me. Just hung up after she blamed me for taking Jeremy to the sauna. Total blackout! And I wouldn't dare try the father. I'm sure they won't even let on if there's going to be a funeral."

"I'm sorry about that," Amanda said, shaking her head. "I can't answer for them. But I did want to know one thing." She took a deep breath: "Did you have an argument with Jeremy?"

"Not really."

"But a few witnesses say they heard you arguing with him."

West's cheeks flushed and he gripped the sides of the chair he was sitting in.

"Okay," he said. "Yes. I was angry at him because he told me... I saw him with that young Mexican fellow... and I knew what had happened. A 'last fling,' and he said like it was just a joke. I didn't think so and it made me furious. So I guess I yelled at him. Said some awful things and then I got my stuff out of the room and left. That's why. You can ask the management. They saw me go. And—" He stopped suddenly, his voice trembling. "It was the very last thing I ever said to him! Do you know how rotten that makes me feel? Awful words! And now he's gone. It didn't mean anything. Makes me feel responsible. Like I cursed him to die! And it was my fault. We never should have gone to that place!"

"I'm really sorry for you, Archie," she said, knowing that her words were entirely useless. Ever the diplomat, she thought—always reassuring, covering up, and deflecting. Suddenly she thought of the joke she once heard in Washington at State headquarters: "You know how they refer to a female ambassador? 'Miss Direction!'" Whoever thought of that pun had a nasty view of women diplomats... but she had to admit it sometimes fit her job description. But why did she think of that now? Was she trying to evade the thought that the murder would never be solved?

"You didn't tell me if the police have arrested someone? Have they?" Archie asked, standing up and hoisting his back pack over one his shoulder.

"This is all I know. They've accused that young Mexican boy you saw him with. They recovered the wedding ring in his possession; apparently he stole it. He confessed to that, but claims he didn't kill your friend."

"Can I get the ring back sometime?"

"No, I doubt very much if you can. It's their only evidence."

"And will they convict him. Do you think he did it? I don't believe it."

"I can't say. But I can let you know."

West shot her a dubious look, picked up his knapsack, and took a step toward the door.

"I guess I should thank you."

"I suppose so," Amanda replied, feeling that she had done nothing to merit anyone's gratitude.

"Goodbye, then," he said, and walked out into the waiting room dragging his bag behind him.

A few last bands of light entered the window behind her, touching a corner of the office wall and floor indicating approaching evening. The crowds of tourists would soon begin their stroll along the Malecon. There might even be a few already sitting in beachside cafés, bottles of beer with lime wedges jammed onto the brim in front of them. Or a margarita selected from a rainbow of flavors on offer. Down at Los Muertos Beach, she could imagine families packing up their towels, umbrellas, and water toys, hauling their reluctant children out of the sea. Only the most devoted sun worshippers would remain, steeping their already bronzed bodies in the remaining ineffective rays. It was a time of day she normally loved, when the whole city returned home from scattered activities: adventure tours, boat trips to view whales and seals, snorkeling, horseback riding, and bus excursions to the back country villages and a stop at an (inevitable) tequila factory. Friends, families, or solitary individuals like herself would slowly gather together into a seeming endless and aimless stroll back and forth along the Malecon, listening to the sounding sea crash invisible against the rocks, watching the few persevering pelicans hanging against the pale horizon ready to make one last plunge into the dark water. Everyone contemplating the meals they would enjoy—but not just yet—at one of the open-air restaurants along the beach.

Tonight, however, she felt sad and depressed, and the thought of a long traipse home in the lingering heat, watching the day pack itself away again in order to greet the night time crowds, only made her more unhappy. She wondered if she was experiencing the notorious burn-out that friends in the Service were always discussing, or that she had, herself, once felt at the conclusion of her years assigned to the embassy in Indonesia and the inevitable end of a relationship she had known would never last beyond her departure. Or maybe it was like the exhaustion that weighed on her during the third summer at State in Washington during her stint at Foggy Bottom, walking back to the metro along the steaming streets of the city, through the thick, polluted air, back to the apartment she shared only with her loneliness. Sometimes she felt as if part of her identity was left behind in the post she had just departed. What would be left, she wondered, at the end of her career?

But tonight she knew it was something else that was bothering her. Not fatigue with the routine that she and Nando performed every day of filling out forms, talking to anxious tourists or helping visa applicants. Bureaucracy could be boring and endless, but she had shuffled most of that onto his shoulders recently. No, she knew it was her feeling of failure and inadequacy and sorrow, a confusing muddle of noxious emotions. Up to now she had not allowed herself to feel grief at the senseless death of Jeremy Blackman. She had refused to reflect on the perpetual bickering of his parents, nor had she really focused on how little they seemed to care about him in their preoccupation with inflicting pain on each other. But now she could no longer suppress these feelings. And she worried about the young Mexican boy who would surely be charged with murder. Because she couldn't disregard the suspicion that someone else might be guilty. An opinion she guessed that Officer Perez shared with her.

She wondered how the Mexican system would judge Herrera. Would his parents even hire a competent lawyer to defend him? She thought she knew the answer, and that worried her even more. Not that it was her responsibility. How could it be? But would he fare better in the United States, where the power and influence of prejudice and corruption so often effaced the precision and technologies of justice and its elaborate protocols—its delusions of fairness? All of her experience abroad and every counsel of her training could be summarized up in one admonition: be cautious about making comparisons. They would never be free of distortion and prejudice. But she couldn't help thinking: two unfortunate boys—one, the victim of a brutal murder and the other, the target of a corrupt investigation—two boys, bound together in some sort of inexplicable injustice! How could she help but feel caught up in their tragedy?

She got up slowly, balancing herself with one hand on the desk; with the other, she picked up her briefcase-like purse. She knew she needed to leave the office and put these thoughts behind her. It was futile to worry so much about something that didn't concern her. There was some comfort in knowing that just getting through the next few days would allow her anxiety to dissipate. It always did. She knew from experience that the sharpest fears or feelings of guilt were always blunted and dulled by time passed. Of course, something could always provoke their return in a shudder of recollection. Or a bad dream. But those too would pass away quickly.

She needed a vacation, from the relentless routine and from her imagination—that annoying conjure of her loneliness. No doubt about it. More than anything, she needed some time away from all this.

Two days later, as the duties of the office forced her to concentrate on the small and predictable complaints from tourists who had lost credit cards or misplaced passports, and one excited couple protesting a particularly egregious misrepresentation in an Airbnb contract, there were long stretches of time when she allowed her preoccupation with the case little attention. These were problems she could solve. As she had expected, the tedium of paper work and listening to petty inconveniences eased her most anxious thoughts except when some unexpected spur sent an intense surge of emotion through her body... and then she would remember why she was upset. And it would be like rousing from sleep in a nervous sweat, and then recalling the end of a dream so disturbing that it had forced her awake. Why was it, she wondered, that intense physical feelings always seemed to announce the recollection of memories that distressed her? She only knew that she couldn't control such emotions.

Toward the middle of the day, just as she was trying to decide if she was hungry enough to wander over to the small restaurant nearby for a quick lunch, Nando buzzed her on the intercom. She could hear the nervousness in his voice:

"It's the American Embassy in Mexico City. Someone there wants to talk to you."

"Put him through," Amanda said, resisting the urge to ask if her assistant had any idea of the purpose of the call. As if she didn't know perfectly well! She had responded to the Ambassador's email the day before, but with only the briefest details. And now she was sure he would be angry. It had been a mistake not to keep him fully informed.

After several clicks as the lines were switched around, a woman asked: "Is this Amanda Pennyworth? The Ambassador wishes to have a brief conversation with you."

"Of course," Amanda answered, "I can speak to him now."

"No. Sorry. That's not what I meant. I'm the First Secretary here in Mexico City. We would like for you to come to the Embassy and clear up a few issues that have come to our attention recently. Would you please plan to arrive tomorrow at 2:00? I'm certain you can find a flight. And if there are any complications, please inform us as soon as possible."

"I understand," Amanda said. "I'll book a flight immediately."

The line went dead, but despite what she said so glibly, Amanda didn't understand. And the "few issues" had sounded to her as if the First Secretary was reading from a script... or perhaps a memo written by a lawyer. And the caller hadn't even bothered to reveal her name. That couldn't be good. But no need to speculate about the reason for her summons. She would know soon enough.

She pushed the button on the intercom and spoke to Nando, asking him to find her a flight to Mexico City that would arrive before noon the next day, or failing that, something this evening. She could always stay in a hotel if need be, and perhaps she might spend the next night anyway.

"If you get me a flight this evening, Nando, please find me a hotel near the Embassy. And in any case, book a room for tomorrow night as well." There was no reason she shouldn't spend an evening or maybe two in a city she loved to visit.

Ten minutes later, Nando appeared at the door of her office and entered.

"I have your reservations, Señora. You leave tomorrow morning at nine and arrive in Mexico City an hour and a half later. I found you a hotel near the Embassy for the evening. You should have plenty of time to check in if you want before your meeting, but I arranged for a late arrival if you prefer."

He handed her several sheets of paper.

"There are bar codes on each of them, so all you have to do is appear at the airport and then the hotel."

"Thanks, Nando. I hope you don't mind my taking another day. I know it's been difficult."

"Not at all, Señora. Have a pleasant time in Mexico City. You can depend on me."

"Yes, I know."

The following morning, Amanda rose from a difficult night of worried anticipation. She showered, ate a light breakfast, and arrived at the airport by 7:30. The Aeroméxico flight was only half full, and she was happy to have an empty seat next to her. After hurriedly drinking a cup of weak coffee, she pulled a pad of paper from her briefcase and set it on the slim drop-down tray in front of her. She was sure that the upcoming meeting had something to do with the murder and quite certain the Ambassador wanted to know details of the case—her impression of its possible resolution. And so she made a list, something she often did to organize her thoughts. At the top of the blank sheet, she wrote and underscored a header:

Reasons to Commit Murder

Then she wrote: <u>MOTIVES</u>:
1. Jealousy (not envy)
2. Some obstacle to happiness
3. An obstacle to wealth
4. An obstacle to position
5. Hatred
6. Revenge
7. A vendetta
8. Momentary uncontrolled rage (irrational)
9. Anger (rational)
10. Desperation
11. Safety for oneself
12. Security for others
13. Self defense
14. To cover up another crime
15. Something else?

She was amazed when she contemplated the extent of her catalogue: so many possibilities, and she had never really considered it. But she also realized that motives alone wouldn't explain anything. They had to be paired either with the energy of some strong emotion: a compulsion, a momentary, irresistible feeling—or perhaps something calculated: a plan or an accidental opportunity. Murders didn't just happen because they seemed reasonable to the killer. There had to be opportunity: and perhaps some chance to get away with it. Although she wasn't sure that always mattered.

Thinking about Jeremy Blackman's death, in terms of the list, however, nothing added up. If his boyfriend was the perpetrator, then the first reason might fit. But she was convinced he was innocent. Would you kill someone you loved over some casual transgression? And the fact they had openly argued about it made her doubt anything more happened. As for the young Mexican who had been charged, the only motive that made any sense was guilt to cover up another crime. Way down on her list! But stealing the ring from the finger of someone unconscious did not necessitate a murder. Unless the victim woke up during the robbery. But the coroner had said there were no signs of a struggle. And she couldn't imagine that the slightly built boy described to her by Perez could hold his own in a fight against someone considerably older and larger, let alone kill his opponent. The puzzle just deepened. The only possible answer was "Something else." Whatever that was would probably remain a mystery forever. She tore the sheet off and crumpled it up and stuffed it in her empty coffee cup to hand to the airline attendant.

Arriving at the airport in Mexico City, she walked down the long corridor from the end of the gangway and then followed the signs directly to the metro station located inside the terminal because she carried an overnight bag; no need to wait for luggage. She didn't have to rush either since the airport line went directly to the Embassy area after a few stops. Entering the gleaming orange subway car, she found an unoccupied space and sat down, holding the handle of her bag to prevent it from rolling away as the train twisted and turned out of the airport and under the city.

It was only slightly after eleven when she emerged into the pale sunlight of the Insurgentes metro station and walked north toward the Embassy. As she approached the entrance, it struck her, as it had during her first visit to the city, how squat and functional-looking that square building appeared. If it had a countenance, it was a face that expressed a malign indifference to the world around it, she thought, returning a blank, alien stare to the animated streets it overlooked. The long, narrow windows, separated by protruding oblong stone slabs reminded her of the arrow slits in medieval castles where archers could shoot down on besieging soldiers. The Embassy seemed to be the bully on the block. She wondered if the aggressive appearance was by chance or maybe the intentional message of the architects: someone's fantasy of impenetrability and power.

Given that she was slightly early, she stopped for a coffee at the Starbucks that was situated like an annex of American culture just adjacent to the entrance. There was a Starbucks in Puerto Vallarta, but she rarely patronized it, preferring the Italian coffee shop located on the Malecon about halfway home to her apartment from the office. But today the bitter, over-roasted and burned taste of the double espresso she ordered reminded her of home. "Quality control," she said to herself, walking slowly away from the counter, as she took her first sip through the plastic lid. She sat down on a stool by the window to look out at the pedestrians and cars passing by. It wasn't a café in the European sense; nothing like Paris where one could nurse a small cup all day until it turned cold watching the elegant and the ordinary as they paraded along the sidewalk. But this would do until her meeting.

Several minutes before her appointment, she picked up her case, shoved the paper container into the trash bin by the door, and walked out onto the sidewalk. Passing by the uniformed soldiers and between the concrete barriers arranged like carefully ordered tombstones, she entered into the front lobby and passed through the metal detector. She picked up her bag when it emerged from the luggage scanner. What a thankless, boring job, she thought, for an attendant to stand all day, peering at people entering and leaving on their way to somewhere with a purpose; something like a museum guard but without the fine art to contemplate. She wondered how often they were allowed to take a break.

She rode the elevator up to the third floor with an escort to the Ambassador's Office. When she identified herself, his secretary motioned toward a conversation area with a leather couch, two arm chairs and a table strewn with American and Mexican newspapers.

"Coffee while you wait?" the assistant asked.

"No. But thank you. I just stopped at Starbucks."

"Good choice! Most of us go there. Better than what we serve here anyway. But if you change your mind, there's a machine and cups on the cabinet behind you. I'm sure you know how to work it. I'll tell the Ambassador you're here."

Amanda scarcely had time to relax before the inner

door opened and the Ambassador stepped halfway out. Smiling, he extended his hand and said, "Please come in, Consular Pennyworth. And thank you for making the trip on such short notice."

She stood up and followed him into a large, sunny office dominated by an immense wooden desk. A row of sharpened pencils were laid out on the right. In the exact center lay an open file and next to it a long yellow legal pad. Behind the desk to the left was an American flag and on the back wall in a spot that would be directly over his chair the Seal of the United States.

When they were both seated, he began: "You probably know why you're here." He waited.

"Yes, I suppose this has to do with the murder in Puerto Vallarta."

"Indeed," he continued, glancing down at the papers. He paused to read something.

"It seems that there have been some complications to the case I want to discuss with you. Maybe you are unaware. And, I will be frank with you, there have been stories in the press back home. You know that they can be as tenacious as a tiger when they get hold of something that makes the Service look bad. Don't want this to get into some committee of Congress. Of course, attention will fade away eventually. But, unfortunately," he paused, "I've also received a personal complaint about you. And I'm wondering just how you want to respond."

"Can I ask who and what they said?"

"Well, you can ask, but I'd prefer to keep their names confidential if you don't mind."

Amanda didn't mind because she thought it had to be one of the Blackmans. Who else?

"It appears that you haven't followed this case as diligently as you should. You know that the Mexican police are sometimes inefficient. Did you keep up pressure on them? And I mean without annoying them."

Amanda was furious, because, if anything, she had been too *close* to the investigation. But the Ambassador didn't need to know that.

"They have arrested a suspect," she said, calmly, "... although I'm not sure he's guilty."

The Ambassador ignored her response: "And there's something about your attitude. Have you been under a lot of stress lately?"

Amanda glared at him for a moment and then forced herself to smile: "No, not particularly. The job is not difficult. Just that this case is troubling."

"How long have you been at your present assignment?" he continued.

Amanda realized that he was not listening to her responses but instead simply following down a list of bullet points that he or an assistant had written out. It suddenly worried her that he would spring some sort of surprise question at the end.

"I've been in Puerto Vallarta two years or so."

"Have you had a vacation recently?"

"I've taken a weekend or two, here and there. Nothing extended."

"Then perhaps you would like to take some time off."

"I don't think so. No. I'm fine. And it would inconvenience the Consulate."

"That's not a problem at all. And I think it would do you good to get away for a spell. Perhaps two weeks, even a month back in the States. See your family? I understand your parents live in Chicago. Any siblings nearby?"

The last thing that Amanda wanted was a family reunion, but she hesitated to contradict him: "I suppose..."

"In fact, I think I will have to insist."

"But what about the Consulate? My assistant is quite competent, but he could never handle everything that comes up. And there are official duties and then documents to sign."

"That's already taken care-of," he said, looking down at his script. "We'll send someone temporarily to take over your post while you're gone. And whether you visit your family or not isn't really my concern. That was just a suggestion."

She understood that her furlough wasn't a suggestion but an order. Nothing gained by arguing.

"All right," she said, trying to sound cheerful. "I'll make arrangements to leave. It'll be in three or four days at the earliest. In the meantime, if you want to send in my relief, I can instruct him or her about the special duties of the office. I appreciate your concern."

"Then it's settled. Are you spending the night in the city?"

"I thought I would."

"Good. Change of setting. That's a promising start. And I'll send your replacement the day after tomorrow."

He closed the file and stood. She understood this as an unsubtle invitation to leave. She also realized that the meeting had been over before it began: just a pantomime performance to ease her out gently. Was this the first step to being recalled to Washington or even issued some sort of reprimand and then farmed out on a new and diminished assignment? She wondered what the Blackmans had said to arouse such suspicions—it had to be them. Surely she didn't like them, but she had tried to be polite and helpful—not let her feelings show. Perhaps in some very strange way they blamed her for the death of their son. Preposterous, of course. But grief could distort reason and that odd couple was anything but reasonable.

Emerging from the Embassy into the afternoon sunlight dimmed by clouds that smudged the sky like streaked erasures, she hailed the first taxi that approached and asked the driver to drive her the short distance to the Anthropological Museum. She would have at least two hours to wander among the amazing collection of pre-Columbian objects. Immersed in their strange and exotic beauty she hoped to suppress the fear that her career was at that very moment being discussed in some sterile conference room, her employment file passed around a table of unknown bureaucrats, a panel of supervisors shaking their heads in disappointment, and her fate defined by the application of abstract rules by people who didn't know her.

The taxi stopped in front of the museum just before three. She paid and entered the huge modern structure. Once inside and her bag stowed in a locker, she followed no particular direction but just wandered through artifacts of history and centuries of culture: statues on pedestals and cases of pottery in earth-colored glazes, glancing at the strange physiognomies, clay gods, and stones inscribed with hieroglyphics and etched faces. What should have been absorbing took a measure of concentration, but she did not have the energy to focus. Her worries kept blurring her vision until finally she found herself standing in front of a huge stone calendar. Something about this monumental sculpture made her pause to stare at its vivid symmetry and the grotesque face chiseled in the center. Something about it made a connection and jerked her back from her aimless and self-absorbed wandering. Before such amazing craft and strange, ominous brilliance, she thought: how silly and insignificant were her worries. She realized she needed to sort out and untangle her loneliness and feelings of inadequacy from the threat she felt to her career and the murder at the gay sauna. Damn the Blackmans for complicating her life!

In the hour that remained, she decided to find the Mayan Codex, the collection of vivid drawings and writings that had, in her last trip to the museum, evoked such an impression of wonder. When she finally stood before the glass display cases, she had the same reaction and spent the remainder of the short time before closing studying the brilliantly colored books, and speculating, as she always did, about what other beautiful objects had been destroyed in the brutal conversion of such mysterious and alien civilizations to European ways.

Just at five, she walked out the front door, found a taxi, and gave the driver the address of the hotel that Nando had booked for her. It was close to the Embassy so the drive, again, was brief, even in the crowded streets of rush hour.

The hotel was large and modern with an open reception area, and off to the left and down a few steps, a sunken bar. No doubt there was also a restaurant some-where, but she had no desire to dine in a hushed and expensive atmosphere on bland international fare. After she settled into her room and had a quick shower, she went back out onto the crowded street. The Zona Rosa, the quarter of the Embassy and location of her hotel, was like a much larger version of the area around her apartment in Puerto Vallarta—filled with small restaurants, gay bars, art studios, small shops, and tourists looking for entertainment. She felt very much at home strolling along the pedestrian streets, pausing to look into shop windows and reading the menus of restaurants that were beginning to post their evening specials.

For the first time that day she felt really relaxed. Perhaps it was being immersed in the familiar that allowed her to appreciate her surroundings. If only for tonight, she promised herself, she would try to forget the brief and ominous inquisition of the Ambassador. But perhaps he got one thing right, she thought: a vacation might be a welcome change from the routine of her job and the extraordinary demands made on her attention by the unresolved murder case. She would have ample time to think about that because she knew for certain that the Mexican courts would move slowly in their consideration of the charges against the Herrera boy. In any case, tonight she intended to have dinner—something exotic—and then several stiff drinks.

The place she finally chose was a Korean establishment. She hadn't realized the extent of that community settled in this quarter, but it became apparent from the numerous store fronts and restaurants that displayed Korean flags and names. It was early yet, especially for Mexico, but she was hungry, so she chose a small café. Inside, a crowd already occupied most of the small tables. The thick, smoky atmosphere made her eyes water. This was precisely what she needed, she said to herself.

After a meal of dumplings and spicy barbecued beef

she went back outside and strolled through the area that was, if anything, even more animated now that it was evening. She wasn't particularly sure where she might stop for a drink, but she knew that any choice would be arbitrary. Meandering back, finally toward the hotel, she decided to try the bar there. It was convenient and safe and she was beginning to tire.

To her surprise, the establishment was dark, noisy, and crowded. She found a stool against the counter and ordered a strawberry daiquiri. While she waited, she turned around and surveyed the room. Most of the clientele looked to be North American or European, probably guests at the hotel, although there were a few who looked to be Mexican businessmen. She was not surprised that these men were dressed formally unlike the foreigners who wore open shirts and jeans. The few women seated at tables or standing in groups seemed to be attached to a couple. It made her feel, suddenly, alone again.

She turned back when she heard the barista place the drink down and said: "Señora." She took a sip of the thick, red liquid through a straw and then set it back on the bar.

"I couldn't help noticing," someone on her left said.

She turned her head and looked at the man who was standing next to her. "Noticing what?" she asked.

"Well, two things. That you are by yourself and very probably an American."

"I could be waiting for my husband; and I might be Canadian or even English." she replied.

"True. But I'll take my chances."

She turned around now to face him. He was obviously not an American; she could detect some sort of Germanic intonation in his few brief words, but that could mean Swiss or Austrian, or something else, even Dutch. He was tall, edging upward from middle age she estimated, with receding dark hair and a very weathered face—not exactly handsome, but pleasant looking.

"Do I hear a hint of something German in your accent?" she asked.

"So you're curious too. That's good. And yes, I'm Danish. Actually I'm attached to our Embassy here."

"Is it nearby?"

"Yes, fairly close. And since I was in the area. Just stopped by for a drink."

He paused and leaned in closer after a particularly loud burst of laughter from one of the groups of men standing at the other end of the bar. That disturbance and the vague thumping background of music gave him two choices: to shout over the ambient noise or move nearer. He chose to lessen the gap between them.

"May I buy you a drink?"

"I haven't even finished this one yet," she laughed. "Aren't you jumping the gun?"

"Oh you Americans have such strange ways of talking. Always something about guns and violence. But no, it would give me pleasure."

"Okay, but only if you tell me your name first."

"Dietrich."

"Well, Dietrich, I will accept another frozen daiquiri."

He signaled to the bartender and continued. If he noticed that she withheld her own name, he pretended not to.

"And what brings you to Mexico City? It's pleasure, I hope."

"It's always a pleasure to be here," she said, "but business is the occasion." She noted that the bartender had already replaced her half-filled glass with another.

"If I might ask...?"

Amanda laughed: "I have to confess, I'm in your business."

"So you're a diplomat?"

"Very junior. Just visiting my Embassy here."

"Well then," he said, "we have much in common."

She looked more carefully at him and, for a moment, thought she might continue this banter to where it would inevitably lead. He was handsome enough in a rugged way and persistent. She might even sleep with him; it would be so easy just to invite him to her room here in the hotel. What would be the harm? Just a night of pleasure away from home, an experience she could insulate from the routine of her life, except, of course, from everything but the memory of it which she might come to regret. Yet she wondered if giving in to temptation was an attempt to evade her fear of missing out—a fear of life passing her by in the solitary profession she had chosen... to prove to herself that she was still attractive and on the game. But for how long would a brief fling make her forget that her career was in serious jeopardy? And how could a sexual encounter distract her from thinking about the unsolved—unsolvable—mystery that accosted her? Damn the way her thoughts raced! Was she that desperate?

"You seem very quiet all of a sudden," he said, touching her arm briefly. "As if you're not completely here."

"I was thinking."

"About?"

"About whether or not I should sleep with you."

He placed his hand on her shoulder: "Oh my! You do shoot straight!" he said, laughing at his own joke. "And the verdict?"

"Permanent injunction."

He looked puzzled and then understood: "But I haven't even entered a plea."

"I'm afraid your case has already been tossed out of court! Rule of preemption. Were you planning to file a motion?"

"Well, perhaps I was. And now I think you've judged me too quickly."

"I'm sorry. Really sorry. It isn't you; it's me. I think you're an attractive man. Very. And I'll enjoy talking to you if that's okay. But nothing more than that for me tonight. I hope you're not offended."

"Not at all," he said, withdrawing his hand. "I'm just impressed with how frank you Americans can be."

"Most of us aren't. Just me and just tonight."

"So something has happened?"

"Yes, it has. You're very observant."

"And it's bothering you? You would like tell me about it, no?"

"Yes, I think I just might." What was the harm in that, she thought? And maybe if she laid out a narrative of the events of the past week or so, put all the events in order, and laid out the evidence such as it was, things might become clearer to her. Not that she expected any insight from him; just an audience to listen as she assembled the pieces of the story. Far better to confide in a stranger whom she would never see again.

CHAPTER 10

The next morning Amanda woke with a slight head-ache—too many mixed drinks—but with a feeling of immense relief nonetheless. She knew that if she had followed her initial impulse and brought Dietrich to her room, he would still be lying next to her in the disheveled bed, the object of her regret and a silent partner in the morning performance of quick and clumsy partings.

She remained still for a moment, planning her day: a shower, breakfast in the hotel dining room, and then the metro to the airport. Her plane did not leave until noon, but there was no time for shopping. Even if she wanted to, the stores wouldn't open until ten at least; maybe even later. What did she need anyway, except some extravagant distraction? What she did require was to return to Puerto Vallarta and then make plans for her vacation. More and more she was considering a trip to Santa Monica to visit her old college roommate. And anyway, it was Los Angeles. She was sure that the city held some sort of key to the mystery.

Last night, talking to Dietrich and responding to his prodding, and formulating her own arguments, she had persuaded herself that the murderer had to be one of the Americans. Herrera just couldn't be guilty. So it must be Jeremy Blackman's roommate, implausible as that seemed, or maybe there was a connection to that unpleasant older man—she had forgotten his name for a moment. And maybe the person she and Perez and interviewed in the marina area, although she doubted that. But then again maybe she was completely wrong and silly to involve herself in what the Mexican police were surely more competent to deal with than she was? And what in the world was the motive?

Back in Puerto Vallarta in her office that afternoon, she greeted Nando and asked him to step into her office. She pointed to a chair and when he was seated, she began: "I hope this won't cause any difficulties for you. In fact, I'm sure it won't. But in a few days, I'll be leaving for a week or so. I'm not sure exactly where I'll go; I have to decide that; probably Los Angeles."

"A vacation, Señora?"

"You might call it that. But, in any case, the Embassy in Mexico City is sending out a temporary replacement. It wouldn't be fair to put all the burden on you, and there are always official documents you couldn't sign. So he—and I assume it will be a man—should arrive soon. I'll stick around long enough to help him adjust to the routine here, but that shouldn't take more than a day or two."

She hesitated and Nando looked at her curiously: "Is there something wrong, Señora?"

"You know me too well, Nando. Yes, there is. I'll be frank with you. The Embassy is very unhappy about the murder case here. There have been some complaints about our role—my role, I mean. I'm not sure who contacted the State Department and it doesn't really matter. It happened. I suppose they think that sending me away will make the protests disappear. I doubt that, but it's what they decided. As to what happens next, I don't know."

"You can depend on me, Señora."

"I know that, Nando. And I'll let you know shortly about plane reservations... when I decide where I'll go."

"Certainly," he said, standing up. "I hope this will go well for you."

"Thank you," she said.

He walked out of the office and back to his desk. Amanda thought about him for a moment; there was something about the way he expressed his confidence in her that made her immensely sad... and then angry. She had to do something quickly before this situation destroyed her career. At worst, she might even be removed from the Service, but more probably, just a series of unpleasant postings: Washington never fired anyone; they just assigned you to oblivion. Reluctantly, she picked up her calendar and began to calculate the best time for her vacation. In her agenda she had also kept the phone number of her best friend from college who had invited her several times to visit Santa Monica. Yes, that would be perfect. Why not? She would surprise her by accepting.

Punching out the number on her cellphone, she was delighted when Stephanie answered immediately.

"Your long lost and now very forlorn roommate calling," she announced.

"Amanda! How nice! Are you in town?"

"Not yet, but I'm hoping to be. That invitation of yours. To visit. Is it still valid? Did you actually mean it? Or is there someone currently occupying your hospitality?"

"If you're asking me if I've found myself a partner since we last talked, the answer is, regretfully, no! So I've still got lots of room in my life for a guest."

"Then I'd like to come. In a few days if that's possible."

"It is."

Stephanie hesitated and Amanda knew what she would ask next, so she continued: "You are probably curious. As you can guess, I'm in trouble."

"A man?"

"Well, of course. There are always men involved, aren't there? But it's my job mainly. I'm being put out to pasture for a couple of weeks. To graze among the civilians!"

"Sounds serious."

"It could be. But I'll tell you about it when I get there."

"Do you have a reservation yet?"

"No, I wanted to check with you first."

"When you do, plan to arrive sometime around noon if you can and take an Uber or Lyft from the airport. I'm not that far and, well, who knows about traffic, even at that hour: it's Los Angeles. It's just easier for me not to fight the freeway both directions."

"Will do. And it'll be wonderful to see you, Steph. Old times."

"And to catch up."

Amanda hung up and decided to make the plane reservation herself. She wasn't sure if this would be on the Consular tab or hers, but she didn't want to fight an audit.

She suddenly wondered if they had made prisoners pay their way to exile in Siberia. She laughed at the awful idea. Where did such crazy thoughts come from? Came from reading too many Russian novels, no doubt.

She located a number of possible flights and made a reservation three days forward with a return a week later. The Ambassador had been vague about the length of time she should spend away from the office, but she was certain it would be a very bad idea to linger too long while her replacement settled in. Who knew if this might be a way of easing her out? She was not willing to let that happen without a fight. Puerto Vallarta was a great assignment and she had welcomed it, even though all the responsibility of the office fell on her shoulders alone.

The next morning, when she arrived at the Consulate, there were several people in the waiting room: a couple with a young daughter overdressed in a pink outfit with matching pink sneakers in the way Mexican mothers sometimes indulged their fantasies about childhood. Sitting next to them, and looking very uncomfortable, was an American man, obviously so, who looked relieved when he saw her enter. He stood to greet her, but she continued on to Nando's desk, leaned down, whispered something to him, and then entered her office and closed the door. She knew she was being abrupt and unwelcoming, but what sort of greeting did she owe to the man who might well steal her job?

After a minute or so, she spoke to Nando on the intercom.

"Is that Mexican couple waiting for me?"

"Yes, Señora. They are having trouble with a visa application. I've done what I could, but they need you."

"Okay. Why don't you apologize to them; tell them I'll be with them in a moment, but then send in the American. Let's get this over with."

A moment later there was a knock on her door and, without waiting, he walked in. Amanda came around her desk to shake hands and motioned for him to sit.

"I'm Mark Sommers," he said. "I guess you've been expecting me. The Ambassador—"

"Ah yes," she cut him off. "My temp."

He said nothing and Amanda studied his face. Her first impression was his soft, bland appearance: a surprising pallor, little masculine angularity, but a kind of puffiness in his cheeks and hands, like over-proofed dough—the "sponge" as the Brits called it on their popular cooking shows. Perhaps she was accustomed to seeing Mexican men and their dark skin... But when he began to speak, the unpleasant image disappeared; he had a pleasant and animated voice.

"I realize this is a bit awkward for you, Ms. Penny-worth," he began. "I'm not aware of all of the circum-stances, but I assure you that this is just a temporary assignment for me. I have no intention of moving from the Embassy in Mexico City. The Ambassador promised me. I'm in the Consulate there and... I really don't want another assignment."

Amanda understood exactly what he meant: Puerto Vallarta would represent a demotion, a stint in a bywater that would interrupt his progress up through the Civil Service ranks.

"I appreciate your replacing me for a couple of weeks," she said, much relieved. "I'll be going to California for a vacation. And I can assure you that the work here is easy enough and mostly routine. Nando, out front, whom you've already met, is a marvel of competence, and he can handle most issues. As for the rest, you've got Consular experience so it won't even be a stretch. Most of the problems come from tourists and occasionally an expat. As a small place, we also have our share of business arrangements and economic issues to facilitate too. Nothing too complicated. But you could always put those on hold until I return."

He was quiet for just a minute, but Amanda guessed what was coming next.

"There was some discussion around the Embassy. Hope you don't mind my asking. But was there something about a murder case? An American? Is that settled?"

"Yes and no. I won't bother you with the details, but the police have arrested a suspect. I'm sure you know how the process works in Mexico with the judge and all. So it's just a matter of time. They won't want you to be involved."

She did not add that she was very dissatisfied with what she feared would be a dreadful mistake: a false accusation, a trifling defense, and then the conviction of the wrong person.

"All right," he said.

"And have you got a hotel? I don't know where you want to live: the marina area perhaps, around here, Old Town, or the Zona Romantica? That's where I am."

"Already found an apartment very close to the office. Nice place too with a view of the ocean."

"Perfect. Nando can make a list of some decent restaurants in the area. And then you'll be all set. Why don't you make yourself at home; listen in to the business of the day."

"Thank you, Ms. Pennyworth. Under the circum-stances..."

"It's Amanda, please."

"Okay. And I'm Mark."

"Welcome, then."

Two days later, Amanda found herself standing among a milling crowd on the sidewalk of the passenger private pickup lot at LAX, Los Angeles, waiting for her Uber ride to arrive. Every time a new vehicle pulled in, she was tempted to rush forward, and then checked her cellphone once again for the description of the car which she knew very well would be a silver Toyota. Stephanie had told her how to navigate this new app she put on her phone, but it was something she hadn't done before and it made her nervous. Too long away from the States, she told herself, because everyone else seemed calm and completely unconcerned.

Her ride finally appeared and she hesitated for a moment. Was this like a taxi or like a friend picking you up? But she decided to sit in the back, and the car drove off, joining the slow stream of traffic inching north toward Santa Monica. The distance was short, just as Stephanie assured her, and they arrived twenty minutes later in front of the three-story apartment house where she lived. Amanda had been to Los Angeles before, but it always struck her how green and lush the older parts of the city appeared. Huge fig trees with their immense twisted trunks shaded the street in front of the dingy stucco building where they stopped. The neighborhood had the feeling of a small town, set far away from the noisy rivers of traffic that crisscrossed the LA basin, cut deep like drainage ditches or flowing over on raised motor aqueducts. She was about to ask the driver for the fare price and then she remembered; everything was done on-line in this new gig economy, including a tip, in the hands-off electronic world where trade and barter were just impulses bouncing around distant cell towers.

Standing in front of the building, she pressed the call button next to her friend's name and, after a minute, the lock on the front gate buzzed. She walked inside the small courtyard surrounded by balconies with a disused and dusty flower bed at the center. Stephanie had just emerged from her apartment on the second floor and waved her up.

"Take the stairs on your left. Do you need help with your suitcase?" she shouted.

"I can manage," Amanda called back and then climbed up the dark staircase.

"I won't apologize for the size of the place," Stephanie said, leading her into the apartment. "At least it's bigger than our dorm room and you'll have your own privacy. Best of all, it's only five blocks from the beach; I consider that my front yard. I go down every chance I get for coffee and to watch the sandlot volleyball games. And the surfers when the wind is up."

"Sounds like an idyllic life."

"Well with work and all and commuting, it's just a Los Angeles life. Anyway, I hope you'll really enjoy yourself: the beach, some great museums—you can take Uber—and just relax. I won't ask you to explain what happened if you don't want to."

"I'll tell you, eventually," Amanda said, cautiously. "But not just yet. There's time, and I have to confess, my own thoughts are still pretty confused."

"I'm all sympathetic ears."

"Sounds great. There's only one thing I need to do. I want to set up a couple of interviews, or maybe better, two visits without forewarning."

"Something to do with work?"

"Something to do with a murder."

"Sounds intriguing... and dangerous! So you *are* mixed up in something then! I just knew it."

"I'll tell you later. Right now, I'd love to walk down to the beach. I'll buy you dinner if you can suggest a place."

"I can, and one with a good view of the volleyball players. It's the sun and surf scene. You won't believe the guys."

"Probably not, but I'll try my best. Just let me change out of these travel clothes and we can go."

For the rest of the weekend, Stephanie led Amanda to her favorite LA spots: the Griffith Observatory and the Getty Museum, both of them with commanding views of the city. From opposite ends, each looked over the enormous sprawl, spread like a skirt sewn with a thousand silver eyelets dazzling in the afternoon sun, that stretched down to the sea and back up against the peaks of the San Gabriel Mountains. The vastness of it made her momentarily homesick for the tiny strip of beach and quaint Old Town of Puerto Vallarta. She wondered if her assignment there... or anywhere else was finished. Of course she had to return, but would it be to pack up her life and career in return for something entirely new in some anonymous American city like this one? Maybe what she could find out here would provide the answer. It was a long shot, but...

If anything, the time to relax, share old stories with

Stephanie, and wander around Santa Monica just sharpened her impatience. When Monday arrived with the possibility of embarking on her investigation and following up on the desperate hope that she could find out something that would rescue her career, she was ready to test whether her better instincts outweighed the temptation to make hasty judgments. She decided she would visit Archie West and the enigmatic Aaron Arlington. Thinking about Archie, she realized that he had good reason to be furious with Jeremy Blackman, despite his denials. After all they had argued, and the victim had in his drunken stupor betrayed his lover. Although she still doubted it. And the other man had no apparent motive at all and that intrigued Amanda even more. Something about him wasn't what it seemed. So she determined to visit him first.

When she told Stephanie of her plan, she saw a look of disapproval spread over her friend's face.

"I've got two really serious objections," she said. "I'm sure you don't want to hear, but I don't think you should do it... at least not alone. What if he *is* the murderer? Have you thought of what he might do? And anyway, you said he lives in Glendale. That's an hour from here at best. How will you know if he's home or in town or hasn't moved away if you don't contact him first? You're doubling the risks and the bother. Just inviting trouble. I don't see it."

Amanda wanted to sound confident: "I have to, Steph. I'll just take my chances. And if I fail, well, that's that."

"You're being very casual."

"I was hoping you would say *brave.*"

"The best I can muster is impulsive. Or maybe reckless."

"Okay. I'll have to settle for that."

The next afternoon, Amanda set out on the long trip to Glendale. It wasn't yet rush hour, but the freeway was jammed and the ride took almost an hour. She timed it to arrive around 5:00, hoping to find Mr. and Mrs. Arlington at home. The Uber driver pulled up in front of the address she had noted from the list she kept of all of the suspects. Sitting for a moment in the car, she studied the house. It was a two-story ranch with a peaked front roof extending over a two-car garage. It looked as if this might also support the arched vault over a cathedral entranceway. The double cement driveway left little room for lawn or garden, but a brick path in the center led down to the street from the front door. There was no sidewalk. Who walked anymore, she thought. The narrow strip of property on either side of the house was planted with short palms. Opposite and beginning on the other side of the street, the emerald green grass and huge pine trees of a city park extended down a steep slope.

Leaving the car, she walked up the front path to the door and pressed the illuminated button to her right. She could hear chimes sound from inside, but no one appeared. She tried again and once more there was no response. She turned and made her way slowly down the walk and then across the street and into the park. To her right there were several wooden benches overlooking a large play area with slides and swings. Beyond that, there was open space that continued down the hill to a distant roadway whose muffled whisper of traffic she could hear. If she wanted to watch the house, she would have to stand or, better, sit twisted around on one of the benches. Either way would be uncomfortable and she needed to be careful not to attract attention. Anyone watching her watching might become curious about her interest in the house behind her.

She sat down and looked out over the playground. Shading her eyes in a gesture that felt like a salute, she could see children climbing up the stairs of a covered metal slide and then shooting out from the base, then to run around and clamber up again. Three or four women were standing nearby casually surveying these energetic antics. A man approached the area, holding the hand of a young boy until he broke loose and ran for one of the swings. In the center of the park, several dogs were racing around barking, nipping at each other, and then running circles around a cluster of their owners who seemed to be deep in conversation. One of them stepped aside every minute or two to throw a ball or Frisbee. Almost at the far-left edge, a couple outfitted in tights were stretching and bending in what looked like standing yoga positions. Amanda watched as more people entered the park: several more with dogs that lunged into the pack once freed from their leashes and more parents and children. Three joggers passed in front of her on a gravel path. She could hear bits of their broken conversation.

She shut her eyes and relaxed as the late afternoon sun warmed her face. The sounds of the activity around her cradled her thoughts and lulled her anxiety about her mission. And then, for a moment everything seemed to disappear and she felt herself falling gently into a kind of half-sleep. She felt pleasantly dizzy until a sudden draft of cool air woke her.

She wasn't sure how long she had dozed: a few

minutes—or had a lifetime of thoughts and memories raced through her mind? The sun had shifted slightly down toward the bottom of the park, shaded now by two immense pine trees. But nothing else seemed to have changed. Except that now this scene of utter normality, relaxation and routine made her feel depressed and out of place. What was she doing here? Why was she pursuing this fruitless search? Stephanie was right, although she hadn't said it exactly: this was a fool's errand, and quite possibly a very dangerous one. She needed to go back to Puerto Vallarta; reclaim her job; and be done with amateur detective work. Look at her now! Her persistence had brought her to the brink of a stupid mistake. She knew if she tried, she was sure she could convince the Ambassador to give her another chance. More than anything, she needed to put an end to this obsessive behavior.

She pulled her cellphone out of her purse and scrolled to the Uber app. As she did, she turned around to glance at the house behind her, just one last check to be sure. But immediately she saw that something had changed. There was a dark blue SUV parked in one half of the driveway. Someone had arrived.

Some sudden automatic impulse compelled her to stand, cross the street, and approach the house. Some inner compulsion demanded that she talk to whomever was inside. How could she not continue after all this? No matter what? She had already come too far to turn back, and she wanted to know.

She walked up the edge of the driveway to the front door, rang the bell, and then waited. The door opened quickly and a middle-aged woman dressed in a black business suit gazed out, obviously curious.

"Yes," she said in a brusque monotone that suggested impatience and perhaps suspicion. "How can I help you?"

"Is Mr. Arlington at home?"

"May I ask what this is about?"

"I'm Amanda Pennyworth. I'm here on official State Department business. I'd like to talk to your husband if he's here." Of course, this was a lie, but how else could she break through the woman's caution?

"I'm afraid he's not in right now. I can give him a message if you like."

"If you expect him soon, I can wait. It's really rather important. And I know he will want to talk to me."

"All right," the woman said hesitantly. "I expect him any minute. Come in then."

She backed away from the door and led Amanda through the huge arched foyer and then to the right and into a large living room. Amanda had the immediate impression that the furnishings were the creation of an interior decorator: all in good taste but with no distinct savor. The color of the walls was a soft blue framed with white trim, like Wedgewood. Pleated chintz drapes in a shade of darker ivory hung at the side of a large bay window that looked across to the park. The furniture: a white sofa with carefully placed pillows, several arm chairs in primary colors, and the hanging abstract prints seemed to be the work of someone's bland imagination, a design featured in a home improvement magazine for anonymous consumption: clean, crisp and boring: something that might be pictured in *House Beautiful*. To Amanda, there was something dishonest and dissembling about so much order and symmetry, with nothing of the accidental or surprising that she believed made a room look lived in. And certainly not like the disheveled cheerfulness of her own apartment. The only personal objects seemed to be a cluster of photographs perched on the mantel above a fireplace of creamy marble streaked with irregular black veins.

"Just a moment," Mrs. Arlington said. "I'll text my husband and see where he is. Hopefully he'll be here soon and then you can finish your business."

As she typed out a message, Amanda studied her. She was a woman that someone might call handsome, using the masculine adjective to indicate that she was attractive, but with nothing really sensual about her. Tall, with her dark hair cut short and swept back, and a pale complexion, this severity extended to the stiff way she held herself.

"Please have a seat," she said but remained standing. Amanda thought for a moment that this invitation would create a kind of unspoken differential between them. But it didn't matter to her. She settled onto the end of a couch near the fireplace.

"Would you like a glass of water, perhaps?" the woman said.

"Yes, please. That would be fine."

Without another word, Mrs. Arlington left the room. Amanda stood up, walked over, and casually glanced at the photographs on the mantel. They were various poses of the same boy, some as a child and then a teenager. Nothing beyond it. She concluded, they must have a son, perhaps still in high school.

Mrs. Arlington returned with two glasses on a small silver tray which she placed next to a bowl of artificial fruit on the ceramic top of a coffee table in front of the couch.

"I see that you have a son; what nice pictures," Amanda

said as she sat down again.

Mrs. Arlington inhaled audibly and something momentarily transformed her as a look of despair flashed across her face. Clearing her throat and throwing back her shoulders, she said, "That's Sammy. He's no longer with us."

"Off at college?"

"No. Passed away."

"Oh, I'm so sorry," Amanda blurted out. "I didn't mean to..."

"Died about five years ago in a traffic accident. The other driver was drunk but he survived. Someone else's son lived while my..."

Amanda was shocked at hearing this detail. Why was she told this detail, unless Mrs. Arlington couldn't help herself?

"That's terrible. It must be awful for you."

"You can't imagine what it's like to lose a son, cut down by someone else's son. I wonder what they might feel if..." She sat down at the other end of the couch, picked up a glass of water, and then set it down again without drinking.

Amanda could think of nothing to say. How would words of consolation from a stranger lessen this woman's grief—pain that her blunder had aroused? She decided then that she had to leave. She had bullied her way into this woman's misery and she needed to depart immediately. This had all been a terrible mistake.

"I'm so sorry. I think I'll go now. I don't want to intrude any longer. I can leave my telephone number; just ask your husband to call me, will you? I'll send for an Uber."

She was about to pull her cellphone from her purse

when she heard the front door bang open. Aaron Arlington rushed into the living room, his face flushed with anger.

"What the hell are you doing here?" he almost shouted when he saw Amanda. "Get out!" And then turning to his wife, he said, "Why did you let her in? What have you told her?"

"I haven't said a word. What do you think?"

"Good. Now Miss Meddler. You may leave quietly and we will just assume you were never here."

Amanda stood up. She was furious to be dismissed in such a brusque way. The man was obviously hiding something. She had to say something. So she took a chance.

"Did you know that your husband is gay?" she blurted out, looking at his wife.

Mrs. Arlington responded almost immediately: "Don't make me laugh. Aaron? Gay?" Her façade of indifference to Amanda had disappeared, and her eyes flashed with anger. "Do you think you can intimidate us with such groundless accusations?"

"Then why was he at the Olympiad Sauna in Puerto Vallarta two weeks ago? Do you know what sort of place that is?"

"Of course she knows," Arlington broke in.

"Then why did you go? What purpose could you possibly have if you're not gay?" Amanda was baffled but then she saw Mrs. Arlington look furtively at the photographs on the mantel. There had to be some connection. One boy's life for another. She had said it. And now Amanda was sure. So she chanced a question, something so far-fetched that she almost regretted saying it: "Does it have something to with your son? His death? It does, doesn't it?!"

"How would you know about that?" Arlington demanded, taking a step toward her. "You can speculate all you want—in the safety of your own home! Now it's time to leave."

"But if you're not gay, there has to be some other reason you went to the sauna that day. I'm sure it has something to do with that boy who was murdered." Amanda knew she was grasping at intangibles, things imaginary and illusory that would disappear the moment she touched them, but she couldn't help herself.

"I think you murdered Jeremy Blackman," she continued. "There's no other reason for you to be there. That's it, isn't it? But why did you do it? What was your relationship to him? And to your son?"

"I never met him in my life," Arlington said, giving her a menacing look and moving even closer.

Amanda thought for a moment that he would strike her. It took all of her will power to resist bolting: "You haven't answered my question. In fact, you're evading it."

"I'm not evading anything. You need to leave before I call the police... or throw you out myself."

"The police," Amanda said, surprised at her own calm. "The police. That might be a good idea. I may not know the exact details of what you did, but they will certainly be interested in what I have to say. Do you want a squad car parked in front of your driveway... neighbors suspecting."

"Tell her, Aaron," Mrs. Arlington said in a small, almost hysterical voice. "Go on. Tell her. What harm can she do now? Who's going to believe such a pathetic, unattractive, aging..."

"Maybe you're right, Emily," he interrupted. "You know, I think I will. I suppose I'm running a risk, but why not? What's to lose anymore? I don't care since it's over." As he said this, he seemed to relax and a look of contentment and perhaps pride swept over his face.

"Sit down, Ms. Pennyworth, and I'll tell you a story that no one will ever believe should you chose to repeat it. A fanciful story without any proof or evidence. A fantasy invented by a frustrated amateur sleuth! I'll bet you already have a reputation. Following me here. Prying. Who would do that? Except that I know you'll realize that it's the truth when I tell you, and it will haunt you forever knowing it because there's nothing you can do about it. Unless you prefer to leave now. Are you really sure you want to hear this? Which will it be? Make your choice."

Amanda returned to the couch and sat down without a further word; her inquisitive eyes told him to continue. Mrs. Arlington also sat down abruptly, her gaze unfocused as if she was suddenly witnessing some internal drama.

"Okay, you guessed right," he began. "I don't know how, but you stumbled on the truth. It was completely a chance occurrence. Do you believe in chance? Or fate? I think I do now. And sometimes I can even believe in justice. Not the decisions of courts or police investigations, of course, not them—but something much larger, something rare. Like the Fates intervened. Anyway, chance happened twice. In the first instance—in the beginning: wasn't it chance that the Blackman kid should be driving that night, drunk and weaving around, speeding, and then smashed into my son's car? Wasn't that chance? And what are the odds that the airbag would go off but not protect him? Or that the other car struck exactly in the spot where it did? That the ambulance didn't arrive in time? Chance, yes! Chance was stalking my son at that intersection!"

"Aaron, please stop," his wife cried. "That's enough! I can't take it."

He glanced at her and then continued: "But it happened and the little bastard that did it survived while my son died. And he was barely hurt; just a few broken bones. Of course they charged him with drunk driving, but his parents—mother I think—hired a clever lawyer and got him off. Just took his license away temporarily and said it was a regrettable accident. There were no witnesses and he claimed that my son ran a stop sign. We couldn't prove otherwise. So what could we do?

"You know those memorials the kids put up at the spot of an accident? Flowers, balloons, mementoes from his friends, pictures, even stuffed animals sometimes. Well, maybe I could have forgiven that Blackman kid if he had left something, anything to show he was sorry and admit his guilt. But no, nothing. Nothing! No token; not a shred of regret, just the silence of a stunted conscience. Not even a fucking teddy bear. You know, I studied his face... watched him from the back of the courtroom during his hearing. I'll never forget how he looked as he sat there and lied and lied. He never knew I was there, or who I was, but I followed every devious word.

"And then chance intervened again... yes chance came 'round again. I could hardly believe it when Emily and I went to Puerto Vallarta for a vacation a few weeks back. I never would have ventured into that Zona Romantica place except that someone gave me advice about a jewelry shop specializing in silver and I wanted to buy something nice for her. And when I came out of the store, there they were! The two of them, that Blackman kid and his little boyfriend, giggling and laughing and having a great time of it. Oh, I recognized him immediately and I heard his name because his friend kept saying 'Jeremy this, Jeremy that.' I was sure it was him: and there he was! I couldn't believe it! Delivered to me by good luck!

"It made me furious just to see him alive and happy, when my own son... so I followed the two of them. Didn't know what I was going to do. He was obviously drunk, staggering around, and his friend was helping him out. When they headed into that sauna, I waited awhile outside; couldn't make up my mind what to do, and then decided to go in too. I'm not sure what I intended: to confront him, maybe; beat him up? Who knows; I sure didn't.

"I've never been in such a place in my life. It was... I can't describe it; it made me sick; and I hardly knew how to act. So I just watched at first. But I was determined. I wandered around for a while and pretended not to notice some of the Mexican guys staring at me. It made my skin crawl. Must have been prostitutes, but I ignored them. But I couldn't find him. And then I eventually wandered into the steam room. I hadn't noticed it before off in the back and downstairs. And there he was, lying on a bench, out cold. I could just barely make out who it was, except I knew. I tried shaking him to wake him up, I just want to let him know how much I hated him... tell him what he had done to us: ruined my son's life and our lives. But he just moaned and, then, I don't know what came over me. I put my hands around his throat and pressed and pressed. And the harder I pressed, the angrier I got. He struggled a bit; tried to push me off, but it was over almost immediately.

"It was dark and I could barely see for the steam, but I

felt an elastic band with a key on his wrist and I took it. When I got out of the room I waited for a moment, trying to decide what to do. And then it occurred to me that I should make it look like a robbery. So I examined the key again. It had a number on it: a room or a locker. I wasn't sure which, but I tried to locate the cubicle first. I had to be cautious because his friend could have been inside, so I waited and listened and then knocked quietly, ready to disappear around the corner if someone opened the door. But the room was empty so I slipped in. I took his pesos from his pants—he only had a few—and emptied everything out of his wallet to make it look like a robbery. I only left is ID so his parents to know as soon as possible and suffer like we did.

"And then I checked out. Told Emily everything when I got back. Now who doesn't believe in chance, I ask you?"

Amanda was stunned by this story and by Arlington's recital of the details. So much could have gone wrong, but it hadn't. He had taken terrible chances. But chance... chance in the face of such determination! Everything made sense now.

And now she also remembered something Sargent Perez had told her just in passing about the autopsy... yes— that the boy, Jeremy, might have once been in an auto accident. If she had only known then... but how could she? It was information without significance until now. Something that became a clue only in retrospect—when the mystery was solved—like some things in the past itself that made sense when they were truly past and understood. Only a fictional detective ever tallied up such hints before their time. And what good was imaginary sleuthing to her?

"So you admit to murder?" she said.

"No, I admit to committing a just act, not murder. I made things whole again."

"And you think you can get away with it? After all, the Mexican police know you were there at the sauna. And you clearly have a motive and opportunity."

"Maybe I did... But where's the proof? You may know the details, but, of course, I'll deny everything I've told you. Even say that I'm gay if necessary and went there to pick up someone... and Emily will back me up. She'll describe how painful it is to be the suffering wife who's had to live for years with the terrible secret of a faithless, bisexual husband and his amorous adventures. They'll believe her."

"But there's the connection to your son. Isn't that evidence?"

"No, just a coincidence. That's all there is to it, and I'm willing to risk it."

"Except that you told me a story that makes complete sense. All the details fit. You can't deny that!"

"Of *course* I'll deny it! Yes, it's a story that might make sense to you and your overactive imagination, but to no one else. Who will believe your fantasy? You don't have enough. You need other evidence—fingerprints, DNA, witnesses, and you haven't got anything. I know I'm taking a chance by telling you, but it's worth it for someone else to know. Just to see that horrified look on your face—your anger and frustration because you know I'm right and you can't do anything about it. And if you think that the United States would extradite me to face a Mexican court on the flimsy word of some petty, junior bureaucrat, some storyteller... you know that won't happen."

Mrs. Arlington had been listening carefully and his confidence seemed to restore her energy.

"Perhaps you should leave now, Ms. Pennyworth," she began calmly, but her voice rose as she stood up. "There's nothing more for you to learn here. I'm sorry you bothered, but it's futile, isn't it? I know that what happened won't bring my son back, my beautiful, handsome boy. But it's over. *Really* over now. Now go!"

Amanda could think of nothing more to say but stood and walked out of the room. She looked back at the couple, mute custodians standing at either end of the mantel bearing sad witness to the pictures of their son. For a moment, she felt sympathy for them. But sympathy for a murderer and his accomplice? Even if enacted in an uncontrolled rage or revenge or whatever you wanted to call it, it was still murder. But now she had no idea what she was going to do.

When her Uber ride finally delivered her back to Santa Monica, she was exhausted, with that unearthly feeling that she could not focus her eyes, and the world seemed a confusion of images melting into each other. She climbed up the dark steps to the landing cautiously and then made her way to the apartment door and walked quietly inside without knocking. Stephanie was in the kitchen.

"I've been so worried, Amanda! And I wasn't sure about waiting for dinner, but here you are. My God! You look terrible; as if you'd seen a ghost!"

"It's a lot worse than that. I just lost an argument to a murderer."

"Then you need a drink. I'll get you something really strong."

"Or two."

CHAPTER 11

Ordinarily, several stiff drinks on an empty stomach would have slowed her pulse and lulled her into a state of suspended perception, a pleasant two steps sideways from an unpleasant reality. But tonight the alcohol made Amanda feel tense and focused instead. She had promised to explain what happened after dinner, but when the time came, she just said: "I'm sorry, Steph. I can't. It's just too much for me to talk about tonight. I've got to think about what to do. Maybe in the morning."

"Sure, if you're up before I leave for work. Except I'm guessing that you won't be. Was it really that bad? Just tell me that and I won't ask anything more."

"If by bad you mean knowing something awful and not knowing what to do about it, then bad has skipped over worse to worst."

"I get it. Okay. I won't pry."

"That's why you're a friend, Steph."

"And now, unless you want another drink, you

probably ought to eat something and then to go to bed. Maybe you can dream a solution. I know that happens to me sometimes."

"I think I will, but I'm afraid I'll dream a dilemma; probably get chased by some monster and faced with a fork in the road, but instead of being able to choose, I'll just stand paralyzed and not know which way to turn as he bears down on me." Amanda tried a laugh, but it just came out as a feeble snort.

"He! So it *is* about that man," Stephanie said.

"Enough! You said you wouldn't pry. And it's not about a fork in the road either. Or maybe... maybe it is now that I think about it. Anyway, I don't think I could eat anything. I'll just say good night."

Amanda retreated into the small study where she slept on a futon. It took almost all of her strength to pull it into position and spread out the sheets. Peeling off her clothes, she lay down and turned off the light. Perhaps she would have to get up in the middle of the night, but she was too exhausted to brush her teeth or perform any of the rituals that were usual before bed. Sleep was what she needed most.

The next morning when she woke, it was after nine. The sun was streaming into the room making it stuffy and close, and giving her a slightly fuzzy feeling. Or, she wondered, was it the drinks from last night? She lay still for a moment until a jumble of discomforting thoughts about yesterday's events came rushing back to her. She sat up abruptly and then went out into the living room.

Stephanie had already gone and when she passed into the kitchen, she found a brief note: "Had to leave for work.

Hope you're feeling better, love, Steph."

Amanda rummaged around in the refrigerator and made herself some coffee and a slice of toast. After she ate, she showered and dressed. All the while, she tried not to think about what she would do next, but when she finished, she returned to the office, pushed the futon back into place, and sat down at Stephanie's desk. Picking up her cellphone, a pencil and the top sheet of a post-it pad, she opened her travel app. It would be expensive to book a one-way trip back to Puerto Vallarta, but she would have to let her later return flight expire. She had to get back today, if possible.

There was no difficulty finding a flight for early that afternoon although the price made her wince. She decided to leave immediately. Better to wait nervously in the airport than to pace around the apartment. She packed up her clothes, set her suitcase by the door and then she found a sheet of paper to write a note:

"Steph: Sorry I had to leave so abruptly, but I guess you will understand. I apologize for not telling you what happened yesterday, but I'll let you know everything—all the details—soon. As for the rest of my vacation, I'd love to come back. Maybe we can drive up north somewhere. I'm getting awfully tired of palm trees.

Love, Amanda.

p.s. I did the dishes and put the sheets in the laundry basket in your room."

Back in Puerto Vallarta, after only a short flight delay, she arrived at the Consulate just as Nando was about to leave for the evening. He was obviously surprised to see her:

"Señora, you are back… but…"

"Yes, Nando. Is Mr. Sommers around?"

She already knew the answer because she could see into her darkened office that he had gone.

"No, he generally leaves early. Usually by three or so."

"Why does that not surprise me?"

"But weren't you supposed to be away for two weeks?"

"I had to come back, Nando. I've got to talk to the police… Sergeant Perez. It's really urgent, but I guess I'll wait until tomorrow morning. Is everything okay here? My replacement? Is he working out?"

"He's not you, Señora."

"I'll take that as a compliment, Nando. And now I'm going straight home to my apartment. Don't tell him I'm here when you see him tomorrow." She gestured toward her office.

"Of course not. But will you be back at work soon?"

"Maybe sooner than you think."

The next morning, Amanda arrived at the police compound slightly after nine. She had barely slept that night, with her mind racing so fast that she outran any dreams—at least she could remember nothing except the discomfort of confusion and fatigue. She did her best, although she was not clever with make-up, to cover up what she knew was her exhausted look, a face that must show premonitions of old age and its delicate decay and thinning of her features: lines appeared that she had never noticed before and the tissue paper flesh of her check sagging.

When she arrived at the compound, she stopped at the

reception desk. "Would you please tell Sergeant Perez that I wish to speak to him?"

"He's not here yet. I expect him soon. Will you wait, Señora?"

Amanda thought for a second and then declined. She didn't want to face Captain Gonzalez accidentally.

"I'll come back. When you see him, tell him I was here. I'm from the American Consulate. He'll know who I am."

She walked out and across the parking lot and onto the sidewalk outside. There was a small restaurant across the street and she chanced going in for a cup of coffee, hoping that none of the policemen who might be present would recognize her. Maybe there was no reason for her caution; perhaps she was merely constructing scenarios of imagined difficulties—the erratic heartbeat of her imagination. But she was aware that what she was going to tell Perez would be explosive and perhaps unbelievable. It would contradict the case that she knew was being compiled against the Mexican boy and, what was worse, complicate everything, maybe even set off an international incident. And her job was precisely to prevent such things from happening.

"Café negro," she told the young woman who materialized in front of her.

She watched as several cars and then a taxi turned into the compound, but she couldn't see who entered the building.

This was a silly idea, she said to herself, suddenly. She took a twenty peso bill from her purse, dropped it on the table, and started to leave.

"Señora, your coffee," the woman said just as she was putting the cup down.

"Okay," Amanda replied, and slumped back onto her

chair. For the next ten minutes she sat almost transfixed by indecision. When she finally picked up her coffee it was already cold and bitter.

She reluctantly pulled herself up and crossed the street and into the compound. When she entered the reception area, the officer behind the counter nodded and picked up the telephone. A few minutes later, Sergeant Perez walked through the swinging doors of the entry and into the hallway.

"Señora. You are back. I had called the Consulate, but they said you were still on vacation. I have news."

"And so do I, officer. But I doubt we will be singing the same hymn."

"Señora?"

"I mean I'm sure our news will contradict."

"Then come back inside, please. We can go into one of the offices where we can be private."

She followed him back through the open work space and down a corridor to a small room. He opened the door and motioned for her to sit down. It looked like another interrogation room—perhaps it was, but she didn't mind; she had a lot to confess.

"I've found the murderer," she began, without waiting for him to sit down. "And I'm certain about it. I know I should lay out the evidence first and then try to convince you by building up a case, but I need to be blunt, so I'll just tell you. I traveled to Los Angeles and was going to talk to Blackman's boyfriend again, but I decided first to visit that older American man Aaron Arlington and his wife. We interviewed him together, you'll remember. Well, he told me everything. He murdered the boy. It's a complicated and strange story, but I believe it's true. And he had a strong motive too. Jeremy Blackman killed his son in an auto accident. It was entirely by chance that he encountered the two boys here in Puerto Vallarta and then followed them into the sauna. He took the gamble, but no one thought anything strange about him. After he strangled Jeremy, he staged it to look like a robbery; took some money and whatever out of his wallet just leaving one item so you could identify him easily. I can give you more details, but that's the bare outline of the story. Maybe you will believe me or maybe not. But I should also tell you that he will deny everything. I think he told me to taunt me—thinking... knowing... I could do nothing. But he's wrong. I intend to go to the Ambassador. I plan to make trouble for him."

Perez looked surprised and then determined. "But, Señora, something is already started here. In fact, I think it's already finished. The judge has agreed to take the case of Herrera. Because he is young, the penalty will not be severe, if anything at all, and because the judge knows that the evidence is weak. But what has started can't be stopped now."

"But it has to be. He isn't guilty!"

"Who is without guilt? There is some guilt at least. You forget the robbery of the ring. As you said yourself, you can prove nothing. And the embarrassment to the judge and the police would be very serious. Do you really think that the Americans would arrest that man and send him here to face a murder charge that had already been settled? No, that will not happen. You Americans would never agree."

"But..."

"There is nothing to do, Señora. Even if I could

persuade Captain Gonzalez, at best he would just shrug his shoulders and at worst he would be in a fury. I am very sorry for you to know what you know because now you must share that man's guilt. Please accept my apology, but I cannot change what has already been decided."

"So a killer remains loose?"

"He will not kill again, am I right?"

"Probably not. But where is justice?"

"Is there justice in my country or in yours? I'm sure you have your doubts about that."

Amanda was about to object but hesitated because she knew that Perez was right, and yet she felt determined to try.

"I still plan on telling the Ambassador."

"If you must. That is your decision. And maybe I am wrong, but I think he will not like it. I should not be giving you advice. But I think it is sometimes better that the real truth between countries should be hidden. Isn't that your job, to hide what might hurt... you diplomats?"

Amanda laughed bitterly: "What makes you such a philosopher, Sergeant Perez?"

"It's not philosophy I'm speaking, but experience. Too many times I've seen the innocent perish before a judge or the guilty escape through a bribe or influence. And do you think you are any better? I am sorry to be blunt, but are you? You Americans? With so many in prison for practically nothing. Really?"

Amanda started to protest, but knew that her objections were more than met by a prejudicial system that incarcerated more young men than anywhere else in the world. She knew the statistics. What was the point of arguing a losing proposition?

"I will still have to see the Ambassador."

"Yes, I'm sure you will do what you must. And I thank you for the information. And I will tell Captain Gonzalez, of course. If it is a good day and he has eaten well and no one has crossed him that morning, perhaps he will be not be terribly angry with me. But I know how most of his days go. So I'm not hoping."

"One last thing and then I'll leave. Did you suspect the American?"

"Not really. But I was sure it wasn't the boy we arrested."

Amanda stood up and reached out to him. "I think you are an honest and truthful man," she said.

He grasped her hand with both of his. "I am delighted to know you, Señora; you represent what is best in your country. And I hope you will stay with us."

"That's up to the Ambassador," she replied. "And right now I'm not optimistic. I plan to make trouble."

Amanda left the police compound immediately and took a taxi to the Consulate. When she arrived, Nando was already facing a room crowded with waiting clients. They looked up anxiously as she entered.

Nodding to him, she walked straight into her empty office—Mark had not arrived yet—and then picked up the intercom.

"Nando, this is important. I want you to call the Embassy and make an appointment for me. Tomorrow: midday. Tell the Ambassador's secretary or whoever you speak to that it's an emergency. Don't accept 'no.' And then find me a flight to the city. Late tonight or early tomorrow morning. I'll stay as long as I can today to help out with that crowd out front. But, I'm curious, some reason why there are so many?"

"Yes, Señora, right away. And I think we have so many guests because there was a story in the local paper about possible changes to US visa policy."

"Do we have any official messages about that?"

"Nothing yet. But perhaps there is some discussion in the American newspapers. You know how carefully we here in Mexico follow such things. And worry about them."

"So it's only rumors so far."

"Yes, rumors."

"And you must have the phone number of Mark Sommers. Please call him and ask him not to come in today. You can tell him I'm back for a few days."

By evening, Amanda was exhausted. Her plans for the next morning were set and the Ambassador had agreed to see her for a "brief appointment." She suspected he was already displeased, but she had no choice. Leaving the office, it was already dark. There was no hurry about returning to the apartment, so she walked slowly along the Malecon, looking into familiar stores and restaurants, stopping once to join a circle of tourists who were taking turns photographing themselves next to a couple dressed up as an Aztec warrior and his consort. Everything seemed normal in this evening processional except that she felt anything but normal. Who else among the hundreds enjoying themselves with an evening stroll would be traveling the next day to accuse someone of murder? Could anyone tell, from looking at her, the importance of that mission? What would they say if they knew?

Tension could sometimes make her ravenous, but

tonight she didn't bother with a restaurant and only made a cup of tea and toast in her apartment when she got home. She laid out her clothes for the next day, set the alarm for early—although she thought she would wake when first light crept around the frame of curtains drawn against the window of her bedroom—and went to bed.

She tried to relax, but every noise from the street, every murmur of wind that rattled the slatted blinds, the dog barking in the garden opposite, a car door slamming somewhere, an indistinguishable shout from far off, the cooing of a dove, even the quiet whirr of the overhead fan—all of the sounds that usually soothed her into sleep tugged her back to consciousness. And yet, she was half-aware of dreaming, of thoughts that raced through her mind, gathering up uncomfortable memories and the unpleasant emotions that accompanied them. In spite of herself, she recalled times when she had been embarrassed, or had made some clumsy mistake, or failed at something, and a feeling of shame swept over her. If this accounting of her life defined her, then what had she accomplished, she thought? Were these disturbing thoughts a foreboding of something she feared would happen tomorrow? Some unforeseen failure? Some weird prophecy? And what future might she have after she confronted the Ambassador? Putting him on the spot with news he didn't want to hear?

She reached over and turned on the light to look at the small round clock on the table beside her bed. Only an hour had passed and she was already bathed in a cold sweat of worry. She sat up and said out loud: "Stop it, you idiot!" as if speaking her silly command could chase away unwanted memories and unfounded fears. Consciously deciding to remember happy times, she thought back to the wonderful, raucous years of college and the times she and Stephanie had double-dated and then, across the cozy dark of their dorm room, laughed and giggled about the boys they knew. It hadn't been all bad since then and she had been happy enough with the men she met. Nothing worked out permanently, however, not even the relationship with Morelos, the Mexican policeman she had gotten to know so well here. If only he hadn't been transferred to Oaxaca, it surely would have continued and become something more.

She thought of Stephanie's friendly welcome again and the Santa Monica apartment but then slipped back to the trip to Glendale and the Arlingtons. And looking at the defiant smirk of a murderer. Damn the way one mental image piled onto another! A memory came, innocent at first to put her off-guard and then suddenly down and down she was dragged into darker thoughts until what was really bothering her slammed her in the face.

She propped up her pillows, reached over for the mystery novel she had been reading—a page or two each night—and balanced it on her lap. She tried to concentrate but the words seemed to blur and her recollection of the story was dim; she couldn't even remember who had died—and she realized that she didn't care.

She wasn't conscious of dozing off, but woke suddenly to the light from the lamp glaring, as if someone had just switched it on. She turned it off and fell back into a deep slumber that only ended with the piercing sound of the alarm the next morning.

She arrived at the airport by nine for her flight and was in Mexico City traveling on the metro toward the

Embassy by noon. Being in motion, moving toward some sort of resolution, and acting, just *doing* something, had calmed her, and she was actually looking forward to confronting the Ambassador. She had no illusions about what how he would react, but she had to try.

Entering the Embassy once more through the elaborate security and then following her escort up to the Ambassador's Office, Amanda began to feel her anxiety return. Perhaps it was the trappings of power that unnerved her: all of the layers of accumulated authority with the soldiers in the foyer, the guards, the formality and symbolism attached to the building. Maybe she was making a terrible mistake. But she had come too far, already. And now she knew she would have to try very hard not to let nervousness show in her voice.

The Ambassador made her wait, and she sat for a half hour in the reception area in front of his office trying unsuccessfully to read a travel magazine, not even really seeing the pictures. Finally his secretary indicated that she could go in. This time she noticed that the Ambassador did not open the door for her. In fact, he remained seated at his desk when she entered and just looked up briefly to nod at her.

She sat down and began: "Thank you very much for seeing me, Ambassador Baldwin. I know you are very busy."

"Yes, I am... very," he said. "And if it's something more about the murder in Puerto Vallarta, I've been informed by the local police that the case is being resolved and already turned over to the court. Were you going to tell me that? What else could you have to add that was so important?"

"That he didn't do it. Herrera, the boy they've charged. He didn't do it. I have proof. It was an American."

She hadn't intended to burst out with her information before she prepared him. But she couldn't help herself.

"And just how do you know it was an American?"

"Because he confessed to me. I just got back from Los Angeles. I went to confront him and his wife. It's a complicated story, but he told me everything: the how and the why. And she confirmed it."

"As it happens, I'm quite aware of your recent activities. And I'm not interested in hearing your so-called facts," the Ambassador interrupted. "I don't care what you think you've discovered. Maybe you have found something circumstantial. But would it ever be convincing? And what makes you think you can fly around interrogating American citizens? Are you trying to cause an international incident?"

"How do you know...?"

"Do you think I'm not informed about what you've been up to? I received a long telephone call yesterday from a lawyer in Los Angeles representing the persons you say you interviewed. Threatened a lawsuit. Do you think you can just burst into someone's home and accuse them of murder?"

"But the truth..."

"I'm afraid that's irrelevant and certainly beside the point. The Mexicans would never admit a mistake; they've gone too far already. And I suppose you don't have any tangible evidence, do you? Something that would convince all the layers of bureaucracy that would have to sign off on reversing something that is so far along? And do you realize how many undersecretaries for Whatnot and Wherefore would have to agree for the US government to intervene?"

"I only know that Arlington was present at the sauna and that he had a strong motive. And that he confessed to me."

"That's what you say. And he will no doubt deny every word. In fact, he did deny it, and vehemently so, according to his lawyer. Claims you made up some crazy story and threatened him and his wife. Do you think that anyone will believe you? Certainly not the Mexican police. They're quite satisfied they have the culprit and wouldn't be happy to be contradicted. They sent me a progress report on the case just a day ago. And you must know that extradition for a crime is very, very rare—especially to Mexico—and you can't do it on flimsy circumstantial evidence or the whim of some hysterical..."

He stopped—glared at her and then, leaning forward, his voice softened as if he had just finished reading chapter and verse from the cruelest jeremiad and was now ready to offer a few soothing words of redemption.

"I think you need to go back to Puerto Vallarta, Ms. Pennyworth, and do the job you were assigned to do. I suppose you imagine you've been helping, but you aren't. Sometimes—and I'll be frank with you—we have to accept situations where we can't act. We may know something, or think we know it, but can't say so because of some larger responsibility. And you know exactly what that reason is: good relations with Mexico. Frankly, I'm surprised that you don't see this more clearly. And a little disappointed. Being a diplomat isn't the same as being a policeman. We have different standards of conduct and different purposes. If I were a detective, I would want to pursue evidence wherever it led—and if it hurt and disrupted and angered, so be it. But for us—and I mean everyone down to the very lowest Embassy employee—our task is to cover up disputes, smooth things over, smile even when we are compromising our principles and personal beliefs. You *do* get that, don't you?"

Amanda ignored his remark about low employees: "But what about the victim's parents? Don't we owe them the truth? I promised them! Shouldn't they know who killed their son?"

"Just what kind of truth do you have in mind, Counselor Pennyworth? Your fantastic story? How will that help them? How will it ease their pain to know the name of a murderer who can never be prosecuted? Even if you told them, it would mean compounding grief with frustration. Sometimes it's better just to be done. To let things alone that can't ever be mended. I know there's that illusion about 'closure,' and resolution. People say foolish things about it, like it's some sort of ritual that has to happen. Like on some TV cop show. But this isn't television; it's the real world of compromises and mendacities. Do you really believe that knowing will erase their grief? Will it be anything but frustrating?"

He paused and looked down as if reading down a list of arguments and then continued to point two: "And as for your promises, you have no right to make them. You can't obligate the Foreign Service of the United States on a personal whim!"

Amanda shook her head and said, "I don't know. Perhaps they could bring a civil suit? Wrongful death or something? If they can't try him for murder here at least drag him into court back home? That would be something."

"So you're giving legal advice now too? Really! You're

grasping at straws and you have to realize it; ideas that become unfeasible the moment you consider them seriously. You can only make things worse for everyone." He stopped for a minute and looked away.

"But what about the boy who's going to be tried for a crime he didn't commit? Doesn't that bother you?"

"*Many* things bother me. A great many things. I see terrible injustice everywhere I look, but do you suppose I can prevent it? I try where I can to make a small difference, but that's not my job or yours!"

"That's so cynical," she said softly, wondering if she was pushing too hard, going too far.

"I'm not cynical," he replied. "I'm a diplomat, doing what I have to do. And you will do what you have to do also if you wish to remain in the Service."

He fell silent for a moment with the briefest of smiles, as if he had just won an argument, and then began again: "You realize, don't you, that this isn't about a murder anymore. Or a false conviction. Or a killer that gets off. It's about your trying to prove a point. Aren't you just making yourself the center of attention? You would be the only witness... and a witness to what? Your own ego trip? Your own delusions? I think you need to stop. For your own sake."

Amanda shook her head. "No, it's not that... I..."

He was silent.

She felt she had to push this to the end. "Are you instructing me to stop?"

"I think it would be best for your future if you did." He paused and then resumed, tapping the file that lay open on his desk. "I've been reading your evaluations and the various yearly reports about you. It seems that you do a good job when you want to, when you aren't distracted, but sometimes you are headstrong and jump into things that don't concern you. I'd say it was an overactive imagination. Nonetheless, I'm going to give you another chance. Go back to your job, forget about this, and be the representative of what is best in us."

"But how can it be our best to overlook justice? To allow a murderer to go free? What's more important than justice?"

The Ambassador paused for a moment and then turned to look out the window, as if some motion had caught his eye. "Justice? Well, justice matters, of course it does, but in our world, there are other things that matter more. Like policy... good relations... diplomacy... peace. Did I mention policy already?"

"And is it the best in us to overlook a crime?"

"Well, I wouldn't put it exactly that way, but yes, sometimes it is. Do you think that I always agree with every word that comes down from the State Department? My God, no! Of course not. Sometimes it makes me furious. But it's not in my job description to make decisions and *certainly* not in yours. We carry out what others decide to the best of our ability. Sure, here and there, if I have the chance, I try to do what I believe is right. After all, not everything we do comes on order from Washington. There's always some wiggle-room for initiative and nuance. Sometimes a gray area between the black and white. But a great deal of what I do comes on order, directly from Foggy Bottom, no matter what I might advise. And in this job, you need to convince yourself that following policy is the best and *only* recourse. Otherwise you will be miserable. You get that, I'm sure."

"But that's so awful," she interrupted. "To sacrifice an individual truth to some vague general precept."

"It isn't vague—just the way things are. Look, Amanda, I sympathize with you. I understand that you want to make things right. But there are circumstances when that just can't be. You need to leave this alone. Accept the fact that it's in everyone's best interest to drop this and drop it now."

"Except, of course, for the murdered boy and his parents."

He ignored her and continued: "And if you want to keep your position, you'll have to behave as if you believe it too. Otherwise... Now I think I've made myself clear. You can close the door on your way out."

He closed the file, pushed it aside, and leaned down to open a lower drawer of his desk. Amanda sat still for a moment, and then he glanced up at her again.

"Now!" he ordered.

During the trip back to Puerto Vallarta, Amanda kept rehearsing her grim conversation with the Ambassador, wondering if she had been more forceful—insisted—then perhaps he might have acted on her evidence or at least listened to her explanation. But he didn't even seem curious. And his brusque dismissal, treating her as if she was a secretary asking for a day off with some frivolous excuse, offended her deeply. As for his attitude toward diplomacy: how furious that made her! And yet she suspected that he might be right: Wouldn't truth always have to be sacrificed to good relations no matter the individual cost? This was something she had always known about her job even if it wasn't in her daily thoughts.

Nor had anyone during her training made the point explicitly. But she knew. *Everyone* in the Service knew without being told, and they all accepted it.

True enough, she sometimes had to act in ways that seemed wrong to her or even immoral. And she understood in a kind of general way that relations between countries were like great tectonic plates scraping against each other, pushing with enormous force that always threatened to erupt into some disastrous incident. Her small role as well as the larger task of the Ambassador was to mediate the possible damage—release the pent up and dangerous energy and direct it elsewhere. Of course she understood that. And she knew in this instance that condemning the Mexican police and judiciary for injustice and a hasty and wrongful conviction was about as serious an accusation that anyone could make. And it would be just as fruitless to accuse an American of murder with no evidence other than coincidence to back it up.

What she knew and what she could prove existed at opposite ends of possibility. She had, indeed, come to that fork in the road she imagined, pursued by dark necessity and with a choice that had to be made. But this time it wasn't in a dream but very real. She could sacrifice her career and inform the Blackmans with who knows what consequences? She had promised them, but that was before... Or she could face up to the Ambassador's cynical truth: that nothing could be done except inflict more harm. And maybe he was right: all of this had become about herself, just as he said.

Finally home in her apartment late that evening, she sat in the semi-dark thinking over the last few hours. Only days ago, she had said to Perez, almost bragged, that she was free while he was bound up in a bureaucracy where his superiors made all the decisions. But what was she thinking? Her position was like his; perhaps even worse: just an insignificant stitch in a fabric of obligations and policies.

Picking up the telephone, she made two calls. The first was to Nando. When he answered, she could hear the ruckus of his family in the background. "Nando," she began. "I'm going to go out of town again. I still have time on my vacation—a week, at least, I think, and I'm going to make good use of it. Can you and Mark Sommers manage?"

"I'm sure I can," he replied.

Amanda was certain she knew what he meant: that he could cope with her absence however little her replacement contributed.

"Was your trip to Mexico City successful?" he asked after a pause.

"No, it wasn't. I'll explain when I get back."

"All right, Señora. Have a good vacation. And don't worry."

Her second call was to Stephanie in Los Angeles.

When she answered, Amanda didn't bother to identify herself, speaking as if their conversation had never ended: "Steph, I still have another week of vacation. Can you join me? I'm thinking we could go up to Seattle. Hike in the mountains maybe. Or maybe Vancouver. Can you get off work?"

"I'll try. Sure. But you? No more detective work? Really Amanda? Is this to be believed? Are you finally going to pack away your magnifying glass, your Junior Federal Agent Fingerprint Kit, and all your disguises? Fake mustache, beard and wigs? Seriously? Are you done with all of that? And…"

"Steph… stop! Just say yes, please. I'll book a hotel and get back to you. And maybe you're right: no more detective work… for now."

When she hung up, she closed her eyes to dull her senses, to concentrate on what she had just promised her friend: whether she meant it or not. Her first thought came like the opening words of a confession: she admitted that she wasn't being completely honest, certainly with herself. But who ever was? Was that an excuse? That we all sinned against truth? Despite her frustration with this case and the stab of fury she felt at the injustice of it all, if something came her way again, reached out to involve her, might she say yes? Maybe she would… but at what cost again? And there was the Ambassador's chilling question—his accusation: had this really become about her? Was she too wrapped up in herself to consider some greater principle? Had she been wrong to follow her instinct to a place where even the police were reluctant to go? There was only one thing she knew for sure now: that she possessed secret knowledge that could ruin people's lives—her own included. She had never doubted herself like this, facing choices that had such terrifying implications.

Stirring from her meditation, she looked around the small, cozy living room of her apartment, at the familiar disharmony of clashing reds and greens and browns that she had grown to love. As she peered into one corner and then the next, someone observing her might wonder as if she was searching for something, as if looking for the answer: whether or not to tell Mr. and Mrs. Blackman everything she knew… and throw all of this away. Just one call would set things in motion that she couldn't stop. She looked at her cellphone lying on the table in front of her, the light of the nearby lamp reflecting something indistinct and shadowy on its glass face. She reached down to pick it up.

ABOUT
ATMOSPHERE PRESS

Atmosphere Press is an independent, full-service publisher for excellent books in all genres and for all audiences. Learn more about what we do at atmospherepress.com.

We encourage you to check out some of Atmosphere's latest releases, which are available at Amazon.com and via order from your local bookstore:

The Embers of Tradition, a novel by Chukwudum Okeke

Saints and Martyrs: A Novel, by Aaron Roe

When I Am Ashes, a novel by Amber Rose

Melancholy Vision: A Revolution Series Novel, by L.C. Hamilton

The Recoleta Stories, by Bryon Esmond Butler

Voodoo Hideaway, a novel by Vance Cariaga

Hart Street and Main, a novel by Tabitha Sprunger

The Weed Lady, a novel by Shea R. Embry

A Book of Life, a novel by David Ellis

It Was Called a Home, a novel by Brian Nisun

Grace, a novel by Nancy Allen

ABOUT
THE AUTHOR

James Gilbert is a historian and novelist. While a professor at the University of Maryland, he published eleven books on American culture, concentrating especially on World's Fairs and the religious and social controversies of the 1950s. One of his histories was selected a New York Times Notable Book. He has lived and taught abroad in Paris, and with year-long Fulbright Fellowships in Australia, Germany, and the University of Uppsala, Sweden, where he received an honorary doctorate degree.

Since turning to fiction writing, he has published a book of short stories and three novels: The Key Party,

Tales of Little Egypt, and Zona Romantica, the first in a series of mysteries set in Puerto Vallarta, Mexico where he has been a frequent visitor. Murder at the Olympiad is the second novel in this series with Amanda Pennyworth as the amateur detective.

He currently lives in Silver Spring, Maryland, outside of Washington, D.C. Find out more at his website, jamesgilbertauthor.com.

CPSIA information can be obtained
at www.ICGtesting.com
Printed in the USA
BVHW041800021121
620550BV00007B/379